NEW YORK REVIEW BOOKS
C L A S S I C S

FAMILY LEXICON

NATALIA GINZBURG (1916–1991) was born Natalia Levi in Palermo, Sicily, the daughter of a Jewish biologist father and a Catholic mother. She grew up in Turin, in a household that was a salon for antifascist activists, intellectuals, and artists, and published her first short stories at the age of eighteen; she would go on to become one of the most important and widely taught writers in Italy, taking up the themes of oppression, family, and social change. In 1938, she married Leone Ginzburg, a prominent Turinese writer, activist, and editor. In 1940, the fascist government exiled the Ginzburgs and their three children to a remote village in Abruzzo. After the fall of Mussolini, Leone fled to Rome, where he was arrested by Nazi authorities and tortured to death. Natalia married Gabriele Baldini, an English professor, in 1950, and spent the next three decades in Rome, London, and Turin, writing dozens of novels, plays, and essays. *Lessico famigliare* (*Family Lexicon*) won her the prestigious Strega Prize in 1963 and *La famiglia Manzoni* was awarded the 1984 Bagutta Prize. From 1983 to 1987, she served in the Italian parliament as an Independent (having left the Communist Party), where she dedicated herself to reformist causes, including food prices and Palestinian rights.

JENNY McPHEE is a translator and the author of the novels *The Center of Things*, *No Ordinary Matter*, and *A Man of No Moon*. She is the director of the Center of Applied Liberal Arts at New York University and lives in New York.

PEG BOYERS teaches poetry and translation at Skidmore College and at the Columbia University School of the Arts. She is the executive editor of *Salmagundi Magazine* and the author of three books of poetry published by the University of Chicago Press. One of those books, *Hard Bread*, is based on the life of Natalia Ginzburg.

FAMILY LEXICON

NATALIA GINZBURG

Translated from the Italian by
JENNY McPHEE

Afterword by
PEG BOYERS

NEW YORK REVIEW BOOKS

New York

THIS IS A NEW YORK REVIEW BOOK
PUBLISHED BY THE NEW YORK REVIEW OF BOOKS
435 Hudson Street, New York, NY 10014
www.nyrb.com

Originally published in Italian in 1963 as *Lessico famigliare*
by Giulio Einaudi Editore

Library of Congress Cataloging-in-Publication Data
Names: Ginzburg, Natalia, author. | McPhee, Jenny, translator. | Boyers, Peggy,
   1952– writer of afterword.
Title: Family lexicon / by Natalia Ginzburg ; translated by Jenny McPhee ;
   introduction by Peg Boyers.
Other titles: Lessico famigliare. English
Description: New York : New York Review Books, 2017. | Series: New York
   Review Books classics
Identifiers: LCCN 2016026803 | ISBN 9781590178386 (paperback)
Subjects: LCSH: Ginzburg, Natalia—Fiction. | Authors, Italian—Fiction. |
   World War, 1939–1945—Italy—Fiction. | Domestic fiction. | BISAC:
   FICTION / Family Life. | FICTION / Historical. | FICTION / Political. |
   GSAFD: Autobiographical fiction.
Classification: LCC PQ4817.I5 L413 2017 | DDC 853/.912—dc23
LC record available at https://lccn.loc.gov/2016026803

ISBN 978-1-59017-838-6
Available as an electronic book; ISBN 978-1-59017-839-3

Printed in the United States of America on acid-free paper.
10 9 8 7 6 5 4 3 2

FAMILY LEXICON

AUTHOR'S PREFACE

THE PLACES, events, and people in this book are real. I haven't invented a thing, and each time I found myself slipping into my long-held habits as a novelist and made something up, I was quickly compelled to destroy the invention.

The names are also real. In the writing of this book I felt such a profound intolerance for any fiction, I couldn't bring myself to change the real names which seemed to me indissoluble from the real people. Perhaps someone will be unhappy to find themselves so, with his or her first and last name in a book. To this I have nothing to say.

I have written only what I remember. If read as a history, one will object to the infinite lacunae. Even though the story is real, I think one should read it as if it were a novel, and therefore not demand of it any more or less than a novel can offer.

There are also many things that I do remember but decided not to write about, among these much that concerned me directly.

I had little desire to talk about myself. This is not in fact my story but rather, even with gaps and lacunae, the story of my family. I must add that during my childhood and adolescence I always thought about writing a book about the people whom I lived with and who surrounded me at the time. This is, in part, that book, but only in part because memory is ephemeral, and because books based on reality are often only faint glimpses and fragments of what we have seen and heard.

AT THE dinner table in my father's home when I was a girl if I, or one of my siblings, knocked a glass over on the tablecloth or dropped a knife, my father's voice would thunder, "Watch your manners!"

If we used our bread to mop up pasta sauce, he yelled, "Don't lick your plates. Don't dribble! Don't slobber!"

For my father dribble and slobber also described modern painting, which he couldn't stand.

He would say, "You have no idea how to behave at the table! I can't take you lot anywhere."

And he said, "Any *table d'hôte* in England would quickly show you slobs the door."

He had the greatest respect for England and believed that civility had found there, more than anywhere else in the world, its greatest expression.

At dinner he'd comment on the people he'd encountered during the day. He was very harsh in his judgments and thought everyone was stupid. For him someone stupid was a "nitwit."

"He struck me as a real nitwit," he would say about some new acquaintance.

In addition to the "nitwits," there were also the "negroes." For my father, a "negro" was someone who was awkward, clumsy, and faint-hearted; someone who dressed inappropriately, didn't know how to hike in the mountains, and couldn't speak foreign languages.

Any act or gesture of ours he deemed inappropriate was defined as a "negroism."

"Don't be negroes! Stop your negroisms!" he yelled at us continually.

The gamut of negroisms was wide. Wearing city shoes on a mountain hike was called a negroism, as was engaging in a conversation on a train with a fellow traveler or in the street with a passerby; or speaking to a neighbor from your window; taking off your shoes in the living room; warming your feet on the radiator; complaining on a mountain hike of thirst, fatigue, or blisters; bringing greasy cooked food on a hike along with napkins to wipe your fingers.

On our mountain hikes only certain foods were allowed: fontina cheese, jam, pears, hard-boiled eggs. And we were only allowed to drink tea prepared on a portable stove by our father. Frowning, he would lean his big head covered in short red hair over the stove while shielding the flame from the wind with the flaps of his rust-colored wool jacket, the pockets threadbare and singed. He always wore that same jacket whenever we were on holiday in the mountains.

Brandy and sugar lumps were, according to him, "negro stuff" and therefore forbidden on our hikes; and we were never allowed to stop for a snack in the mountain chalets as this was considered a negroism. Protecting your head from the sun by wearing a kerchief or a straw hat, or from the rain with a waterproof cap, or tying a scarf around your neck were also deemed negroisms. Such preventive wear was, instead, precious to my mother, and the morning before we left on our hike she would try to slip these things into a rucksack for both our use and her own. If my father laid his hands on any of them, he would angrily throw it out.

While on hikes, wearing our large, rigid, lead-heavy hobnailed boots, thick woolen socks, balaclava helmets, and snow goggles across our foreheads with the sun beating squarely down on our sweating heads, we would stare with envy at the "negroes" who strode easily by in tennis shoes or lounged at the chalet tables eating cream.

My mother called mountain hiking "the devil's idea of fun for his children," and she always tried to stay home, above all when the outing included a meal, since after eating she loved to read the paper and then take a nap on a sofa indoors.

We went to the mountains every summer. We rented a house for three months, from July through September. The houses were usually far from town in some remote location. Every day, our rucksacks on our backs, my father, my siblings, and I went to do the shopping in the village. There were no amusements or distractions of any kind. We children and my mother spent the evenings in the house sitting around a table. My father retreated to a distant part of the house to read, every so often sticking his head into the room where the rest of us were talking and playing together. Frowning and suspicious, he complained to my mother about our servant Natalina who had disturbed certain books of his. "Your darling Natalina, that half-wit," he would say, careless of the fact that from the kitchen Natalina could hear his every word. She was, however, accustomed to hearing herself called "that half-wit Natalina" by him and took not the slightest offense.

On some evenings during our mountain holiday my father would prepare for the next day's hike or climb. Kneeling on the ground, he greased his and my siblings' boots with whale fat; he believed that he alone knew how to grease the boots properly with the fat. A great clashing of metals would then be heard throughout the apartment as he looked for crampons, pitons, and ice axes.

"Where have you hidden my ice ax?" he roared. "Lidia! Lidia! Where have you lot hidden my ice ax?"

He would set off for a mountain climb at four o'clock in the morning, sometimes alone, sometimes with an Alpine guide who was also a friend, sometimes with my siblings. He'd be so worn out the day following these climbs he'd become unbearable. He'd read the paper silently, his face red and swollen, having been burnt by the sun reflecting off glaciers, his lips chapped and bleeding, his nose covered in a yellow cream that looked like butter, his brow furrowed and stormy. Any trifle would send him flying into a terrifying rage. Whenever he returned from these climbs with my siblings, my father announced that his children were "numskulls" and "negroes," and that none of his children had inherited his passion for the mountains—with the exception of Gino. Gino was the eldest and a great climber. Along with a friend he'd completed highly difficult ascents. When my father spoke about Gino and his friend, he did so with a mixture of pride and envy, declaring that he no longer possessed their stamina now that he was getting old.

My brother Gino was, in any case, his favorite and he was gratified by him in every way. Gino was interested in natural history; collected insects, crystals, and other minerals; and was very studious. Gino later enrolled in engineering school and when he came home after an exam reporting that he had received an A, my father would ask, "What do you mean you got an A? Why didn't you get an A-plus?"

And if he did get an A-plus, my father would say, "Oh, it must have been an easy exam."

In the mountains, when he wasn't on a climb or hike that lasted until the evening, my father would go "walking" every day. He left early in the morning, dressed exactly as he would have been for a climb but without ropes, crampons, or his ice ax. He often went walking alone, because we and my mother were, in his words, "loafers, dolts, and negroes." He set off with his hands clasped behind his back, his tread heavy due to his hobnailed boots, his pipe between his teeth. Sometimes he made my mother go with him. "Lidia! Lidia!" he thundered in the morning, "Let's go walking! If you don't, you'll grow lazy always lounging about in the meadows." My obedient mother, her walking stick in hand, her sweater tied around her waist, followed a few paces behind him, shaking her head of curly gray hair that she wore very short, even though my father objected vehemently to the current fashion for short hair—so much so, that on the day she'd had it cut, he'd flown into a rage violent enough to bring down the house.

"You've cut your hair again! What a jackass you are!" my father told her every time she came home from the hairdresser. "Jackass" in my father's lexicon didn't mean someone who was ignorant but someone who was rude or ill-mannered. We children were "jack-asses" when we were either uncommunicative or talked back.

"Frances put you up to it!" my father said to my mother when he saw she'd cut her hair again. Frances, a friend of my mother's and the wife of a childhood classmate of my father's, was in fact much loved and respected by my father. In his eyes her only flaw was having introduced my mother to the short hairstyle. Frances had relatives in Paris, whom she visited often, and one winter arrived home declaring, "In Paris, short hair is in fashion. In Paris, everyone has the sporty look." All winter long, my sister and mother kept repeating, "In Paris, the sporty look is all the rage," trying to sound like Frances who spoke with the soft *r*. They shortened the hems on all their dresses, and my mother cut her hair. My sister didn't cut hers because her hair was beautiful and blond and fell down the entire length of her back—and she was too afraid of my father.

My grandmother—my father's mother—usually joined us on those mountain holidays. She didn't stay with us but at a hotel in the village.

When we went to visit her we often found her sitting on the hotel terrace under a sun umbrella. She was small and on her minuscule feet wore black ankle boots with tiny buttons. She was proud of her small feet, which poked out from under her skirt, and she was proud of her crimped, snow-white hair combed up into a bouffant. Every day my father took her for a "stroll." They went along the main roads because she was old and couldn't manage the trails, especially in her ankle boots with those little heels. He walked ahead, his strides long, his hands behind his back, his pipe in his mouth, while she followed, her dress swishing as she took tiny steps in her tiny heels. She never wanted to take the same road as the day before, always desiring new ones.

"This is the same road we took yesterday," she complained.

Without turning around, my father responded perfunctorily, "No, it's a different one."

But she continued to repeat, "It's the same road as yesterday. It's the same one."

After a while she said, "I have a cough that's choking me to death," but my father pushed on ahead without looking back. "I have a cough that's choking me to death," she repeated, raising her hands to her throat.

She always repeated the same thing two or three times. She said, "That scoundrel Fantecchi insisted on making me a brown dress! I wanted a blue one! I wanted a blue one!" And she angrily struck her umbrella against the pavement. My father told her to watch the sunset over the mountains, but having been seized by an attack of rage at her tailor Fantecchi, she furiously continued to jab the tip of her umbrella into the ground. She came to the mountains only in order to be with us. The rest of the year she lived in Florence and we lived in Turin so we only ever saw each other in the summers. But she couldn't stand the mountains and her dream would have been to go on holiday to the spa towns of Fiuggi or Salsomaggiore, places where she'd spent her summers when she was young.

My grandmother was once very rich but had been impoverished by the Great War. Convinced Italy wouldn't win, and nurturing a blind faith in Franz Joseph, she had insisted on keeping her Austrian investments and so had lost a great deal of money. My father, an irredentist, had tried in vain to convince her to divest of her Austrian interests. My grandmother referred to her money loss as "my misfortune," and in the mornings she despaired over it while pacing up and down in her room and wringing her hands. But she wasn't all that poor. In Florence, she had a beautiful home with Turkish carpets and furniture from China and India because one of her grandfathers—he was called Parente—had been a collector of precious objects. Portraits of her various ancestors hung on the walls, including those of her grandfather Parente and of La Vendée, an aunt who was so called because of her reactionary politics and the fact that she had held a salon for diehards and counterrevolutionaries. There were many more portraits of aunts and cousins called Margherita or Regina, names once common in Jewish families. Among the portraits, however, my grandmother's father was not to be found, and he wasn't to be mentioned either. He was a widower, and after quarreling one day with his two daughters, by then adults, he declared that to spite them he would marry the first woman he met on the street, and he'd done just that. Or, at any rate, that was the family story. Whether or not he did actually marry the very first woman he encountered after walking out his front door, I don't know. In any case, with his new wife he had another daughter whom my grandmother wanted nothing to do with, and whom she referred to with disgust as "Daddy's doll-baby." Occasionally, we would run into "Daddy's doll-baby"—by now a mature and distinguished woman of fifty—while we were on holiday in the mountains, and my father would turn to my mother and say, "Did you see that? Did you see? There went 'Daddy's doll-baby'!"

"For you lot everything is a bordello. In this house you make a bordello out of everything," my grandmother always said, meaning that for us nothing was sacred. The saying became famous in our family and we used to repeat it every time we found ourselves laughing over a death or a funeral. My grandmother had a profound revulsion for animals and went into a frenzy whenever she saw us playing with a cat, saying that we would catch diseases and then infect her with them. "That dreadful creature," she would say, stamping her feet and jabbing the tip of her umbrella into the ground. She had an aversion to everything and a terror of disease. She was, however, incredibly healthy and in fact lived to be over eighty without ever needing a doctor or a dentist. She was always afraid that one of us might trick her into being baptized, since one of my brothers once jokingly pretended to baptize her. She said her prayers daily in Hebrew without understanding a word since she didn't know Hebrew. For those who weren't Jewish, as she was, she had a horror similar to the one she had for cats. My mother was the sole exception, the only non-Jew for whom she ever had any fondness. My mother returned her affection and said of her that in her utter self-absorption she was as innocent and naive as a newborn baby.

According to my grandmother she was very beautiful when she was young, the second-most beautiful girl in Pisa. The first was her friend Virginia Del Vecchio. A man named Signor Segrè arrived one day and asked to meet the most beautiful girl in Pisa so that he could ask for her hand in marriage. Virginia turned down the proposal. He then introduced himself to my grandmother. She also refused him, saying that she didn't want "Virginia's leftovers."

She then married my grandfather, Michele, a man who must have been very sweet and gentle. She became a widow very young. We once asked why she didn't remarry. With a strident laugh and a brutal frankness that we never expected from that querulous and plaintive old lady, she responded, "Come now! And have him eat me out of house and home?"

My siblings and my mother sometimes complained of boredom while on those mountain holidays, staying in isolated houses where there was nothing to do, no social life. Being the youngest, I amused myself with very little and at the time had yet to experience the boredom of those holidays.

"You lot get bored," my father said, "because you don't have inner lives."

One year when we were particularly short of money it looked as if we were going to have to remain in the city for the summer, but at the last minute we rented an inexpensive house with no electricity, only oil lamps, in a village hamlet called Saint-Jacques-d'Ajas. The house must have been very small and very uncomfortable because the whole summer all my mother could say was, "What a dump of a house! How vile a place is Saint-Jacques-d'Ajas!" Our only source of entertainment was eight or ten leather-bound books containing back issues of I'm not sure which weekly magazine with riddles, puzzles, and horror stories. They had been leant to my brother Alberto by his friend Frinco. We lived on Frinco's books throughout that entire summer. Then my mother struck up a friendship with the woman next door. They chatted when my father wasn't around. He said talking with one's neighbors was "a negro thing to do." It turned out, however, that this woman, Signora Ghiran, lived in the same building as Frances in Turin and knew her slightly, making an introduction to my father possible. He was then very kind to her. The fact was that when it came to strangers my father was always wary and suspicious, fearing they might be of "questionable character," but as soon as he discovered even a tenuous connection he was immediately reassured.

My mother could speak of nothing else but Signora Ghiran, and at mealtimes we ate dishes from recipes Signora Ghiran had taught us. "New star rising," my father said every time Signora Ghiran's name was mentioned. "New star rising," or simply "new star," was how my father ironically greeted our every new infatuation. "I don't know what we would have done without Frinco's books or Signora Ghiran," my mother said at the end of the summer. Our return to the city that year was marked by the following incident: After two hours on a bus, we arrived at the train station and took our seats on the train. We suddenly realized that all of our luggage was still on the platform. Raising the flag, the conductor cried out, "The train is departing!" To which my father responded "The hell it is!" with a shout that echoed throughout the entire carriage. The train didn't budge an inch until every last one of our suitcases had been loaded aboard.

Back in the city we had to wrench ourselves away from Frinco's books because Frinco wanted them back. And as for Signora Ghiran, we never saw her again. "We have to invite Signora Ghiran over! How rude we are!" my father would say every so often. But my mother's affections were as erratic as ever, her relationships inconstant. Either she saw someone every day or she never wanted to see them. She was incapable of cultivating acquaintances just to be polite. She always had a crazy fear of becoming "bored," and she was afraid visitors would come to see her just when she wanted to go out.

The friends my mother did see were always the same ones. With the exception of Frances and a few of my father's friends' wives, my mother's friends were young, a good deal younger than she—young women who were newly married and poor. She could give them advice, suggest seamstresses. She had a horror of "old biddies," as she called them, alluding to women who were more or less her age. She had a horror of entertaining. If one of her old acquaintances sent word that she would like to pay her a visit, my mother went into a panic. "That means today I won't be able to go out!" she said in despair. On the other hand, she could take her young friends out with her or to the cinema. They were easy to manage, amenable, and more than willing to maintain a casual relationship with her. If they had small children better yet, because she loved children very much. Sometimes, in the afternoon, these friends would come all together to see her. In my father's language my mother's friends were called the "gabblers." When dinnertime approached, my father would shout from his office, "Lidia! Lidia, have the gabblers all gone home?" At which point a last terrified gabbler could be seen slinking down the hallway and slipping out the front door. My mother's young friends were all very afraid of my father. At dinner my father would say to my mother, "Aren't you tired of gabbling? Aren't you tired of chitchat?"

Sometimes in the evening my father's friends came to our apartment. Like him, they were university professors, biologists, and scientists. On the evenings his friends were coming over, at dinner he would ask my mother, "Have you prepared some refreshments?" Refreshments meant tea and biscuits. Alcoholic beverages were never allowed in our home. Sometimes my mother hadn't prepared anything and my father got angry. "What do you mean there are no refreshments? You can't have people over without offering refreshments! One cannot commit such negroisms!"

The Lopezes—Frances and her husband—and the Ternis were among my parents' closest friends. Frances's husband's name was Amedeo but he was nicknamed "Lopez" from the time he and my father were students together. As a student my father's nickname was "Pom," short for *pomodoro*, a tomato, due to his red hair, but whenever anyone called him Pom he got very angry and only ever allowed my mother to call him that. Nevertheless, when the Lopezes mentioned our family among themselves they referred to us as "the Poms" just as we called them "the Lopezes." No one has ever been able to explain to me why Amedeo was given his nickname, its origin no doubt lost in the mists of time. Amedeo was fat, his head covered in tufts of fine silken white hair; he spoke with the soft *r* as did his wife and their three boys who were our friends. The Lopezes were much more elegant, refined, and modern than we were: their building had an elevator, their apartment was nicer than ours, and they had a telephone, which in those days hardly anyone had yet. Frances, who went frequently to Paris, brought back with her the latest fashions and fads. One year she brought back a Chinese game, in a box with dragons painted on it, called "mah-jongg." They had all learned to play this mah-jongg and Lucio, the youngest Lopez, who was my age, often boasted about this mah-jongg to me but never wanted to teach me how to play: he said it was too complicated and his mother wouldn't let anyone touch the box. Whenever I went over to their apartment, I was consumed with envy at the sight of that exquisite, forbidden box full of mystery.

After an evening spent with the Lopezes, my father would come home exalting to the high heavens their apartment, their furniture, the tea served in beautiful porcelain cups from a trolley. He would say Frances was "in the know," meaning she knew where to find nice furniture and beautiful cups, she knew how to decorate a home and how to serve tea.

It was hard to tell if the Lopezes were richer or poorer than us. My mother said they were much richer. My father said that no, like us, they didn't have a lot of money, it was just that Frances was "in the know" and "not a lummox like you lot." My father, however, felt himself to be extremely poor, especially early in the morning when he first awoke; he awakened my mother as well and said to her, "I don't know how we're going to keep going. Have you seen that the property shares have gone down?" The property shares were always down, they never went up.

"Those vile property shares," my mother would always say and complain that my father hadn't the slightest business sense and as soon as there was a rotten stock, he bought it. She often begged him to consult a stockbroker but this only infuriated him because he wanted, as in all things, to do it his own way.

As for the Ternis, they were very rich. Even so Mary, Terni's wife, was a woman of simple tastes and didn't go out much, spending her days in contemplation of her two children and their nanny, Assunta, who dressed entirely in white. Both Mary and the nanny, who imitated her, made an ecstatic whispering sound: "Ssst! Ssst!" Even Terni made this same sound "ssst, ssst" whenever in contemplation of his children. Actually, he made this sound "ssst, ssst" about everything, about our maid Natalina who was no beauty, and he made the noise whenever he saw my sister and my mother wearing old dresses. He said of every woman he laid eyes on that she had "an interesting face" and that she resembled someone or other in a famous painting. He remained in contemplation of her for a few minutes more, then removed his monocle from his eye and cleaned it with an impeccable white handkerchief. Terni was a biologist and my father greatly respected his work, but he would call him "that moron Terni" because he believed he was a poseur in his personal life. "Terni's a poseur," he would say after every time they met up. He would then repeat, "I think he's a poseur." When Terni came over he would usually come into the garden to discuss novels. He was very cultured, had read all the modern novels, and was the first to introduce us to *À la recherche du temps perdu*. Now that I think about it, I believe he was actually trying to resemble Swann with that monocle and his affectation of discovering in each of us an ancestral link to a famous painting. From his study my father would call out loudly for him to come inside so they could discuss tissue cells. "Terni," he yelled, "come here! Don't be such a moron!" Whenever Terni, making his ecstatic whispering sounds, stuck his nose into the dusty, threadbare curtains in our dining room and asked if they were new, my father would yell, "Don't be such a buffoon!"

The things my father appreciated and respected were socialism, England, Zola's novels, the Rockefeller Foundation, mountains, Val d'Aosta Alpine guides. The things my mother loved were socialism, Paul Verlaine's poetry, music, in particular *Lohengrin*, which she used to sing for us in the evenings after dinner.

My mother was Milanese but her family, like my father's, was originally from Trieste. In marrying my father she'd also married his many Triestine expressions. Whenever she recounted her childhood memories, Milanese dialect mixed into her speech.

Once when she was a small girl walking down the street in Milan she'd seen a man standing rigid and immobile in front of a hairdresser's window staring at a mannequin's head. He was muttering to himself, "Beautiful, beautiful, beautiful. Too long in the neck."

A lot of her memories were like this: simple phrases that she overheard. One day she was out for a walk with her boarding-school classmates and teachers. Suddenly one of the girls broke rank and ran to embrace a passing dog. She hugged it and in Milanese dialect said, "It's her, it's her, it's her, it's my bitch's sister!"

My mother attended boarding school for many years. She had a grand old time at that boarding school.

She acted, sang, and danced in the school productions; she performed in a comedy dressed up as a monkey; she sang in a light opera entitled *The Slipper Lost in the Snow*.

She wrote the libretto and music for an opera. Her opera began like this:

> I am Don Carlos Tadrid
> And I'm a student in Madrid!
> While strolling down via Berzuellina,
> I stopped in my tracks for I'd seen a
> Window in which I spied quite a creature,
> A young and most beautiful teacher!

And she wrote a poem that went:

> Ignorance I thee hail,
> You're my holy grail!
> Happiness is your realm so please
> Let's leave studying to the Maccabees!
> Let's drink, dance, and avoid debate,

>C'mon let's celebrate!
>Now Muse inspire you must,
>What is in my heart do say,
>Tell me the philosopher is bust,
>True love the ignoramus's way.

And she parodied Metastasio:

>If each man's inner stress
>His forehead did express
>How many who by foot travel far
>Would appear to rather go by car.

She stayed at boarding school until she was sixteen. Every Sunday she went to visit an uncle on her mother's side who was nicknamed "Barbison." Turkey was served; after they had eaten, Barbison pointed to the leftovers and said to his wife, "That'll be our breakfast."

Barbison's wife, Aunt Celestina, was nicknamed "Baryte." Someone had told her that baryte was in everything, so she would, for example, point to the bread on the table and say, "See that bread there? It's all baryte."

Barbison was a coarse man with a red nose. "A Barbison nose" my mother would say whenever she saw a red nose. After those turkey lunches Barbison would say in dialect to my mother, "Lidia, you and me, we know a thing or two about chemistry so what's sulfuric acid stink of? It stinks of fart. Sulfuric acid stinks of fart."

Barbison's real name was Perego. Some of his friends had made up this ditty for him:

>Night or day there's no grander feller
>Than Perego and his wine cellar.

Barbison's sisters were nicknamed "the Blesseds" because of their sanctimoniousness.

Another aunt of my mother's, Aunt Cecilia, was famous in the family for a particular remark. My mother was telling her how they'd all been worried something terrible had happened to my grandfather when he'd been very late coming home for lunch. In dialect, Aunt Cecilia promptly asked her, "What did you serve for lunch, rice or pasta?"

"Pasta," my mother responded.

"Good thing you didn't serve rice or there's no saying how long he would have been gone."

My maternal grandparents both died before I was born. Grandmother Pina, my mother's mother, was from a modest family and had married a neighbor. Young, diminutive, and bespectacled, my grandfather was at the beginning of his career as a distinguished lawyer. Every day my grandmother heard him at the front entrance to the building asking the concierge, "Are there any let-ters for me?" My grandfather pronounced each *t* emphatically as if the one word were actually two. This pronunciation impressed my grandmother as a sign of great refinement. She married him because of his pronunciation, and because she wanted a black velvet coat for the winter. It was not a happy marriage.

When she was young my grandmother Pina was blond and pretty. Once she performed in an amateur drama production. When the curtain rose my grandmother Pina was onstage with a paintbrush and easel. She said these words: "I cannot go on painting; my soul cannot be constrained by toil and art; it flies far from here and is nourished by painful thoughts."

My grandfather threw himself into socialism. He was friends with Bissolati, Turati, and Kuliscioff. My grandmother Pina stayed out of her husband's political activities. Because he always packed the house full of socialists, my grandmother Pina used to say bitterly, in dialect, of their daughter, "That girl's going to marry the gasman." They ended up living separately. In the last years of his life, my grandfather gave up politics and resumed his practice as a lawyer, but he slept until five in the afternoon and when clients turned up he would say, "What are they doing here? Send them away!"

At the end of her life, my grandmother Pina lived in Florence.

Sometimes she went to visit my mother who was married by then and also living in Florence. My grandmother Pina, however, was terrified of my father. One day she came to visit my brother Gino—still a babe in arms—who was running a slight fever. My father was nevertheless very worried and in an effort to calm him down my grandmother suggested that the fever was due to teething. My father became furious, insisting that teething did not cause fevers. On her way out my grandmother Pina met my uncle Silvio, who was also coming to visit us. In dialect, she whispered to him on the steps, "Whatever you do, don't say it's the teeth."

Beyond "Don't say it's the teeth," "That girl's going to marry the gasman," and "I cannot go on painting," I don't know anything about this grandmother of mine and no other words of hers came my way. I do remember, however, often hearing repeated in the family this phrase of hers, also in dialect: "Every day it's something, every day something, and today Drusilla's broken her specs."

She had three children, Silvio, my mother, and Drusilla, who was shortsighted and always breaking her eyeglasses. My grandmother died alone in Florence after a life full of sorrow: Her eldest child, Silvio, committed suicide when he was thirty by shooting himself in the temple one night in a public park in Milan.

After boarding school, my mother left Milan and went to live in Florence. She enrolled at the university to study medicine but never finished her degree because she met my father and married him. My grandmother on my father's side was opposed to the marriage because my mother wasn't Jewish and someone had told her that my mother was a devout Catholic and that every time she saw a church she bowed low and made the sign of the cross several times. This was entirely untrue. No one in my mother's family went to church or crossed themselves. So for a while my grandmother was opposed to the marriage, but then she agreed to try to get to know my mother. They met one evening at the theater and watched a play in which a white woman ended up among black Africans and a black woman who was jealous of her, gnashed her teeth and, glaring at her with terrible eyes, said, "White lady cutlet! White lady cutlet!"

"White lady cutlet," my mother would always say whenever she ate a cutlet.

They'd been given complimentary seats for that play because my father's brother, Uncle Cesare, was a theater critic. He was, this uncle Cesare, completely different from my father—calm, fat, and always cheerful. As a theater critic he was not at all caustic and never wanted to say anything bad about a play, finding something positive about each production. When my mother told him that a play seemed stupid to her, he would get mad and say, "Why don't you try to write one yourself." Later Uncle Cesare married an actress, a great tragedy for my grandmother; for many years she didn't want to be introduced to Uncle Cesare's wife because in my grandmother's opinion an actress was even worse than a woman who made the sign of the cross.

At the time he got married my father was working in Florence in a clinic run by one of my mother's uncles, nicknamed the "Lunatic" because he was a doctor who treated the insane. The Lunatic was, in fact, a man of great intelligence, cultivated and wry. I'm not sure if he ever knew what our family called him. In my paternal grandmother's house my mother encountered a retinue of various Margheritas and Reginas who were either my father's cousins or aunts, and she also met the renowned La Vendée who was still alive in those days. As for my great grandfather Parente, he'd been dead for some time as was his wife, my great grandmother Dolcetta, and their servant known as Bepo, the porter. It was known that my great grandmother Dolcetta was small and round like a ball and always had indigestion because she ate too much. She felt sick, vomited, then went to bed, but after a little while they would find her eating an egg. "It's so fresh," she'd say by way of justification.

Great Grandfather Parente and Great Grandmother Dolcetta had a daughter called Rosina. Rosina's husband died leaving her with small children and little money so she moved back into her father's house. The day after she returned, while everyone was at the dinner table, Great Grandmother Dolcetta stared at her and said, "What's wrong with our Rosina today? She's not her usual self."

My mother used to tell us, and at some length, the stories about "our Rosina" and Great Grandmother Dolcetta and the egg because my father wasn't any good at telling stories, always confusing the facts and details, and interrupting himself with his thunderous and prolonged laughter—because memories of his family and his childhood delighted him—making it hard for us to follow him.

Enjoying the sheer pleasure of storytelling, my mother was always greatly cheered up whenever she told a story. She would turn to one of us at the dinner table and begin telling a story, and whether she was telling one about my father's family or about her own, she lit up with joy. It was as if she were telling the story for the first time, telling it to fresh ears. "I had an uncle," she would begin, "whom they called Barbison."

And if one of us said, "I know that story! I've already heard it a thousand times!" she would turn to another one of us and in a lowered voice continue on with her story.

"I can't even begin to count how many times I've heard this story," my father would shout, overhearing a word or two as he passed by.

My mother, her voice lowered, would continue on with the story.

The Lunatic had a madman in his clinic who believed he was God. Every morning the Lunatic said to him, "Good morning, most eminent Signor Lipmann." And the madman responded, "Most eminent, perhaps yes, Lipmann, probably not!" because he believed he was God.

And then there was the famous line from the orchestra conductor, an acquaintance of Silvio's, who while on tour in Bergamo said to his restless or undisciplined singers, "We haven't come to Bergamo on a military campaign but to conduct *Carmen*, Bizet's masterpiece."

My parents had five children. We now live in different cities, some of us in foreign countries, and we don't write to each other often. When we do meet up we can be indifferent or distracted. But for us it takes just one word. It takes one word, one sentence, one of the old ones from our childhood, heard and repeated countless times. All it takes is for one of us to say "We haven't come to Bergamo on a military campaign," or "Sulfuric acid stinks of fart," and we immediately fall back into our old relationships, our childhood, our youth, all inextricably linked to those words and phrases. If my siblings and I were to find ourselves in a dark cave or among millions of people, just one of those phrases or words would immediately allow us to recognize each other. Those phrases are our Latin, the dictionary of our past, they're like Egyptian or Assyro-Babylonian hieroglyphics, evidence of a vital core that has ceased to exist but that lives on in its texts, saved from the fury of the waters, the corrosion of time. Those phrases are the basis of our family unity and will persist as long as we are in the world, re-created and revived in disparate places on the earth whenever one of us says, "Most eminent Signor Lipmann," and we immediately hear my father's impatient voice ringing in our ears: "Enough of that story! I've heard it far too many times already!"

I don't know how my father and his brother Cesare, both devoid of all business sense, could have emerged from that long line of bankers who were my father's ancestors and relatives. My father spent his life immersed in scientific research, a profession that didn't yield much money; in any case, money for him was a vague and confused concept dominated by an essential indifference. The result was that whenever he had to deal with money in any practical way, he nearly always lost it or, at least, conducted himself in such a way that he should have lost it, and if he didn't lose it, and all went smoothly, it was only by pure chance. All his life he was plagued with the anxiety that from one moment to the next he might find himself on the street. It was an irrational worry that dwelled within him along with other dark moods and forebodings, like his foreboding about the future success and fortune of his children. His fear of homelessness weighed on him like a dark mass of black clouds hovering over rocky mountains, yet it never managed to penetrate the depths of his spirit and his essential, absolute, and intimate indifference to money. He would say "a considerable sum" when speaking of fifty lire, or he would say "fifty francs" since his preferred unit of monetary measurement was the franc not the lira. In the evenings, he would go from room to room shouting at us for leaving the lights on but then would go and lose millions of lire, almost without noticing, by casually buying or selling stocks, or by handing over his work to publishers then neglecting to ask for proper compensation.

After Florence, my parents went to Sardinia because my father was appointed to a professorship in Sassari, and for a few years they lived there. They then moved to Palermo, where I was born, the last of the five children. During the war, my father was a medical officer on the Karst Plateau. Finally, we came to live in Turin.

Those first years in Turin were difficult for my mother. The First World War was just over, the postwar cost of living was high, and we had little money. It was cold in Turin and my mother complained about that and about the dark, damp apartment that my father had found for us before we arrived, without having consulted anyone. My mother, according to my father, complained in Palermo, and she complained in Sassari. She always found something to grumble about. Now she spoke of Palermo and Sassari as if they were paradise on earth. In both places she had made many friends, however she never wrote to them because she was incapable of maintaining friendships with anyone at a distance. She'd had beautiful sun-drenched apartments, a comfortable and easy life, and wonderful housemaids. In Turin, at first she couldn't find a housemaid; then one day, I don't know how, Natalina turned up at our apartment and stayed for thirty years. The truth was, even if my mother grumbled and complained in Sassari and Palermo, she'd been very happy there because she had a joyful nature, and no matter where she was she found people to love and to love her. Wherever she was she always found a way to enjoy the places and things around her and to be happy. She was even happy during those uncomfortable, if not actually difficult, first years in Turin in which she often cried because of my father's bad moods, because of the cold, because she missed those other places, because her children were growing up and needed books, coats, shoes, and there wasn't much money. Still, she was happy because as soon as she stopped crying she'd become very joyful, and at home she would sing *Lohengrin*, *The Slipper Lost in the Snow*, and *Don Carlos Tadrid* at the top of her lungs. And later, recalling those years when she still had all her children at home and there wasn't any money, and the price of the property shares was always going down, and the apartment was damp and dark, she always spoke of that time as beautiful and very happy. "The era of via Pastrengo," she would say later to describe those years. Via Pastrengo was the street where we lived then.

The apartment on via Pastrengo was very big. There were ten or twelve rooms, a courtyard, a garden, and a glass-enclosed veranda looking onto the garden. It was, however, very dark and certainly damp because in the bathroom one winter two or three mushrooms sprouted. Those mushrooms were a great topic of conversation in the family. My brothers told my paternal grandmother, who was staying with us at the time, that we had cooked them up and eaten them. My grandmother, even if incredulous, was nevertheless alarmed and disgusted and said, "In this house you make a bordello out of everything."

I was a small girl then and I had only the vaguest memory of Palermo, the city where I was born and then left when I was three years old. I believed, however, that just like my mother and sister, I too missed Palermo terribly. I missed the beach at Mondello where we would go swimming, and I missed Signora Messina, a friend of my mother's, and a little girl called Olga, a friend of my sister's, whom I called "Live Olga" in order to distinguish her from my doll called Olga. Every time we saw her on the beach I would say, "Live Olga makes me blush." These were the people we knew in Palermo and Mondello. Nurturing my nostalgia, or feigning nostalgia, I wrote the first poem of my life, comprised of only two lines:

> Palermino Palermino,
> You're more beautiful than Torino.

This poem was hailed in our family as a sign of my precocious vocation for poetry, and encouraged by my success, I immediately composed two more very short poems about mountains I'd heard mentioned by my siblings:

> Long live Grivola mountain,
> If ever you slide down one.
> Long live Mont Blanc,
> If ever you're zonked.

Of course, in our family writing poetry was a common practice. My brother Mario wrote a poem about the Tosi boys, playmates from Mondello whom he couldn't stand:

> And then the Tosi boys came,
> All nasty, boring, and lame.

But the best and most celebrated poem of all was by my brother Alberto, written when he was ten or eleven and not based on any real event but created from nothing, the product of undiluted poetic invention:

> The old maid
> With no titties
> Had a babe
> She was pretty.

We often recited from *The Daughter of Iorio* at home. But mostly in the evenings, sitting around the table, we recited a poem my mother had taught us, having heard it when she was a child at a charity performance put on for refugees from the Po Valley flooding:

For many days everyone trembled where they stood!
And the elders said, "Mary, Mother of God, this flood is
    rising hour upon hour!
Listen to us children; take your things and leave evermore!
What's that! Depart and abandon the dear old poor!"
The father wouldn't hear of it; and the father was young
    and bold and was not one to be told
That such an aberration should ever again appear;
And that night he said to the mother, "Rosa, my dear,
Put the children to bed and have a peaceful repose,
The Po, a tired-out giant, is calm and in need of a doze.
In his great earth-bed carved by God does he now lie,
So go to sleep; there are many brave spirits such as I,
Many here with strong shoulders who will swiftly rally
To guard the banks and defend all in this poor valley."

My mother had forgotten the rest of it but I don't think her memory of the first part was totally accurate either since in some places, for example, where it goes "and the father was young and bold," the line gets longer without any regard for the meter. But she made up for her memory's imprecision with the emphasis she placed on the words.

Many here with strong shoulders who will swiftly rally
To guard the banks and defend all in this poor valley!

My father couldn't bear this poem, and whenever he heard us reciting it with my mother, he would get angry and say that we were putting on "puppet shows" and incapable of ever doing anything serious.

Almost every evening Terni and some friends of my brother Gino came over. Gino, the eldest, went to the Polytechnic then. We sat around the table and recited poetry or sang

I am Don Carlos Tadrid
And I'm a student in Madrid!

My mother would sing. And my father, who'd stayed in his study reading, would show up every so often at the dining-room door, suspicious, scowling, his pipe in hand.

"Still saying your nitwitteries! Still putting on your puppet shows!"

The only subjects my father tolerated were either scientific, political, or changes "in the department," which meant some professor or other was appointed a post in Turin, unjustly according to my father, since the man was "a dim-wit," or another was not appointed a post in Turin unjustly because he was a man "of great importance." In any case, he deemed scientific subjects, and what went on "in the department," matters beyond our capacity for understanding. At the table, however, he would report daily to my mother about the situation "in the department," and about the progress of his various tissue cultures in petri dishes in the laboratory, and he'd get angry if she demonstrated even the slightest lack of attention. At mealtimes my father ate a lot, but always in such a hurry that it seemed like he ate nothing because his plate was almost immediately empty again. He was actually convinced that he hardly ate anything and had transmitted this belief to my mother who was always pleading with him to eat. He, on the other hand, was always yelling at my mother because he thought she ate too much.

"Don't eat too much! You'll get indigestion!"

"Don't pick at your cuticles!" he would thunder at her periodically. My mother did, in fact, have the habit of picking at her cuticles ever since, as a girl at boarding school, she'd developed a whitlow on her finger that then peeled.

All of us, in my father's opinion, ate too much and would have indigestion. Any dish he didn't like he claimed was unhealthy and indigestible. Dishes he liked he claimed to be healthy and said they "stimulated peristalsis."

If a dish he didn't like arrived at the table he would become infuriated. "Why do you cook the meat like this! You know that I don't like it this way!" If a dish he liked was prepared only for him he got angry all the same. "I don't want things made specially for me! Don't make anything special for me!"

"I eat everything," he said. "I'm not picky like you lot. I don't care in the least about food!"

"One shouldn't talk all the time about eating! It's vulgar!" he would thunder if he heard us talking about one dish or another.

"How I do love cheese," my mother invariably would say whenever cheese was served.

And my father would say, "How monotonous you are! All you do is repeat yourself!"

My father liked his fruit very ripe, so whenever one of us came across an overripe pear we gave it to him.

"Ah, so you give me your rotten pears! What real jackasses you are!" he'd say with a hearty laugh that reverberated throughout the apartment, then he'd eat the pear in two bites.

"Walnuts," he'd say as he cracked them open, "are good for you. They stimulate peristalsis."

"You're monotonous too," my mother would say. "You repeat yourself too."

My father would then take offense. "What a jackass!" he'd say. "You tell me I'm monotonous! What a real jackass you are!"

At home we had ferocious arguments over politics, which ended in tantrums, napkins hurled into the air, and doors slammed so hard the whole apartment shook. That was during the early years of fascism. I still can't understand what they were arguing about so vehemently since my father and siblings were all against fascism. I asked my siblings recently and none of them could enlighten me on the subject, yet they all remembered those fierce fights. It seems to me that my brother Mario, playing devil's advocate with my parents, would defend Mussolini in some way, and this certainly would have enraged my father. Mario and my father always argued because Mario's opinions were consistently at odds with my father's.

My father said Turati was naive and my mother, who didn't think there was anything wrong with naiveté, would nod and sigh and say, "My poor Filippetto." During that period, Turati once came to our apartment when he was passing through Turin. I remember him in the living room, as big as a bear with a round gray beard. I saw him twice: that time and later on, when he had to flee Italy and stayed in hiding with us for a week. I can't remember, however, even one word he said that day in our living room. All I remember is a lot of arguing and debate.

My father always came home enraged whenever he ran into Blackshirts parading in the street or when he'd discovered new fascists among his colleagues at department meetings. "Buffoons! Thugs! What a joke!" he'd say, sitting down at the table. He slammed down his napkin, slammed down his plate, slammed down his glass, and snorted in disgust. He'd express his opinion in a loud voice on the street to some acquaintances who happened to be walking home with him and they'd look around terrified. "Cowards! Negroes!" my father thundered later at home, describing his acquaintances' fear. I think he enjoyed terrifying them by speaking in a loud voice on the street when he was with them. Partly he enjoyed himself, and partly he didn't know how to control the volume of his voice, which always sounded very loud, even when he thought he was whispering.

Regarding my father's inability to control the volume of his voice, Terni and my mother would tell the story of how one day during a reception for professors while they were all assembled in the halls of the university my mother asked my father in a whisper the name of someone nearby.

"Who's that?" my father had yelled so loudly that everyone turned to stare at them. "Who's that? I'll tell you who he is! He's a perfect imbecile!"

In general, my father had no tolerance for jokes, those told either by us or by my mother. In our family jokes were called "little gags," and we loved to both tell and hear them. But my father would get angry. The only little gags he had any tolerance for were the antifascist ones, and then a few from his era that both he and my mother knew and that he sometimes recollected on those evenings with the Lopezes who, of course, by then had heard his little gags many times. My father deemed some of those little gags lewd, even if I'm sure they were very innocent, and whenever we children were present he would only whisper them. His voice would become a loud hum but we could still make out many of the words, one of which was coquette, a term often featured in those nineteenth-century gags and which he, while endeavoring to whisper, pronounced louder than the other words and with a special mingling of malice and pleasure.

My father always woke up at four o'clock in the morning. After getting out of bed, his first concern was to go and see if the *mezzorado* had turned out well. *Mezzorado* was a kind of sour milk he'd been taught how to make by shepherds in Sardinia. It was actually just yogurt. Yogurt wasn't yet fashionable then. You couldn't buy it in dairies and snack bars as you do nowadays. In making his own yogurt my father was, like in so many things, a pioneer. Winter sports weren't fashionable at the time either, and my father might have been the only one in Turin to engage in them. As soon as snow fell, no matter how light, on Saturday evening he took off for Claviere with his skis on his shoulder. Neither Sestriere nor the hotels in Cervinia existed then. My father regularly slept in a mountain hut above Claviere called the Mautino Hut. He sometimes dragged along with him my siblings or a few of his assistants who shared his passion for the mountains. He used the English pronunciation "ski." He had learned to ski as a youth while on a trip to Norway. On Sunday night when he came home he would always claim that the snow had been terrible. Snow for him was always too wet or too dry, like the *mezzorado*, which never turned out just as it should. It always seemed to him either too watery or too thick.

"Lidia! The *mezzorado* didn't set," he would thunder down the hall. The *mezzorado* was in a bowl in the kitchen covered by a plate and wrapped in an old salmon-colored shawl of my mother's. Sometimes it really didn't set and the result was a greenish trickle with marble-white lumps that had to be thrown away. Making *mezzorado* was an extremely delicate process and the slightest thing would spoil it—for example, if the shawl slipped even slightly out of place and a sliver of air seeped in.

"It didn't set again today and it's entirely your Natalina's fault!" my father thundered down the hall at my mother who was still half asleep, her response to him garbled.

Whenever we went on our summer holiday we had to remember to bring the *mezzorado* yeast base, or "mother," which was kept in a small cup, securely wrapped and tied up with string. "Where is the mother? Did you bring the mother?" my father would ask on the train, rummaging through a rucksack. "It's not here! I can't find it!" he'd shout. Sometimes the mother really had been forgotten and he'd have to make it again from scratch with brewer's yeast.

In the morning my father always took a cold shower. Under the water's lash, he'd let out a long roar, then he'd get dressed and, after stirring in many spoonfuls of sugar, he'd gobble down great cupfuls of that cold *mezzorado*. By the time he left the apartment, the streets were still dark and mostly deserted. He'd set out into the cold fog of those Turin dawns wearing a large beret that formed a kind of visor over his brow and a great big raincoat full of pockets and with many leather buttons. He'd go out with his hands clasped behind his back, his pipe in his mouth, his stride lopsided because one shoulder was higher than the other. Almost no one was on the street yet but he still managed to bump into whoever happened to be out then. Scowling, he'd continue on his way with his head lowered.

At that hour no one was at the laboratory yet, with the exception of maybe Conti, his attendant, who was a short, calm, mild-mannered little man wearing a gray lab coat; he was very fond of my father and my father was very fond of him. He sometimes came over to our apartment when a cupboard needed fixing, or a fuse needed replacing, or our trunks needed cording. After years at the laboratory, Conti had learned a great deal about anatomy and during the exams he would drop helpful hints to the pupils and my father would get angry. But later at home my father would proudly tell my mother that Conti knew anatomy better than the students. At the laboratory, my father wore a gray lab coat identical to Conti's and he yelled down the halls just like he did at home.

I am Don Carlos Tadrid
And I'm a student in Madrid!

My mother sang this at the top of her lungs in the mornings while she brushed out her drenched hair. Like my father, she too took a cold shower and she and my father had these spiny gloves that they rubbed themselves down with to warm up after their showers.

"I'm freezing!" my mother would say joyfully because she loved the cold water. "I'm still freezing! How cold it is!"

She'd wrap herself up snugly in her bathrobe and with a coffee cup in hand she'd take a spin around the garden. My siblings were all at school and there was a little peace in the house then. My mother sang while shaking out her wet hair in the morning air. She'd then go to the ironing room to chat with Natalina and Rina.

The ironing room was also called "the wardrobe room." The sewing machine was in there and it was where Rina spent her days sewing. Rina was a home seamstress of sorts. She was good but only for things like turning out our coats and patching our trousers. She didn't make clothes. When she wasn't at our apartment she was at the Lopezes. My mother and Frances passed her back and forth like a juggling ball between hands. She was teeny tiny, almost a dwarf. She called my mother "Signora Maman" and when she ran into my father in the hallway she scampered away like a mouse because he couldn't tolerate her.

"Rina! Rina's here again today!" he'd say, infuriated. "I can't stand her. She's a gossip! And she's entirely useless!"

"But the Lopezes always have her come too," my mother would say as justification.

Rina was moody. When she came to our house after a period of being away, she was very friendly and devoted herself to a thousand tasks—she would plan to refurbish all of our mattresses and pillows, clean the curtains, remove stains from the carpets using coffee grounds as she'd seen done at Frances's house. But she soon got bored. She became sullen and irritated with me and Lucio for hanging around her after she'd earlier promised to take us out for a walk or to give us sweets. Lucio, Frances's youngest son, came nearly every day to our apartment to play.

"Leave me in peace! I have to work!" Rina would say sulkily while she worked the sewing machine and then she'd bicker with Natalina.

"That wicked Rina!" my mother would say on the morning Rina, without warning, didn't show up and no one knew where she'd disappeared to because even Frances hadn't seen her. At Rina's instigation there were mattresses and pillows all undone, their wool stuffing heaped in the wardrobe room, and yellow smears were all over the carpets from coffee grounds.

"That wicked Rina! I'll never have her back!" After a few weeks Rina would come back, cheerful, kind, full of initiatives and promises. And my mother forgot all about her faults and perched herself in the wardrobe room to listen to Rina's chatter as she rapidly worked the sewing machine, tapping the pedal with her dwarfish foot on which she wore a cloth slipper.

Natalina, my mother said, resembled Louis XI. She was small and frail with a long face and her hair was sometimes combed straight and other times had been sumptuously curled with an iron. "My Louis XI," my mother would say in the morning when Natalina would walk into the bedroom, glowering, with a kerchief on her head, carrying a mop and bucket. Natalina made a muddle of her feminine and masculine pronouns.

"She went out this morning without a coat," she'd announce to my mother.

"And who is she?"

"Master Mario. He should say something to him about it."

"He who?"

"He, Signora Lidia, he," Natalina said, pointing at my mother impatiently and rattling the bucket.

Natalina, my mother told her friends, was "a lightning bolt" because she did the housework with extraordinary speed. And she was "an earthquake" because she did it all ferociously while making a racket. She had the look of a whipped dog because she'd had an un-happy childhood. She was an orphan who grew up in either orphan-ages or hospices and then in the service of merciless employers. She had for those old bosses—whom she would tell us used to slap her so hard her head would hurt for days—a profound nostalgia. At Christmas she would send them lavish gilded cards. She even some-times sent them presents. She never had a cent in her pocket, being so generous and extravagant in her spending habits, and she was for-ever inclined to lend money to those friends with whom she went out on Sundays. She never lost that look of a whipped dog. Never-theless, she took out on us, and in particular on my mother, her pen-chant for sarcastic, domineering, and stubborn behavior. With my mother, whom she loved tenderly and who tenderly loved her back, she maintained a surly, sarcastic, and in no way servile rapport.

"It's a good thing he is a woman because otherwise how would he earn a living? He who is good for nothing," she'd say to my mother.

"He who?"

"He, she, you!"

At home, we lived in a recurring nightmare filled with my father's sudden outbursts, exploding as he did often over the most trifling things—a pair of shoes he couldn't find, a book put back on the wrong shelf, a blown-out lightbulb, a slight delay in a meal being served, an overcooked dish. We also lived in the nightmare of the fights between my brothers Alberto and Mario, which also exploded without warning; we would suddenly hear coming from their room the sound of chairs being overturned and banged against the walls, followed by piercing and savage shrieks. By then Alberto and Mario were big, strong teenagers who could do some real damage when punching each other; they came out of their scuffles with bloody noses, swollen lips, torn clothes.

"They're *murdring* each other!" my mother screamed, dropping the *e* in her fright. "Beppino, come quick, they're *murdring* each other!" she screamed, calling my father.

My father's intervention, like all of his actions, was violent. He threw himself between the two locked in combat and smacked them head to toe. I was little and remember being terrified by those three men and their brutal fights. The trivial reasons over which Alberto and Mario frequently fought were much the same as the trivial reasons over which my father exploded in anger—a book or tie not found, wanting to be first in line when it was time to wash. Once when Alberto appeared at school with his head bandaged, a professor asked him what had happened. He stood up and said, "My brother and I wanted to take a bath."

Of the two, Mario was older and stronger. His hands were as hard as iron and when he was angry he went into a nervous frenzy that caused his muscles, tendons, and jaw to become rigid. As a child, he'd been a bit delicate, so my father had taken him hiking in the mountains to toughen him up, which, of course, he did with all of us. Mario had developed an unspoken hatred of the mountains, and as soon as he was able to escape my father's will, he quit going entirely. But in those years he was still obligated to go. Alberto wasn't always the object of Mario's rage. Sometimes Mario's anger was directed at things, especially things that didn't obey the fury of his hands. Saturday afternoon he'd go to the basement to look for his skis and be overcome by an unspoken wrath either because he couldn't find them or because no matter how hard he wrenched the ski bindings with his hands they wouldn't open. Even if they were nowhere near him at the time, Alberto and my father were inescapably implicated in his wrath: Alberto for always using his things; my father for persisting in taking him to the mountains when he hated going, then making him wear old skis with rusty bindings. Sometimes Mario couldn't get his ski boots on. He raised hell in that basement all by himself and from upstairs we heard a great racket. He knocked everyone's skis to the ground, hurled bindings, boots, and sealskins, tore down ropes, smashed out the bottoms of drawers, kicked chairs, walls, and table legs. I remember seeing him one day in the living room sitting peacefully reading the newspaper. All of a sudden he was seized by one of his silent rages and began to furiously rip the paper to pieces. He gnashed his teeth, stamped his feet, and ripped up the paper. That time neither Alberto nor my father was to blame in the slightest. All that had happened was that the bells of a nearby church had begun to ring and their insistent peal had exasperated him.

Once, at the dining table after one of my father's outbursts—not even one of his worst—Mario picked up the bread knife and scraped the back of his own hand with it. Torrents of blood flowed and I remember the terror, the screams, my mother's tears, and my father, who was also frightened and screaming, holding sterilized gauze and iodine.

After he had argued with Alberto and they had come to blows, Mario went around for the next few days "in a pout," or "with the moon," as it was called in our family. He came to the table very pale, with swollen eyelids and teeny-tiny eyes. Mario always had small eyes, narrow and long like the Chinese. But during those "moon" days, his eyes were invisible, reduced to two slits. He didn't say a word. He generally was in a pout because he was convinced that in our family Alberto was always believed to be in the right and he in the wrong. And he thought himself too grown up for my father to still have the right to smack him around.

"Did you see that pout on Mario? Did you see that moon face?" my father would say to my mother as soon as Mario left the room. "What's wrong with that moon face? He didn't even say one word! What a jackass!"

Then one morning Mario was no longer "with the moon." He came into the living room, sat down on the couch, and began to stroke his cheeks with a rapt smile and narrowed eyes. He said, "The Brot shot in the pot." It was one of his little jokes that he liked very much and repeated incessantly. "The Brot shot in the pot. The Brut shut in the put. The Bret shet in the pet. The Brit—"

"Mario," my father yelled, "don't use bad words!"

"The worm squirms to confirm . . ." Mario began again as soon as my father had left the room. He stayed in the living room to chat with my mother and Terni who was his great friend.

"How sweet Mario is when he's in a good mood!" my mother would say. "How charming he is! He's reminds me of Silvio!"

Silvio was my mother's brother, the one who killed himself. In our family, his death was shrouded in mystery. I now know that he killed himself but I still don't really know why. I believe the air of mystery surrounding the figure of Silvio was perpetuated mostly by my father because he didn't want us to know that there had been a suicide in our family, and perhaps for other reasons I'm unaware of. As for my mother, she always spoke joyfully of Silvio, since my mother by nature was happy. She perceived and accepted the good and joyfulness in everything, and elicited the same from everything and everyone, leaving sorrow and evil in the shadows, only scarcely and rarely acknowledging them with a brief sigh.

Silvio had been a musician and a man of letters. He had put to music "Les feuilles mortes" and other Paul Verlaine poems. What little he could play, he played badly. He hissed his tunes while playing the piano with one finger. He'd say to my mother, "Listen, you fool, listen to how beautiful this is." Even though he played so badly, and sang with such a reedy voice, it was nevertheless beautiful to listen to him, my mother said. Silvio was very elegant and dressed with great care. He'd complain vehemently if his trousers weren't ironed properly with a straight crease. He had a beautiful walking stick with an ivory knob, and he went about Milan with his walking stick, wearing a boater and meeting with his friends in a café to discuss music. In those stories my mother told, Silvio was always a happy person. Unaware as I was of the details, his death seemed incomprehensible to me. On my mother's bedside table was a small faded portrait of him wearing his boater and sporting a little mustache with ends that twirled upwards. It sat next to another photograph of my mother with Anna Kuliscioff, both of them wearing veiled hats with feathers and standing in the rain.

In our apartment, another trace of Silvio was his unfinished opera of Peer Gynt stored high up at the very top of a cupboard in large booklets inside folders tied with ribbons. "How witty Silvio was!"

my mother often said. "How charming he was! And his *Peer Gynt* was an opera of great merit."

My mother always hoped that at least one of her children would become, like Silvio, a musician. It was a hope that remained unfulfilled because each one of us proved to be entirely tone-deaf when it came to music and whenever we tried to sing we were always entirely out of tune. Yet all of us wanted to try to sing and Paola, while cleaning up her room in the morning, would repeat in a sad catlike voice snatches from operas and songs she'd heard my mother sing. In order to assert her love of music, Paola sometimes went to concerts with my mother, but my brothers said she was just faking it and that she didn't care about music at all. As for me and my brothers, we were occasionally taken to concerts, but we always fell asleep, and when taken to the opera we complained about "all that music that got in the way of the words." Once my mother took me to *Madama Butterfly*. I brought with me the *Children's Journal* and read it throughout the entire performance, trying to make out the words using the light from the stage and covering my ears with my hands so as not to hear the din.

Still, whenever my mother sang we all listened with our jaws dropped. Once Gino was asked if he was familiar with Wagner's operas. "Of course," he said, "I've heard *Lohengrin* sung by my mother."

My father didn't simply dislike music, he actively loathed it. He loathed any kind of instrument that produced music, whether a piano, an accordion, or a tambourine. Once, just after the war, I was in a restaurant with him in Rome. A woman came in begging for money. The waiter chased her off. My father became furious with the waiter, shouting, "I forbid you to chase off that poor woman! Let her be!" He then gave her some money. The waiter, offended and angry, withdrew into a corner with his napkin draped over his arm. The woman then pulled out from beneath her overcoat a guitar and began to play. My father, after a little while, exhibited signs of impatience, the same signs he would show at the dinner table at home: he fidgeted with a glass, the bread, the utensils, he slapped his napkin across his lap. The woman continued to play, leaning over him with her guitar, grateful to him for having protected her, while long melancholic moans issued forth from the guitar. Suddenly my father exploded. "Enough of this music! Get out of here! I can't stand to hear that sound!" But she continued to play and the triumphant waiter remained quietly in the corner, immobile, contemplating the scene.

Besides Silvio's suicide, there was something else in our family that always remained tinged with a vague mystery, even if it concerned people we were constantly talking about. It was the fact that Turati and Kuliscioff lived together even though they weren't married. I recognize even in this particular mystery my father's way of thinking and his prudishness because if it had been left up to my mother she probably wouldn't have given it much thought. It would have been simpler if they'd lied and told us they were husband and wife. Instead they concealed from us, or at least from me since I was still a child, the fact that they did live together. Hearing their names always mentioned together as a couple, I asked if they were husband and wife, or sister and brother, or what. I always got a confusing answer. Furthermore, I didn't understand where Andreina, my mother's childhood friend and Kuliscioff's daughter, had come from and why her surname was Costa, and I didn't understand what she had to do with Andrea Costa, who was long dead but was nevertheless often mentioned in the same breath with these people.

Turati and Kuliscioff were ever-present in my mother's reminiscences. I knew they were both still alive and living in Milan (perhaps together, perhaps in two different apartments) and that they were still involved in politics and the fight against fascism. Nevertheless, in my imagination, they had become tangled up with other figures who were also ever-present in my mother's reminiscences: her parents, Silvio, the Lunatic, Barbison. People who were either dead or, if still alive, very old and belonging to a distant time, to far-off events when my mother was a child and heard someone or another say, "It's my bitch's sister!" and "Sulfuric acid stinks of fart." These were people impossible to meet now, impossible to touch, and even if I were to meet them and touch them they were not the same as the people I imagined, and even if they were still alive, they were in any case tainted by their proximity to the dead with whom they dwelled in my soul; and they had assumed the step of the dead, light and elusive.

"Oh, poor Lidia," my mother would sigh now and again. This was how she bemoaned her troubles: the lack of money, my father's outbursts, the constant fights between Alberto and Mario, Alberto's insistence on playing soccer instead of studying, her children's sulking and Natalina's too.

I also sulked or threw tantrums. I was, however, still little and my sulking and tantrums didn't bother my mother very much at the time.

"It's itchy. It's itchy!" I'd say in the mornings when my mother was dressing me in those wool sweaters that irritated my skin.

"But these are good-quality sweaters!" my mother said. "They're from Neuberg's. You can't possibly expect me to throw them away!"

Our mother bought our sweaters "from Neuberg's"; a sweater from Neuberg's meant it was of the finest quality and couldn't possibly irritate the skin. Sweaters were bought at Neuberg's. Overcoats were made by the tailor Maccheroni. As for our winter shoes, they were my father's responsibility and he ordered them from a shoemaker named Signor Castagneri who had a shop in via Saluzzo.

I came into the dining room, still sulking over the sweater from Neuberg's. Seeing me sullen and under a dark cloud, my mother said, "Here comes Hurricane Maria!"

My mother hated the cold and this was why she bought all those sweaters from Neuberg's. She hated the cold even though she loved to take that freezing shower every morning. Still, she loathed the cold, that constant penetrating cold of winter days.

"How cold it is!" she'd repeat, putting another sweater over the one she had on and pulling the sleeves down over her hands. "How cold it is! I can't stand the cold!" And she pulled the sweater from

Neuberg's down over my hips while I tried to wiggle out of it. "All wool, Lidia!" she said, mimicking the way an old school friend used to speak to her. And then she said, "Just seeing you in that beautiful warm wool sweater cheers me up considerably."

She also, however, hated the heat. When it was hot she would begin to pant and pull at the collar of her dress. "How hot it is! I can't stand the heat!" she'd say. And my father would respond, "How intolerant you are! All of you are so intolerant!"

When she went away with my father on a trip, my mother brought with her a great quantity of sweaters and dresses made from an extensive variety of fabrics, heavy to light, and with the slightest alteration in temperature she'd change her outfit.

"I can never find just the right temperature," she'd say.

And my father would say, "How boring you are with your heat and your cold! You always find something to complain about!"

In the mornings, I never wanted to eat breakfast. I detested milk and found the *mezzorado* even more disgusting. My mother, however, knew that when I was at Frances's apartment I would drink a full glass of milk at snack time, and the same when I was at the Terni's. Actually, I drank that milk when I was at the Terni's or at Frances's with extreme repugnance; I only drank it out of obedience and timidity because I wasn't at my own home. My mother was convinced that since I liked to drink milk at Frances's, I therefore liked milk, resulting in my being given a glass of milk in the mornings, which I regularly refused to go near.

"But it's milk from Frances's home!" my mother would say. "It's Lucio's milk. It's from Lucio's cow!"

She tried to make me believe that they'd gone to get the milk from Frances's apartment, that Lucio and Frances had their own personal cow, and that the milk at their apartment wasn't bought from the milkman but was delivered every day from land they owned in Normandy, in a rural region called Gruchet.

"It's milk from Gruchet! It's Lucio's milk!" my mother would insist, but since I absolutely refused to drink it, Natalina in the end made me a broth.

I didn't go to school even though I was old enough because my father said that at school one catches germs. All of my siblings had been homeschooled by tutors for their first years of elementary school for the same reason. My mother gave me my lessons. I didn't understand arithmetic and I was incapable of learning the multiplication tables. My mother made herself hoarse trying to teach me. She would take pebbles from the garden and line them up on the table, or she'd use candies. In our family, we weren't allowed to eat sweets because my father said it would ruin our teeth. At home, there were never any chocolates or cakes or cookies because it was forbidden to eat "between meals." The only dessert we ate, and only ever at the dinner table, was a kind of pancake called *smarren* that was introduced to us by I can't remember which German cook. It seemed they were cheap to make and we ate them so often we couldn't stand them. Then there was the dessert that Natalina knew how to make called Gressoney cake, no doubt because she learned to make it when we were in the mountains at Gressoney.

My mother only bought candies in order to teach me arithmetic. But learning arithmetic by way of pebbles and candies only made me dislike the subject even more. My mother took out a subscription to a scholastic periodical called *School Rights and Responsibilities* so that she could learn modern didactic methods. I don't know what she learned regarding pedagogical systems from that journal—perhaps nothing—but she did find a poem that she liked a lot and would recite to my siblings:

> Let's all shout out to say:
> Long live the nobility
> Of a girl's respectability
> When virtue is her way.

While teaching me geography, my mother told me about all the countries my father had been to when he was young. He'd been to India, where he'd fallen ill with cholera and, I believe, yellow fever. He'd been to Germany and Holland. He was also in Spitzberg. In

Spitzberg he had gone inside a whale's cranium to look for cerebrospinal ganglia but couldn't find them. He got covered in whale blood and the clothes he brought back home with him were stained and hardened with dried blood. In our apartment, there were many photographs of my father with whales and my mother would show them to me, but I was always a little disappointed because the photographs were blurry and my father appeared only in the background as a tiny shadow. Nor could you see the whale's head or tail, just this gray and cloudy jagged hill and that was the whale.

In the spring many roses grew in our garden. How so many roses grew I don't know, given that not one of us ever dreamed of watering or pruning them. A gardener came perhaps once a year and it seemed that was sufficient.

"The roses, Lidia! The violets, Lidia!" my mother would say, mimicking her classmate while strolling in the garden.

In the spring, the Terni children would come to play in our garden with their nanny, Assunta, who wore a white smock and white lisle stockings, and she'd take off her shoes and place them next to her on the lawn. Cucco and Lullina, the Terni children, also wore white outfits and my mother put my smocks on them so they could play without getting their clothes dirty.

"Ssst, ssst! Look what Cucco is doing!" Terni would say, admiring his children while they played in the dirt. Terni also took off his shoes and jacket and laid them on the lawn while he kicked around a ball, but if he heard my father coming he put them back on immediately.

In our garden we had a cherry tree and Alberto would climb the tree and eat cherries with his friends, Lucio's brothers and Frinco, the one who leant us the books, an ominous figure in his peaked cap and wool jersey.

Lucio came in the mornings and left in the evenings. In the warm seasons he would always come over to our place because there wasn't a garden at his apartment building. Lucio was delicate and frail and was never hungry at mealtimes. He ate little, putting down his fork and sighing. "I'm tired of chewing," he'd say, speaking with the soft *r*, like everyone in his family. Lucio was a fascist and my siblings made him angry by speaking ill of Mussolini. "Let's not discuss politics," Lucio would say as soon as he saw my siblings arrive. When he was small he had big black sausage curls that hung over his forehead. Eventually they cut his hair and he wore it combed straight back, glistening with brilliantine. He was always dressed like a little man wearing tight little jackets and little bow ties. He'd learned to read at the same time I did, but I'd read a ton of books while he'd read very few because he read slowly and became tired. Still, whenever he was at our place he read too because when I was tired of playing occasionally I would fling myself down on the lawn with a book. Lucio would then go boast to my siblings that he'd read an entire book since they were always teasing him because he read so little. "Today I read two lire," he'd say proudly. "Today I read five lire," and he'd show the price of the book printed on the title page. In the evenings his nanny, Maria Buoninsegni, would come fetch him. She was a wrinkled old woman who wore a mangy fox fur around her neck. She was very devout and she took me and Lucio to church and to religious processions. She was a friend of Father Semeria's and she talked about him all the time. Once, during I can't remember which religious ceremony, she introduced me and Lucio to Father Semeria, who patted our heads and asked if we were her children. "No, they're a friend's children," Maria Buoninsegni responded.

Neither Lopez nor Terni liked the mountains and so my father sometimes went on hikes and made ascents with his friend Galeotti.

Galeotti lived with his sister and nephew in the countryside at a place called Pozzuolo. My mother once visited them there and had a great time. She spoke often of those days in Pozzuolo with the chickens and turkeys and the great meals they had. Adele Rasetti, Galeotti's sister, took many walks with my mother and told her the names of herbs, plants, and insects because everyone in that family was an entomologist and a botanist. Adele gave my mother one of her paintings of an Alpine lake and we hung it in our dining room.

In the morning, Adele got up early either to go over the accounts with the farmer, or to paint, or to roam the fields in order to "herbalize." She was small and thin with a pointy nose and often wore a straw hat.

"How good Adele is! She rises early and paints! She goes herbalizing!" my mother would say admiringly. She didn't know how to paint and she couldn't tell the difference between basil and chicory. My mother was lazy and always full of admiration for active people, and every time she saw Adele Rasetti she began to read science manuals in order to learn something about insects and botany herself, but she soon got bored and it ended there.

In the summer, Galeotti visited us in the mountains with his nephew, Adele's son, who was friends with my brother Gino. In the morning, my grandmother paced back and forth in her room anguishing over what to wear. "Why don't you wear," my mother suggested, "the gray dress with the tiny buttons?"

"No, Galeotti's already seen that one!" my grandmother said, wringing her hands with indecision.

Galeotti barely noticed my grandmother since he was always off conferring with my father about upcoming hikes and ascents. Furthermore, my grandmother, despite her worry over the fact that Galeotti might have seen her wearing "yesterday's dress," couldn't stand Galeotti, believing him to be crude and commonplace, and she was afraid he'd lead my father off some precipice.

Galeotti's nephew was called Franco Rasetti. He studied physics but he also had a mania for collecting insects and minerals, an obsession he passed on to Gino. They came back from hikes with clumps of moss in their handkerchiefs, dead beetles, and rucksacks full of crystals. At the dinner table, Franco Rasetti talked incessantly but always about physics or geology or coleoptera and while he talked he pressed up with his finger all the crumbs on the tablecloth. He had a pointy nose, a sharp chin, a spiky mustache, and his coloring was always slightly lizard-green.

"He's very intelligent," my father often said. "But he's aloof! He's very aloof!" Despite his aloofness, Franco Rasetti wrote a poem once on his way back from a hike with Gino while they were waiting in an abandoned hut for the rain to stop:

> Slow and steady falls the rain
> Over green pastures and black schists.
> Vague shapes appear and remain
> Veiled in the delicate mists.

Gino didn't write poetry and he didn't much like poetry or novels. But this poem he liked a great deal and recited it often. It was long and, unfortunately, I only remember that one stanza.

I, too, thought the poem with the black schists beautiful and was consumed with envy not to have written it myself. It was simple. Green pastures, black schists. I'd seen those things myself so many times in the mountains, but it had never occurred to me that I could do something with them. All I had done was observe them. That's what poems were then, simple and made of nothing, made of things that you observed. I looked around me with watchful eyes. I looked for things that could be like those black schists, those green pastures, and made sure that this time no one would take them away from me.

"Gino and Rasetti are good hikers!" my father would say. "They've climbed the Aiguille Noire de Peuterey! They do just fine. It's too bad that Rasetti is so aloof. He doesn't discuss politics. He's not interested. He's aloof!"

"But Adele isn't. She isn't aloof," my mother said. "She's amazing. She gets up early. She paints! How I wish I were like Adele!"

Galeotti was always cheerful. He was rather short and stout, and wore woolly gray suits. He had a trimmed white mustache, hair somewhere between white and blond, and a tanned face. All of us really loved him. But I don't remember anything else about him.

One day my mother and Terni were standing in the vestibule and my mother was crying. They were saying that Galeotti was dead.

Those words, "Galeotti is dead," have always stayed with me. In my life up until then, no one we were close to had died. From then on death was inextricably linked in my mind to that cheerful figure dressed in gray wool who came to visit us during the summer in the mountains.

Galeotti had died suddenly of pneumonia.

Many years later after penicillin was discovered my father often said, "If there'd only been penicillin in poor Galeotti's day he wouldn't have died. He died of streptococcal pneumonia. Penicillin can cure that now."

As soon as anyone died my father immediately added to his name the word "poor" and he became angry with my mother if she didn't do the same. This addition of "poor" was a long-held tradition in my father's family. My grandmother, when she spoke of her dead sister, invariably said "poor little Regina," and never referred to her in any other way.

Within an hour after his death, Galeotti had become "poor Galeotti." My grandmother was told of his death with great delicacy because she, having always had a great fear of death, was not at all pleased that death was anywhere in her vicinity and among people she knew.

After Galeotti's death, my father said he no longer got much joy out of making ascents. He still made them anyway but not with the same pleasure. He and my mother would talk about the time when Galeotti was still alive as a time of happiness and joy when they were younger and when the mountains still held some fascination for my father, a time when fascism seemed as if it would soon be a thing of the past.

"How cute, how nice Mario is!" my mother said brushing Mario's hair as soon as he had gotten out of bed, his eyes tiny, almost invisible from sleep.

"The Brot shot in the pot," Mario said with a distant smile as he stroked his jaw. It was his way of announcing that he wasn't in a sulk and would consent to chat with my mother, my sister, and me.

"How cute Mario is, how handsome!" my mother said. "He looks like Silvio! He looks like Suess Aja Cawa!"

Suess Aja Cawa was a famous movie actor at the time. Whenever my mother saw the Mongolian eyes and high cheekbones of Suess Aja Cawa on the screen, she would exclaim, "It's Mario! It's really him!"

"Don't you think Mario is handsome?" she asked my father.

"I don't think he's that handsome. Gino's better-looking," my father answered.

"Gino's handsome too," my mother said. "How appealing Gino is! My little Gino! I only like my own children. I only have a good time with my children!"

And when either Gino or Mario had on a new suit made by Maccheroni the tailor, she'd hug him and say, "Whenever one of my sons wears a new suit, I love him even more."

In our family, we had heated discussions over how ugly or good-looking someone was. A persistent topic of discussion was whether a woman named Gilda, the governess in a family we were friendly with in Palermo, was beautiful or not. My siblings maintained that she was ugly, her nose a variation on a dog's snout, but my mother said she actually possessed extraordinary beauty.

"Nonsense!" my father shouted, then laughed one of his thundering laughs that echoed throughout the apartment. "That woman is in no way beautiful!"

And we had endless discussions over whether the Colombos or the Cohens, friends we'd met in the mountains over the summer, were uglier.

"The Cohens are uglier!" my father shouted. "You want to put them in the same category as the Colombos? There's no comparison! The Colombos are better-looking! You're blind if you can't see that! You lot are blind!"

Of his various cousins called either Margherita or Regina, my father would say they were very beautiful. "As a young woman Regina," he'd begin, "was a great beauty."

And my mother would say, "But it's not so, Beppino! She had a jutting chin!"

She'd then demonstrate Regina's protruding chin by sticking out her own chin and lower lip, and my father would get angry. "You don't understand a thing about beauty and ugliness! You say that the Colombos are uglier than the Cohens!"

Gino was serious, studious, and serene. He never hit either of his brothers. He was a good mountain hiker. He was my father's favorite. My father never called him a "jackass." He did say, however, that Gino "didn't lend his gear." Lending an ear in our family was called "lending gear." Gino, in fact, didn't lend much gear because he was always reading and when anyone spoke to him he responded in monosyllables without lifting his eyes from his book. If Alberto and Mario were fighting, he didn't move a muscle but continued to read and my mother would have to call out to him and shake him in order to get him to break them up. While he read he ate bread very slowly, nibbling away at one roll after another. He would ingest almost a kilo of bread after lunch.

"Gino," my father yelled, "you don't lend your gear! You never tell us anything, and don't eat so much bread or you'll get indigestion!"

In fact, Gino often had indigestion: he became red in the face, sullen, and his protruding ears turned fiery red.

"Why does Gino look like that?" my father asked my mother, waking her up in the middle of the night. "Why does he have that pout? Why does he have that moon face? Do you think he's in some kind of trouble?"

My father never could tell by the look on his children's faces if they were suffering from indigestion. He never recognized indigestion when he saw it, suspecting instead mysterious troubles with women, with coquettes as he would call them.

Since Gino seemed to be the most serious, well-mannered, and presentable of his children, my father would take Gino to the Lopezes in the evening sometimes. But Gino had the unfortunate habit of falling asleep after he ate and he also fell asleep at the Lopezes in an armchair while Frances was talking to him. His eyes became small, his head gently nodded, and after a little while he was asleep with his hands on his lap and the trace of a blissful smile on his lips.

"Gino!" shouted my father. "Don't fall asleep! You're falling asleep!"

"You lot," my father would say, "I can't take you anywhere."

On one side there was Gino and Rasetti, the mountains, the "black schists," the crystals, the insects; on the other was Mario, my sister Paola, and the Ternis who detested the mountains and loved stuffy rooms with the windows closed, dimmed lights, and cafés. This latter group loved the paintings of Casorati, the theater of Pirandello, the poetry of Verlaine, Gallimard editions, Proust. They were two incommunicable worlds.

I didn't know yet which side I would choose. They both attracted me. I hadn't yet decided if, in my life, I wanted to study beetles, chemistry, or botany, or if, instead, I would paint pictures or write novels. In Rasetti's and Gino's world everything was clear, everything would unfold beneath the light of the sun, everything was plausible and without mysteries or secrets. The discussions, on the other hand, that Terni, Paola, and Mario had while sitting on the couch in the living room were tinged with mystery and obscurity, arousing in me a combination of fear and fascination.

"What does Terni have to tittle-tattle about with Mario and Paola?" my father asked my mother. "They're always tattling in the corner. What is all this taradiddling?"

"Taradiddling," for my father, meant passing secrets, and he couldn't stand to see people off in a corner talking without his knowing what they were saying.

"They must be talking about Proust," my mother told him.

My mother had read Proust and she, like Terni and Paola, loved his work enormously, and told my father that this Proust was very fond of his mother and his grandmother and had asthma and couldn't sleep and because noise bothered him, he had covered the walls of his room with corkboard.

My father said, "He must have been a jackass!"

My mother hadn't chosen either one of those two worlds but lived a little in one and a little in the other, residing happily in each because her curiosity never let her reject anything but rather fed on all manner of food or drink. Instead, my father looked upon all new and unfamiliar things with menace and suspicion, and feared that the books Terni brought into our apartment weren't "suited."

"Is that suited for Paola?" he asked my mother, leafing through *À la recherche* and reading a phrase here and there. "It must be very boring stuff," he said tossing the book away, to some extent appeased by the fact that it was "boring stuff."

Terni brought us reproductions of Casorati's paintings and my father couldn't stand them. "Dribbledrabs! Doodledums!" he'd say. Painting of any kind didn't interest him in the slightest. He went to art museums with my mother when they were traveling. He would grant old masters like Goya or Titian some legitimacy since they had become universally recognized and exalted. He desired those museum visits to be extremely brief, however, and he didn't let my mother pause in front of the paintings.

"Lidia, come on, let's go!" he said, dragging her away.

When traveling he was always in a great hurry.

My mother also, however, didn't have much interest in painting but she knew Casorati personally and thought him charming. "What a handsome face Casorati has," she often said. Since she thought his face handsome, she also approved of his paintings.

"I've just been to Casorati's studio," my sister said on arriving home.

"How charming Casorati is! What a handsome face!" my mother would say.

"Why the hell is Paola going to Casorati's studio?" my father asked, frowning suspiciously. My father was always afraid that we would get ourselves into "trouble," meaning we would find ourselves entangled in some nefarious love intrigue, and he perceived threats to our chastity everywhere.

"It was nothing. She went with Terni. They went to say hello to Nella Marchesini," my mother explained.

The mere mention of Nella Marchesini's name reassured my father. She was my sister's childhood friend and my father knew her well and respected her. Nella Marchesini studied painting with Casorati and my father accepted her presence at his studio as legitimate. Terni's companionship, on the other hand, would never have reassured him because my father didn't consider him to be a reliable chaperone for us.

"What a lot of time that Terni wastes," he observed. "He'd be better off finishing his work on tissue pathology. I've been hearing about it for a year."

"You do know that Casorati is an antifascist," my mother said.

Over time antifascists were becoming increasingly rare and whenever my father heard of one he was immediately cheered up.

"Ah, he's an antifascist. Is that so?" he said with interest. "But his paintings are such great doodledums! How can anyone possibly like them!"

Terni was very good friends with Petrolini and when Petrolini came to Turin for a series of performances, almost every evening Terni had complimentary seats in the orchestra, which he gave to my mother and siblings.

"How wonderful!" my mother would say during the day. "Tonight we're going to see Petrolini again! And we'll be sitting in the orchestra. How I love to go to the theater and sit in the orchestra. Petrolini is so charming and so witty! Silvio would have liked him a great deal too!"

"Ah, so you're leaving me all on my own again tonight," my father would say.

"Why don't you come too, Beppino?" my mother would say.

"No way," my father yelled. "Imagine me coming to see Petrolini! I couldn't care less about Petrolini! He's a clown!"

"We went with Terni to say hello to Petrolini in his dressing room," my mother said to my father the following day. "Mary came too. They're very good friends with Petrolini."

In my father's estimation, Mary, Terni's wife, was a reliable chaperone and he found her presence reassuring because he harbored for her the highest possible admiration and respect. Mary's presence gave a legitimacy and decorum to those evenings at the theater and maybe even a little to Petrolini himself. Still, my father continued to scorn Petrolini imagining that in order to perform one was required to wear a false nose and bleach one's hair.

"I don't understand why Mary is such good friends with Petrolini," he would say with profound astonishment. "I don't understand why she likes to go see Petrolini so much! I understand why Terni and the rest of you like him because you lot love nitwitteries! How is it that they are such good friends with Petrolini? There must be something shady about him!"

For my father, an actor, and especially a comedian who made funny faces onstage in order to get the audience to laugh, was undoubtedly "a shady character." My mother reminded him, however, that his brother Cesare had lived his life in the company of actors and had married an actress. All those people his brother hung around couldn't have been "shady characters" even if they wore costumes onstage or dyed their hair or mustaches.

"And Molière?" my mother said. "Molière, wasn't he also an actor? You're not going to tell me that he too was a shady character!"

"Ah Molière!" my father said. He had the greatest respect for Molière. "Molière is fabulous! Poor Cesare had a passion for Molière! But you couldn't possibly be placing Molière and Petrolini on equal footing, could you?" he shouted, then laughed one of those thundering laughs of his, heaping on Petrolini his most intense scorn.

Usually it was my mother, Paola, and Mario who went to the theater, and they frequently went with the Ternis who, if they didn't have complimentary orchestra seats as they did for Petrolini, had box seats. They were always the Ternis' guests so my father wasn't able to say, "I don't want you throwing money away on the theater," and instead looked benevolently upon my mother's evening out with Mary.

Nevertheless, my father would say to my mother, "You're always going out and having a good time and leaving me behind."

"But every evening you keep yourself closed up in your study," my mother said. "You don't pay any attention to me. You don't keep me company."

"What a jackass!" my father said. "You know I'm very busy. I don't have time to waste with all of you. And besides, I didn't marry you to keep you company!"

In the evenings my father worked in his study. He corrected the proofs for his books and pasted in illustrations. Sometimes, though, he read novels.

"Is that novel good, Beppino?" my mother would ask.

"Hardly. It's a bore. A nitwittery," my father responded with a shrug.

He read, however, with rapt attention while smoking his pipe and brushing the ashes from the page. When he returned from a trip he always brought home with him a few crime novels that he'd bought at the station bookstalls and would finish reading them in his study in the evening. They were often in English or German, perhaps because it seemed to him less frivolous to read that sort of novel in a foreign language.

"A nitwittery," he said, shrugging his shoulders, and he'd continue reading until he'd read the very last line.

Later, when Simenon's novels began to appear my father became his devoted reader. "He's really not bad, Simenon," he'd say. "He describes that French province really well. He really describes French provincial life very well!"

But during the era of via Pastrengo, Simenon's novels didn't yet exist. The books my father brought home from his trips were small editions with glossy covers showing female characters with their throats slit. My mother, finding them in the pocket of his coat, said, "Will you look at what nitwitteries our Beppino reads!"

Under Terni's influence, an alliance had developed between Paola and Mario that persisted even when Terni wasn't around. As far as I could tell, it was an alliance founded on their worship of melancholy.

Together or separately, in meditative solitude Paola and Mario took melancholic walks at dusk. They read sad poetry to each other, reciting poems aloud in sorrowful whispers.

As I remember, Terni wasn't at all prone to such melancholy. He wasn't especially attracted to silent, abandoned places, nor did he ever take solitary, melancholic walks. Terni lived in a perfectly normal manner at home with his wife, Mary; the nanny, Assunta; and his children, Cucco and Lullina, whom he and his wife spoiled, becoming ecstatic at the mere sight of them. But Terni had introduced into our family a taste for melancholy and melancholic moods just as he had brought us *La Nouvelle Revue française* and the Casorati reproductions. Paola and Mario had welcomed his influence, but not Gino, whom Terni didn't like, Gino disliking Terni just as much. Neither did Alberto, who cared nothing for poetry or painting, having never written another line of verse after "The old maid / With no titties." Playing soccer had become his sole interest. And neither did I because Terni was nothing more to me than the father of Cucco, a friend I played with now and again.

Lost in their melancholy, Paola and Mario exuded a profound intolerance for my father's despotism and for our family's simple and austere habits. It seemed they felt themselves exiles in our family, dreaming of an entirely different homelife and lifestyle. Their intolerance manifested itself in great pouts and moon faces, listless looks and impenetrable expressions, monosyllabic responses, angrily slammed doors that shook the building, and curt refusals to go to the mountains on Saturday and Sunday. As soon as my father left the room, they immediately cheered up because their intolerance was reserved exclusively for him and not for my mother. They listened to her stories and together they recited aloud the poem about the flood: "For many days everyone trembled where they stood!"

Mario wanted to study law but my father had forced him to enroll in business economics, believing—I don't know why—that the law department was not very serious and a law degree wouldn't lead to a secure future. Mario held a silent grudge against him for years. As for Paola, she was generally unhappy with her life and wanted very much to own more clothes. Those she did own she disliked, having deemed them masculine and unflattering. My father insisted our clothes were made by Maccheroni, a man's tailor, who was inexpensive, or at least so my father thought. Sometimes my mother would resort to her seamstress, Alice, but claimed she wasn't any good.

"How I would like a beautiful silk dress!" my sister said to my mother when they were chatting in the living room.

"Me too," my mother said, flipping through the pages of fashion magazines. "I would like a beautiful princess-line dress made of pure silk!"

And my sister said, "Me too!"

But they could never afford to buy pure silk and, in any case, the seamstress Alice would have ruined the fabric as soon as she took her scissors to it.

Paola wanted to cut her hair and to wear high heels instead of those sturdy masculine shoes made by "Signor Castagneri." She wanted to go dancing at her girlfriends' homes and to play tennis. She wasn't allowed to do any of these things. Furthermore, she was practically forced to go to the mountains with Gino and my father on Saturday and Sunday. Paola thought Gino was boring, Rasetti boring, Gino's friends in general all very boring, and the mountains unbearable. Nevertheless, she skied very well, without particular style, they said, but with great courage and determination, attacking the slopes with the vehemence of a lioness. Based on the vehemence and zeal with which she attacked the slopes, I presume she did like to ski and took the utmost pleasure in it despite the fact that she insisted she had the most profound contempt for the mountains, claiming she loathed the spiked shoes, the thick woolen socks, and the little freckles the sun caused to appear on her delicate nose. When she returned from the mountains, in order to make those little freckles disappear she would cover her face with white powder. She wished she'd had a fragile constitution, delicate health, and a lunar complexion like the women in Casorati's paintings. She became terribly irritated whenever she was told she looked "fresh as a rose." When my father saw her white face, having no idea that she'd covered herself in powder, he said she was anemic and made her take iron pills.

Waking in the middle of the night, my father said to my mother, "What moon faces Mario and Paola have. Those two have become thick as thieves. I'm sure that nitwit Terni has turned them against me."

I never did know what it was Terni, Paola, and Mario whispered about to one another on the couch in the living room, but sometimes they spoke of Proust, and then my mother would join their conversations. "*La petite phrase!*" she'd say. "How wonderful it is when he discusses the *petite phrase*! How much Silvio would have liked it too!" Terni would remove his monocle and polish it with his handkerchief in the manner of Swann, while making the sound "Ssst! Ssst!"

"What a great book! What beautiful writing!" Terni would often say, and Paola and my mother would mock him by repeating his words throughout the remainder of the day.

"Nonsense!" my father said, whenever he overheard them as he passed by. "I'm sick of your nonsense!" he repeated, heading for his study, and once he'd arrived there he yelled, "Terni! You still haven't finished your work on tissue pathology! You waste all of your time on nitwitteries! You're lazy and don't work enough. You're a great slouch!"

Paola was in love with one of her university classmates. He was young, small, delicate, courteous, and had a mellifluous voice. They took walks together along the Po and in the Parco del Valentino. He was a passionate Proustian, so they spoke often about Proust, and he, in fact, would be the first to write about Proust in Italy. Debenedetti wrote short stories and literary criticism. I think Paola was in love with him because he was the exact opposite of my father: He was very small and very courteous with a sweet and mellifluous voice, didn't know a thing about tissue pathology, and had never set a foot on a ski slope. When my father learned of their walks he became furious: First, because any daughter of his should not be going on walks with men; and second, because for him a literary man, a critic, a writer, represented the contemptible, the frivolous, even the louche. It was a world he loathed. The walks were banned, but despite the prohibition Paola continued to go on them. Sometimes the Lopezes or other friends of my parents ran into them and, knowing about the ban, told my father they'd seen her. As for Terni, if he ran into her, he certainly never said anything about it to my father because Paola had confided in him on the couch in secret whispers.

My father yelled at my mother, "Don't let her go out! Forbid her to leave!"

My mother wasn't very happy about those walks either, and she, too, was suspicious of the young man because my father had imbued her with his vague and murky repulsion for the world of letters, a world unknown in our family because only biologists, scientists, or engineers ever came over. Furthermore, my mother was very close to Paola and before she started seeing her young man, the two of them used to go out and roam the city for hours looking in shopwindows at the "dresses made of pure silk" that neither one of them could buy. Paola was now rarely free to go out with my mother. Whenever they did go out arm in arm, chatting away, they inevitably ended up talking about the young man and returning home furious with each other because my mother, though she hardly knew him, wasn't as kind or welcoming towards him as Paola would have liked. My mother was totally incapable of forbidding anyone anything.

"You have no authority!" my father yelled, waking her up in the middle of the night.

In this matter, however, he'd shown he didn't have much authority either because Paola continued to take walks with her small young man for years. She stopped only when the relationship ended of its own accord; slowly, as a candle burns out, and not because my father wanted it to, but for reasons entirely beyond his shouts and bans.

My father's rages erupted not only over Paola and her small young man but also over Alberto's studies. Instead of doing his homework, Alberto was always playing soccer, and as far as my father was concerned only mountain sports qualified as legitimate sports. He considered all others, such as tennis, to be frivolous and insignificant or, as in the case of swimming, boring and stupid, especially since he hated the sea, beaches, and sand. As for soccer, he regarded it as a game played by street urchins and wouldn't even call it a sport. Gino was a good student, as was Mario. Paola didn't study but my father didn't care. She was a girl and he believed it hardly mattered if girls didn't study because eventually they would get married. In my case, he had no idea that I had trouble learning arithmetic; only my mother despaired since she was the one teaching it to me. Alberto didn't study at all and my father, who was used to the success of his other sons, was seized by a frightful rage every time Alberto brought home a bad report card or was suspended from school for bad behavior. My father was concerned for the future of all his sons and waking up in the middle of the night, he would say to my mother, "What will become of Gino? What will become of Mario?" As for Alberto, who was still in middle school, my father wasn't so much concerned as panic-stricken. "Alberto is a thug! What a delinquent he is!" He didn't even say "what a jackass Alberto is" because Alberto was far worse than a jackass and his faults seemed to my father to be unprecedented and monstrous. Alberto spent his days on the soccer fields, returning home covered in dirt and occasionally with a bloody or bandaged head or knees. Otherwise, he roamed around with his friends and was always late coming home for lunch. My father sat down at the table and began to bang his glass, his fork, the bread, and we didn't know if he was angry at Mussolini or Alberto who hadn't yet returned home. "Thug! Delinquent!" he said, while Natalina came into the room with the soup. As the meal progressed so did his fury. By the time we were having our fruit, Alberto arrived fresh-faced, flushed, and smiling. Alberto was never moonish, always happy. "Thug!" my father thundered. "Where have you been?"

"At school," Alberto said coolly, "and then I walked my friend home a ways."

"Your friend! You're nothing but a thug! It's past the toll!" One o'clock was for my father "the toll," and the fact that Alberto came home "past the toll" was an outrage.

My mother also complained about Alberto. "He's always filthy!" she said. "He goes around looking like a hooligan! He's always asking me for money! He never studies!"

"I'm going for a minute over to my friend Pajetta's place." "I'm going for a minute over to my friend Pestelli's." "Mother, could you lend me two lire?" Whenever he was home, these were the things Alberto said and not much else. It wasn't because he was uncommunicative. He was, in fact, the most communicative among us, expansive and cheerful. It was just that he was almost never home.

"Always with Pajetta! With Pajetta! With Pajetta!" my mother said, pronouncing that name with a special furious rapidity, perhaps in order to indicate the rapidity with which Alberto fled our apartment. Two lire was a small sum even then, but Alberto asked for two lire many times during the course of the day. My mother, sighing, opened the drawer in her bedside table with a key. Alberto never had enough money. He got into the habit of selling books from the apartment and slowly our shelves began to empty. Every so often my father wouldn't be able to find a book and, so that he wouldn't get angry, my mother told him that she had leant it to Frances, but she well knew that the book had in fact wound up at some used-book stall. Alberto also sometimes took a piece of the family silver to the pawnbroker and my mother, not finding a coffeepot, would begin to cry.

"Listen to what Alberto's done!" she said to Paola. "Listen to what he's done to me. I can't tell your father. If I do, he'll scream his head off!"

She had such a terror of my father's anger that she searched in Alberto's drawers for the pawnbroker's receipt and sent Rina to buy back her coffeepot in secret without telling my father.

Alberto was no longer friends with Frinco, who disappeared into the mists of time along with his leather-bound books of horror stories, and he wasn't friends anymore with Frances's children either. Alberto's friends at the time, his schoolmates Pajetta and Pestelli, were, in fact, studious. My mother always said that Alberto chose friends who were better than he was.

"Pestelli," my mother explained to my father, "is an exceptional boy. He comes from a very good family. His father is the Pestelli who writes for *La Stampa*. His mother is Carola Prosperi," she said admiringly, trying to present Alberto in a positive light to my father. Carola Prosperi was a writer whom my mother liked. She was convinced Carola Prosperi couldn't possibly belong to the treacherous literary world since she also wrote children's books. Furthermore, her novels for adults were, my mother always claimed, "very well written." My father, having never read Carola Prosperi's books, shrugged.

As for Pajetta, while still a boy in short pants at middle school, he was arrested for distributing antifascist pamphlets in the classrooms. Alberto, one of his closest friends, was summoned to the police station and interrogated. Pajetta was sent to a reformatory for minors, and my mother, admiringly, said to my father, "You see I always said so, Beppino. You see, Alberto has always chosen his friends well. They are inevitably more impressive and more serious than he is."

My father shrugged. He too, however, admired the fact that Alberto had been interrogated at the police station and for a few days refrained from calling him a thug.

"A hooligan!" my mother said, when Alberto came home after playing soccer, dirty, his blond hair soaked in mud, his clothes ripped. "A hooligan!"

"He smokes and drops his ashes on the floor!" she complained to her friends. "He lies on the bed without taking his shoes off and soils the bedcover! He asks for money and whatever I give him is never enough! He was so adorable when he was little!" she lamented. "He was so sweet and gentle! A lamb! I dressed him all in lace and he had those beautiful curls! Now look what's become of him!"

Alberto's and Mario's friends made only rare appearances at our home. Gino, instead, was always having friends over in the evening. My father would ask them to stay to dinner. He was always inviting people to lunch or dinner even if there wasn't enough food to go around. On the other hand, he was always afraid that we would "scrounge lunches" at other people's homes. "You scrounged a lunch off Frances! I don't like it!" And if one of us was invited over to someone else's home for a meal, and complained the next day that this person was annoying or disagreeable, my father would immediately protest: "Disagreeable! But you scrounged a lunch off him!"

Our dinners usually consisted of broth made from Liebig's beef-stock cubes, which my mother adored but Natalina always made too watery, followed by an omelet. Gino's friends shared these monotonous dinners with us while listening, as they sat around the table, to my mother's stories and songs. One of these friends was named Adriano Olivetti, and I remember the first time he came over to our apartment he was wearing a soldier's uniform because he was doing his military service then. Gino was also doing his military service and he and Adriano shared the same dormitory. At the time, Adriano had an unkempt and curly ginger-colored beard and tawny-blond hair that curled up at the nape of his neck. He was fat and pale and his uniform fit badly over his round, fat shoulders. I've never seen anyone wear that gray-green outfit with a pistol at the waist more awkwardly and less martially than him. He had a pronounced melancholic air about him, which was perhaps because he didn't like being a soldier in the least. He was shy and quiet, but when he did speak he talked for a long time in a low voice and said confusing and enigmatic things while staring off into space with his small blue eyes, at once cold and dreamy. Adriano seemed the embodiment of what my father defined as a "lummox" and yet my father never called him a lummox, or a dolt, or a negro, never aimed in his direction any of these words. In wondering why, I suppose my father may have had a deeper psychological understanding than any of us suspected and was able to see in the guise of that clumsy boy the man who Adriano would later become. But my father also may have refrained from calling him a lummox because he was aware that Adriano liked to go to the mountains and because Gino had told my father that Adriano was an antifascist and that Adriano's father was a socialist and also a friend of Turati's.

The Olivettis had a factory that made typewriters in Ivrea. Until then, we'd never known any industrialists. The only industrialist ever mentioned in our family was Lopez's brother Mauro who lived in Argentina and was very rich. My father had plans to send Gino to work for Mauro's company. The Olivettis were the first industrialists that we saw up close and I was impressed by the idea that those advertisement posters I saw on the street depicting a typewriter on railroad tracks speeding past a locomotive, sheets of paper flying from its carriage, were directly linked to the Adriano in the gray-green uniform who shared our bland broths in the evenings.

When his military service was finished, Adriano continued to come to our apartment in the evenings. He became ever-more melancholy, shy, and quiet because he was in love with my sister, Paola, who barely noticed him then. Adriano had an automobile. He was the only person we knew who had an automobile. Even Terni, who was so rich, didn't have one. Whenever my father had to go out, Adriano immediately offered to accompany him in his automobile and my father became furious since he couldn't stand automobiles and also because he couldn't tolerate, as he often reminded us, acts of kindness.

Adriano had many brothers and sisters, all of them with freckles and red hair, which might explain why my father, who also had freckles and red hair, felt such an affinity for them. It was well known that they were very rich but they nevertheless lived simply, dressed modestly, and brought old skis with them to the mountains just as we did. They did have, however, a lot of automobiles and they were always offering rides to this place or that. Whenever they were driving in the city and saw someone old walking with a tired gait, they would stop and ask if the person would like a lift. My mother was constantly saying how good and nice they were.

Eventually we also met their father, who was a short, fat man with a white beard. Beneath that beard was a handsome face of fine and noble features lit up by blue eyes. While speaking, he would either play with his beard or with the buttons on his vest. He had a high-pitched voice, whiny and childish, almost a falsetto. Perhaps because of his white beard my father always called him "old Olivetti" even though he and my father were more or less the same age. They had socialism and their friendship with Turati in common, and they regarded each other with mutual esteem and respect. Nevertheless, whenever they met they both wanted to speak at the same time and so they shouted—one short and one tall, one with his falsetto voice and the other with his thunderous voice. Olivetti's conversation was sprinkled with references to the Bible, psychoanalysis, and the sayings of the prophets, things that weren't remotely a part of my father's world and about which he hadn't formed any particular or profound opinion. My father felt that old Olivetti was very intelligent but that his ideas were in a great muddle.

The Olivettis lived in Ivrea in a house called the Cloister because in the past it had been a friars' cloister. It had woods and vineyards, cows, and a stable. Every day they used cream from their cows to make cakes. Ever since our father wouldn't allow us to stop and eat cream in the mountain chalets, we had developed a keen desire for it. We hadn't been allowed to eat cream because my father was afraid of Malta fever. Since the Olivettis owned their own cows there was no risk of Malta fever, so whenever we visited them we gorged ourselves on cream.

Still, my father told us, "You mustn't always be getting yourselves invited to the Olivettis'! You mustn't scrounge!"

We subsequently became obsessed with not appearing to scrounge. Once when Gino and Paola had been invited to spend the day in Ivrea, despite the Olivettis' insistence they refused to stay to dinner or to accept a ride home in their automobile and instead had to wait for the train in the dark and on empty stomachs. Another time, I took a trip in the car with the Olivettis and we stopped for lunch in a restaurant. While they all ordered tagliatelle and steaks, I ordered a soft-boiled egg and later told my sister that I'd ordered just the egg "because I didn't want Mr. Olivetti to spend too much." The old engineer heard about this and was very amused and would frequently laugh about it, and ringing in his laughter was all the joy of being very rich, knowing he was very rich, and discovering that there was still someone who didn't know he was very rich.

When Gino finished at the Polytechnic, two choices were available to him: either he could go work with Mauro, the one with the company in Argentina whom, imitating the Lopez children, we familiarly called "Uncle Mauro" and with whom my father had been carrying on a diligent correspondence for months regarding Gino's future; or he could work at the Olivetti factory in Ivrea. Gino chose the latter option.

So Gino left our home and went to live in Ivrea. A few months later he announced to my father that he'd met a girl there and had become engaged to marry her. My father was seized by a terrifying fury. Whenever one of us announced to him that we planned to get married, he was seized by a terrifying fury, no matter who the chosen person might be. He always found some pretext for his wrath. Either he questioned our chosen one's health or claimed the person had too little or too much money. My father forbade us to marry every time, but to no avail since we married all the same.

Gino was sent to Germany to study German and to forget. My mother urged him to go see Signora Grassi in Freiburg. Signora Grassi was my mother's childhood friend, the one who said, "All wool, Lidia! The violets, Lidia!" In Florence, Signora Grassi had met a bookseller from Freiburg and married him. He read Heine to her and she taught him to love violets, and she had also taught him to love "all wool" fabric, having brought some with her to Germany after the First World War when pure wool was not to be found.

Returning to Freiburg after the war, the bookseller had exclaimed, "I don't recognize my Germany anymore!"

It was a saying that remained famous in our family and every time my mother didn't recognize someone or something she would repeat it.

That summer my father kept up a considerable correspondence

with Gino in Germany, and with the Lopezes, the Ternis, and Signor Olivetti, mostly regarding Gino's marriage. To the Ternis, the Lopezes, and Signor Olivetti my father wrote that they should do all they could to dissuade Gino from getting married at twenty-five, his career hardly begun.

"I wonder if he's gone to see Signora Grassi," my mother would say that summer whenever she thought of Gino, and my father would become furious.

"Signora Grassi! I couldn't care less if he's seen Signora Grassi! You'd think all Germany had to offer was Signora Grassi! I will not let Gino get married under any circumstances whatsoever!"

Gino, however, did get married as soon as he returned from Germany just as he had said he would. My father and my mother went to the wedding. But my father, waking in the middle of the night, would say, "If only I'd sent him to Mauro in Argentina instead of to Ivrea! Who knows, perhaps in Argentina he wouldn't have married!"

We moved and my mother who had always complained about the apartment on via Pastrengo now complained about the new one. The new apartment was on via Pallamaglio.

"What an ugly name!" my mother would say. "What an ugly street! I can't abide these streets—via Campana, via Saluzzo! At least on via Pastrengo we had a garden!"

The new apartment was on the top floor overlooking a square where there was a big ugly church, a paint factory, and public baths. Nothing seemed more squalid to my mother than looking out her window and seeing men with a towel under their arms on their way to the public baths. My father had actually bought the apartment because he said it had cost little and, though unattractive, had some advantages: it was big, had many rooms, and was very near to the train station.

My mother said, "What does it matter if we're near the station? We never go anywhere."

Something must have improved in our economic situation because money receded as a topic of conversation. To listen to my father, the property share prices continued to go down and by this point I thought they must have been swallowed into the depths of the earth. Nevertheless, my mother and my sister increased the number of outfits they had made for them. We now had a telephone like the Lopezes. The phrases "high cost of living" and "rising food prices" were never mentioned anymore. Gino lived with his wife in Ivrea. Mario had a job in Genoa and only came home on Saturdays.

After much discussion and indecision, Alberto had been sent away to boarding school. My father had hoped he would take this severe punishment badly, repent, and change his ways. My mother, however, said, "You'll see how much you'll love it! You'll see how much fun you'll have! You'll see how much you'll love boarding school. I loved my boarding school and had so much fun there!"

Alberto went to boarding school very happily, as he did everything. When he came home for holidays he would tell us how at his school while they were sitting at the table eating an omelet, suddenly a bell would ring and the headmaster would come into the dining hall and say, "I am here to inform you that one does not cut an omelet with a knife." The bell then rang again and the headmaster disappeared.

My father no longer went skiing, though he continued to use the English spelling of the word. He said he was too old. My mother, who didn't ski and stayed at home, had always said, "Abominable mountains!" But now she regretted that my father didn't ski anymore.

Anna Kuliscioff died. My mother hadn't seen her for many years, but she'd been happy to know she was still around. She went to Milan to attend the funeral with her friend Paola Carrara who, as a young women, had often gone to Kuliscioff's place as well. My mother brought back a black-bordered book containing homages to Kuliscioff along with pictures of her.

After many years, my mother had the opportunity to visit Milan once again, but no one she knew lived there anymore and her relatives were all dead by then. She found the city greatly changed for the worse, even ugly. She said, "I don't recognize my Germany anymore!"

The Ternis had to leave Turin and went to live in Florence. Mary left first with the children. Terni stayed on for a few months. "What a shame you're leaving Turin!" my mother said to Terni. "What a shame Mary has left! And I won't see the children anymore. Do you remember the garden at via Pastrengo when you played ball with Cucco? And Gino's friends came over and they played Steps? It was wonderful!" Steps was a game in which one person stood facing the trunk of a tree and would turn around suddenly. The others had to take steps towards him only when he wasn't looking or they were out of the game.

"I don't like this apartment!" my mother said. "I don't like via Pallamaglio! I liked having a garden!"

But her melancholic mood quickly passed. She got up in the mornings singing and went to order the day's groceries. She then got on the number seven tram and rode it to the end of the line and back again without ever getting off.

"How nice it is to ride the tram!" she'd say. "It's much nicer than riding in an automobile!"

"Why don't you come too?" she said to me in the morning. "Let's go to Pozzo Strada!"

Pozzo Strada was the terminus for the number seven tram where there was an open space with an ice-cream kiosk, a few apartment houses on the city's periphery, and, in the distance, wheat and poppy fields.

In the afternoon she read the newspaper while lying on the couch. She said to me, "If you're good I'll take you to the cinema. Let's see if there's a film 'suited' for you." It was she who wanted to go to the cinema, however, and, in fact, she went anyway, either alone or with her girlfriends, even if I had schoolwork to do. She rushed home afterwards because my father came back from the laboratory at half past seven and she wanted him to find her at home when he returned. If she wasn't at home he would wait for her on the balcony until she came back out of breath and holding her hat.

"Where the hell have you been?" my father shouted. "I've been worried. I bet you've been to the cinema again today! You spend your life at the cinema!"

"Have you written to Mary?" he asked her. Now that Mary had

gone to live in Florence letters from her periodically arrived at the apartment and my mother never remembered to write back. She loved Mary very much but she never liked to write letters. She didn't even write to her children.

"Have you written to Gino?" my father yelled at her. "Write to Gino! Shame on you if you don't write to Gino!"

I came down with something and was ill for most of the winter. I had an ear infection and then a sinus infection. For the first few days I was ill, my father took care of me.

In his study he had a small cabinet he called "the pharmacy" where he kept a few medicines and instruments he used to treat his children, or friends, or his friends' children. These included tincture of iodine for cuts and scrapes, methylene blue for sore throats, a *bir* for whitlows and felons. A *bir* was a rubber tourniquet that was tied tightly around the afflicted finger until it turned a turquoise color. The *bir*, however, was always missing from the "pharmacy" whenever it was needed and my father would shout throughout the apartment, "Where is the *bir*! Where have you put the *bir*!"

He'd say, "What slobs you lot are! I've never seen anyone as slobbish as you are!"

Usually the *bir* was found in his desk drawer.

He would, on the other hand, get angry if anyone asked him for health advice. He would take offense and say, "I'm not a doctor!"

He wanted to treat people but only on the condition that they didn't ask to be treated.

One day at lunch he said, "That nitwit Terni has the flu. He's in bed. Damn. I'm sure it's nothing, but I'll have to pay him a visit."

"How Terni exaggerates!" he said that evening. "He's fine. He's in bed wearing a woolen vest. I never wear woolen vests!"

"I'm worried about Terni," he said a few days later. "His fever won't go away. I'm afraid he has a pleural effusion. I want Stroppeni to examine him."

"He has a pleural effusion!" he shouted out one evening as he searched every room in the apartment for my mother. "Lidia, what do you know, Terni has a pleural effusion!"

He had brought Stroppeni and all the doctors he knew to Terni's bedside.

"Don't smoke!" he yelled at Terni who was by then on the mend and getting a bit of sun on the balcony at his apartment. "Listen, you mustn't smoke! You smoke too much, you've always smoked too much! You've ruined your health by smoking like a fiend!"

My father himself smoked like a Turk, but he didn't want others to smoke.

During the time his friends or his children were ill my father became very mild-mannered and kind, but as soon as they were well again he resumed his bullying.

My illness was serious and my father stopped treating me immediately, calling in all of his trusted doctors. In the end, I was taken to the hospital.

So that I wouldn't be frightened, my mother tried to convince me that the hospital was the doctor's home and that the other patients were his children, or cousins, nieces, and nephews. Out of obedience I believed her, but at the same time I knew that it was a hospital, and on that occasion as on many others in the future, truth and lies became all mixed up for me.

"Your legs are skinnier than Lucio's," my mother said. "Now Frances will be happy!"

Frances, in fact, used to compare my legs to Lucio's and fret over how thin and pale his legs looked in his white socks held up by black velvet garters.

One evening, I heard my mother talking with someone in the front hall and then heard her open the linen closet. Shadows flitted across my glass-paneled door. During the night, I heard coughing in the room next to mine, the room Mario slept in when he came home on Saturdays, but it couldn't have been Mario because it wasn't Saturday, and it sounded like the cough of an old, fat man. When my mother came into my room the following morning she told me that a man called Signor Paolo Ferrari had slept in the next room and that he was old, tired, sick, had a cough, and I was not to ask him too many questions.

Signor Paolo Ferrari was in the dining room drinking tea and when I saw him I immediately recognized Turati who had once come to visit us while we were living on via Pastrengo. But since they told me his name was Paolo Ferrari, I obediently believed he was both Ferrari and Turati; once again truth and lies were mixed up for me.

Ferrari was old and big as a bear with a trimmed gray beard; his shirt collar was very wide and he knotted his tie as if it were a piece of string. His small white hands were leafing through a volume, bound in red, of Carducci's poetry when suddenly he did something odd. He picked up the book made in Kuliscioff's memory and wrote a long dedication in it to my mother, then signed it "Anna and Filippo." I was more confused than ever; I didn't understand how he could be Anna, not to mention Filippo, if he was, as they said, Paolo Ferrari.

My mother and father seemed very happy he was staying with us; my father didn't fly into his rages and we all spoke in lowered voices. Whenever the doorbell rang, Paolo Ferrari rushed down the hall and closed himself into a room at the back of the apartment. It was usually either Lucio or the milkman at the door because during that period people we didn't know rarely came to our apartment. Signor Paolo Ferrari rushed down the hall as best he could on his tiptoes, his great bear shadow traveling along the walls.

Paola said to me, "His name isn't Ferrari; it's Turati. He has to flee Italy. He's in hiding. Don't tell anyone, not even Lucio."

I swore not to say anything to anyone, not even to Lucio, but whenever he came over to play I had the overwhelming desire to tell him. Lucio, however, wasn't even mildly curious. Whenever I asked him about things going on at his home, he inevitably told me that I was a "busybody." The Lopezes were all very secretive; they didn't like to talk about family matters, and this is why we never knew if they were rich or poor, or how old Frances was, or even things like what they'd eaten for lunch.

Offhandedly, Lucio said to me, "There's a man in your apartment with a beard who rushes out of the living room whenever I go in."

"Yes," I said, "that's Paolo Ferrari!"

I wanted him to ask me more questions but Lucio didn't ask me anything else. He was using a hammer to hang up artwork he'd made and given to me as a present. It was a painting of a train. All his life Lucio had been passionate about trains. He always ran around the room making noises and whistling like a locomotive and at his place he had a huge electric train set his uncle Mauro had sent to him from Argentina.

I said to him, "Don't bang like that with the hammer! He's old, sick, and in hiding! He mustn't be disturbed!"

"Who?"

"Paolo Ferrari!"

"Do you see the tender," Lucio said. "Do you see that I also painted the tender?"

Lucio was always talking about the tender. By this point in our lives, he bored me. We were the same age and yet he seemed so much younger. Nevertheless, I didn't want him to leave. When Maria Buoninsegni came to take him home, I became desperate and begged that he be able to stay a little while longer.

My mother arranged for me and Lucio to go down into the square with Natalina. She said, "So you can get a little air." But I knew it was so that Maria Buoninsegni wouldn't run into Paolo Ferrari in the hall.

At the center of the square was a little patch of grass surrounded by a few benches. Natalina sat on a bench swinging her short legs and big feet. Lucio ran all around the square pretending to be a train making noises and whistling. When Maria Buoninsegni arrived wearing her fox, Natalina was all smiles and kindnesses. She held Maria Buoninsegni in the highest esteem though Maria Buoninsegni barely gave her the time of day. Maria Buoninsegni spoke to Lucio in her polished and prized Tuscan accent. Since he'd been perspiring she made him put on his sweater.

Paolo Ferrari stayed at our place, I think, for eight or ten days.

They were strangely calm days. I heard them talking often about a motorboat. One evening, we ate dinner early and I understood that Paolo Ferrari had to leave. During his stay he'd always been calm and cheerful, but that evening at dinner he seemed anxious and kept scratching his beard. Then two or three men wearing raincoats arrived. Adriano was the only one I recognized. He'd started to lose his hair and now his square-shaped head was nearly bald except for a halo of blond curls. That evening his face and scant amount of hair looked as if they'd been whipped by a sudden wind. His eyes were fearful, resolute, and excited. I saw those eyes two or three times again in my life; his eyes took on that look whenever he was helping someone to escape, whenever there was danger, and whenever someone had to be transported to safety.

Paolo Ferrari said to me in the hall while they were helping him to put on his coat, "Don't ever tell anyone I was here."

He left with Adriano and the others wearing raincoats and I never saw him again because he died in Paris a few years later.

The day after, Natalina asked my mother, "Do you think that boat has taken her all the way to Corsica by now?"

Hearing what she said, my father flew into a rage at my mother. "You went and confided in that half-wit Natalina! She's a half-wit! She'll get us all locked up!"

"But no, Beppino! Natalina knows she mustn't say anything!"

A postcard arrived sometime later from Corsica with greetings from Paolo Ferrari.

Over the following months, I heard that Rosselli and Parri, the ones who had helped Turati escape, were arrested. Adriano was still free, but they said he was in danger and should come hide at our apartment. Adriano hid in our place for several months. He slept, as Paolo Ferrari had, in Mario's room. Paolo Ferrari was safe in Paris but in our family everyone was tired of calling him Ferrari and called him by his real name.

My mother said, "How nice he was! How much I liked having him here!"

Adriano was not arrested but he left the country, and he and my sister, being engaged, wrote to each other. Old Olivetti came to my parents to ask, on his son's behalf, for my sister's hand in marriage. He came from Ivrea on a motorcycle wearing a peaked cap and many newspapers over his chest. He was in the habit of layering himself with newspapers whenever he rode his motorcycle in order to shield himself from the wind. He asked for my sister's hand quickly and then stayed for a while sitting on the couch in our living room fiddling with his beard and talking about himself: how he'd begun his factory with very little money, how he'd educated every one of his children, and how he read the Bible every night before going to sleep.

My father then flew into one of his rages at my mother because he was against the marriage. He said that Adriano was too rich and too obsessed with psychoanalysis—as were, for that matter, all of the Olivettis. My father liked the Olivettis but he found them a bit extravagant. And the Olivettis said we were too materialistic, especially my father and Gino.

After a while we realized we weren't going to be arrested, and neither was Adriano, who returned from abroad and married my sister. As soon as she was married, she cut her hair. My father didn't comment because now he could no longer tell her what to do, he could no longer forbid her from doing anything or order her to do something. Still, he soon enough started to yell at her again and he even started to scream at Adriano. He thought they spent too much money and used the automobile too frequently to go between Ivrea and Turin. When they had their first child he criticized their child-rearing methods, telling them that the child should be kept in the sun more often or he would get rickets.

"They'll give that child rickets!" he yelled at my mother. "They never keep him in the sun! Tell them to keep him in the sun!"

He was also afraid that they would take their child, when sick, to witch doctors. Adriano didn't believe much in real doctors and once when he had sciatica he went to a Bulgarian for aerial massages. He then asked my father what he thought of aerial massage and if he'd heard of the Bulgarian. My father knew nothing about the Bulgarian and was outraged by the very idea of aerial massage.

"He's surely a charlatan! A witch doctor!"

And when the child came down with a small fever, he worried. "They won't take him to one of those witch doctors, will they?"

He loved that child, Roberto. He thought he was beautiful and laughed whenever he saw him because he thought he was the spitting image of old Olivetti.

"It's as if I'm looking right at old Olivetti!" my mother would also say. "He looks exactly like the old engineer!"

Whenever Paola came from Ivrea, the first thing my father would say to her was, "Tell me about Roberto!"

He always said, "Roberto is beautiful!"

Paola had another child, a girl, but he didn't like her. When they brought her to see him, he barely looked at her. He said, "Roberto is much more beautiful!"

Paola was offended and scowled. When she left, my father said to my mother, "Did you see what a jackass Paola was?"

During the first years Paola was married, my mother cried often because Paola had left home. My mother and Paola were very close and told each other a great many things. My mother never told me anything because I seemed too young to her and also because I didn't "lend my gear."

I went to the middle school then and my mother no longer taught me math. I still didn't understand math but my mother couldn't help me because she couldn't remember middle-school math.

"She doesn't lend her gear. She doesn't talk!" my mother said about me. The only thing she could do with me was take me to the cinema. I, however, wasn't always willing to go with her, despite her pleas.

"I don't know what the mistress wants to do! Let me see what the mistress wants to do!" my mother would say when talking to her friends on the telephone. She always called me her "mistress" because I was actually the one who decided what we did in the afternoons, if we would go to the cinema or not.

"I'm bored!" my mother said. "I have nothing to do anymore, there's nothing more for me to do in this place. Everyone has left. I'm bored!"

"You're bored," my father responded, "because you have no inner life."

"My dear little Mario!" my mother said. "Thank God it's Saturday. My dear little Mario is coming!"

Mario, in fact, came home almost every Saturday. In the room where Ferrari had slept, he would open his suitcase on the bed and with meticulous care unpack his silk pajamas, his toiletries, his Moroccan leather slippers. He always had new things that were elegant and beautiful, as well as suits made from English fabrics.

"All wool, Lidia," my mother said, touching the suit fabric. "Ah, you too have your little things," she said, repeating what my aunt Drusilla used to say.

Stroking his jaw, Mario still said "The Brot shot in the pot" whenever he sat down briefly with me and my mother in the living room. But he was soon on the telephone, speaking in a lowered voice while making mysterious engagements.

"Goodbye, Mama," he said from the front hall, and we didn't see him again until dinner.

Mario rarely brought his friends home, but even when he did he wouldn't bring them into the living room. Instead, he shut himself up with them in his bedroom. These particular friends seemed decisive and determined, and Mario, too, now always seemed decisive and determined. It was as if he cared for and thought about nothing else besides his career and the business world. He was no longer friends with Terni and he no longer read either Proust or Verlaine; he only read books about the economy and finance. He no longer came with us on holiday, instead spending his holidays abroad on tours and cruises. He went off on his own and sometimes we didn't even know where he'd gone.

"Where do you think Mario is?" my father would ask after some time had passed and Mario hadn't written. "We no longer know anything about him. We never know what the hell he's up to. What a jackass!"

We knew, however, from Paola that Mario often went to Switzerland, but not to ski. He hadn't put a ski on his foot from the day he left home. In Switzerland, he had a lover who was very thin and couldn't have weighed more than thirty-five kilos. He only liked women who were extremely thin and very elegant. Paola said this one took a bath two or three times a day; Mario also did nothing but take baths, shave, and douse himself in lavender water since he was chronically worried that he might be dirty and stink. Everything disgusted him, much the same as it did my grandmother. Whenever Natalina brought him coffee, he inspected the cup thoroughly to make sure it had been cleaned well enough.

Every so often my mother would say, "How happy I would be if he were to marry a nice, smart girl!"

And my father immediately flew into a rage. "Married, sure! That's just what he needs. I don't want Mario to get married under any circumstances!"

My grandmother died and we all went to Florence for her funeral. She was buried in the family tomb there with our grandfather Parente, with "poor little Regina," and with all the many other Margheritas and Reginas. My father now called her "my poor little mother," his tone full of affection and compassion, but when she was alive he'd always treated her as if she were a bit of a fool—much the same way he treated all of us. Now that she was dead her defects seemed innocent and childish, deserving of pity and sorrow.

My grandmother left us her furniture. My father said the furniture was "very valuable." My mother, however, didn't like it. Piera, Gino's wife, also said that it was very beautiful. My mother was somewhat taken aback since she trusted Piera who, my mother said, was very knowledgeable about furniture. But my mother found it too big and heavy. There were armchairs my grandfather Parente had imported from India made of dark wood full of tiny holes, with elephant heads carved on the armrests. There were some small black-and-gold chairs—from China I think—and a great many knick-knacks as well as porcelain figurines, silverware, and dishes decorated with a coat of arms that had once belonged to our Dormitzer cousins who'd been made barons after lending money to Franz Joseph.

My mother was afraid that Alberto, when home from boarding school on his holidays, would take some of my grandmother's things to the pawnshop. So she had a glass-front cupboard made that could be closed with a key and placed all the little porcelain figurines inside it. She said, however, that my grandmother's furniture was not right for our apartment, that it was cumbersome and wouldn't make a good impression.

Every day she repeated, "That furniture clashes with via Pallamaglio!"

So my father decided we should move and we went to live on the Corso Re Umberto in a rather run-down and not very tall building that overlooked the avenues of the Corso. Our apartment was on the ground floor and my mother was once again very happy because she felt nearer to the street and could come and go without having to climb up or down stairs. "I can even go out," she said, "without a hat." Her dream had always been to go out "without a hat," something my father had forbidden her to do.

"But in Palermo," my mother said, "I went out without a hat!"

"In Palermo, in Palermo! In Palermo was fifteen years ago! Look at Frances! Frances never goes out without a hat!"

Alberto left boarding school and came back to Turin to finish his high-school degree. He got excellent marks on all of his exams and graduated with honors. We were all shocked.

"See, I told you so, Beppino," my mother said. "You see, when he wants to he can really study!"

"And now what?" my father said. "Now what are we going to do with him?"

"But what are you going to do about Alberto?" my mother said, repeating what my aunt Drusilla always used to say. My aunt Drusilla also had a son who didn't study and my mother, in turn, used to say to her, "But what are you going to do about Andrea?" Drusilla was the one who said, "Ah, you too have your little things!" Occasionally she'd come with us on holiday in the summer and rent a house near ours. She'd show my mother her son's clothes and say, "You know Andrea too has his little things." As soon as Drusilla arrived in the mountains, she would go to the barn where they sold milk and say, "I would be willing to pay a bit more if you would bring me my milk slightly earlier than the others." In the end, they brought her milk at the same time as they brought ours, but they still made her pay more for it.

"But what are you going to do about Alberto?" my mother repeated the entire summer. That year Drusilla wasn't with us because she'd given up coming to the mountains a while ago, but my mother could still hear her voice echoing in her ears. When asked, Alberto said he intended to study medicine. He said this in a manner that was both resigned and indifferent, shrugging his shoulders. Alberto was a tall youth, thin and blond, with a long nose. Girls liked him. Whenever my mother searched his drawers for the pawnbroker's receipts, she found a heap of letters from girls along with their photographs.

Alberto didn't see Pestelli anymore because he'd gotten married. Nor did he see Pajetta. After Pajetta got out of reform school he was arrested again, tried at the special tribunal, and sent to a prison in Civitavecchia. Alberto now had a new friend called Vittorio.

"That Vittorio," my mother would say, "is a very smart boy, very studious! He's from a very good family! Alberto is a rapscallion but he's always chosen his friends well." Even after having graduated from high school, Alberto was still, in my mother's lexicon, "a hooligan" and "a rapscallion"—a word I still don't know the precise meaning of.

"Thug! Delinquent!" my father yelled when Alberto came home at night. He was so used to yelling at him for coming home late that he yelled at him all the same even when he happened to come home early.

"Where the hell have you been out so late?"

"I accompanied a friend home for a ways," Alberto always responded in his cool, soothing, cheerful voice.

Alberto chased after working girls but he also chased after girls from good families. He chased after all girls and liked them all, and because he was kind and lighthearted, he also, out of kindness and lightheartedness, flirted with girls he didn't like. He enrolled in medical school. My father taught him in his anatomy course, and didn't like this at all. Once my father was showing slides and in the darkness of the classroom saw a lit cigarette glowing.

"Who's smoking?" he shouted. "Who is that son of a bitch smoking?"

"I am, Papa," Alberto responded in his notoriously soothing voice, and everyone laughed.

Whenever Alberto had to take an exam my father was in a bad mood from the moment he woke up. "He's going to embarrass me! He hasn't studied at all!" he said to my mother.

"Wait, Beppino!" she responded. "Wait! We don't know yet."

"He got an A," my mother told him.

"An A?" my father said, flying into a rage. "An A! They gave it to him because he's my son! If he weren't my son, they would have failed him." And he became angrier than ever.

Alberto later became a very good doctor, but my father was never convinced it was true. And when my mother or any one of us became ill and expressed the desire to have Alberto examine us, my father broke into one of his thunderous laughs. "Alberto, sure! Do you think Alberto knows anything?"

Alberto and his friend Vittorio strolled up and down the Corso Re Umberto. Vittorio had black hair, square shoulders, and a long, prominent chin. Alberto had blond hair, a long nose, and a short, disappearing chin. Alberto and Vittorio talked about girls. They also, however, talked about politics because Vittorio was a political conspirator. Alberto didn't seem to be at all interested in politics. He didn't read the papers or offer his opinion, and he never participated in the arguments that still sometimes erupted between Mario and my father. Alberto was, nevertheless, attracted by conspirators.

Since the time he and Pajetta, still in short pants, were first friends, Alberto was drawn to conspiracies but never took part in them. He liked to be the friend and confidant of conspirators.

My father, when he ran into Alberto and Vittorio on the Corso, greeted them with a cold nod. It never remotely occurred to him that of the two one was a conspirator, the other his confidant. Furthermore, the people that my father was used to seeing in Alberto's company filled him with suspicious contempt. He was also convinced that conspirators didn't exist anymore in Italy. He thought he was one of the few antifascists left in the country. The others were those he used to see at Paola Carrara's, my mother's friend who had also been a friend of Kuliscioff.

"Tonight," my father said to my mother, "let's go over to Carrara's place. Salvatorelli will be there."

"How marvelous!" my mother said. "I'm so curious to hear what Salvatorelli has to say!"

And after having spent an evening with Salvatorelli in Paola Carrara's small living room full of dolls, because she used to make dolls for a charity she worked for, my father and my mother felt somewhat comforted, even though perhaps nothing new had been said. Many of my mother's and father's friends had become fascists, or at least they were not as openly and vocally antifascist as my parents would have liked them to be. So as the years passed, my parents felt themselves ever-more isolated.

Salvatorelli, the Carraras, and the engineer Olivetti were, for my father, among the few antifascists left in the world. To him they signified another way of life, which appeared to have been swept off the face of the earth. They preserved for him memories of Turati and that entire era. Spending time with these people allowed my father to breathe a breath of fresh air. There was also Vinciguerra, Bauer, and Rossi who all had been shut up in prison for years for having conspired long ago against fascism. My father thought of them with a mixture of veneration and pessimism, believing they would never be freed. There were the communists, but my father didn't know any of them except for Pajetta. He remembered Pajetta as a child in short pants and as a reckless little adventurer, and associated him with Alberto's bad behavior. At the time, my father didn't really have a well-defined opinion about the communists. He didn't believe there were any conspirators in the new, younger generation, and if he had suspected that there were, he would have thought them crazy. In his opinion, there was nothing, absolutely nothing to be done about fascism.

As for my mother, she had an optimistic nature and was waiting for a dramatic turn of events. She was waiting for someone, someday, somehow to "topple" Mussolini. My mother went out in the morning saying, "I'm going to see if fascism is still on its feet. I am going to see if they've toppled Mussolini." She picked up rumors and hearsay in the shops and deduced from them comforting signs. At lunch, she said to my father, "People are very unhappy. They can't take it anymore."

"Who told you so?" my father shouted.

"I was told," said my mother, "by the greengrocer."

My father snorted disdainfully.

Every week Paola Carrara received the "*Zurnàl de Zenève*" (this is how she pronounced the French title of the *Journal of Geneva*). Her sister, Gina, and her brother-in-law, Guglielmo Ferrero, lived in Geneva, having emigrated long ago for political reasons. Every so often Paola Carrara went to Geneva to visit her sister, though sometimes they took away her passport so she wasn't able to go.

"They took away my passport! I can't go visit Gina!"

They would eventually return her passport and then she would go, coming home after a few months full of hope and reassuring news.

"Listen, listen to what Guglielmo told me! Listen to what Gina told me!"

Whenever my mother wanted to reinforce her optimism, she went over to Paola Carrara's place. Sometimes, however, she would find her in a foul mood sitting in her living room in the semidarkness among the dolls, beads, and postcards. Either they had just taken away her passport or the latest issue of the "*Zurnàl de Zenève*" hadn't arrived yet and she was convinced it had been sequestered at the border.

Mario left his job in Genoa, made a deal with Adriano, and was hired by Olivetti. At heart, my father was happy but before being happy he got angry fearing that Mario had been hired because he was Adriano's brother-in-law and not on his own merits. Paola now lived in Milan. She'd learned to drive a car and went back and forth among Turin, Milan, and Ivrea. My father disapproved of her never staying in one place for very long. None of the Olivettis, for that matter, ever stayed still in one place. They were always in their cars— and my father disapproved.

Mario went to live in Ivrea. He rented a room there and spent his evenings with Gino discussing the factory's problems. Mario's relationship with Gino had always been distant but in that period a friendship grew between them. Still, Mario was bored to death in Ivrea. In the summer Mario had gone to Paris. He'd gone to visit Rosselli and had asked to be put in contact with the Justice and Liberty group in Turin. He had suddenly decided to become a conspirator.

Mario came to Turin on Saturdays. He was the same: mysterious, meticulous in hanging up his clothes inside the dresser, in placing his pajamas and silk shirts in the drawers. He didn't stay long at home. He put on his raincoat in a decisive and determined manner and went out, and we knew nothing about him. My father ran into him one day on the Corso Re Umberto along with someone he recognized, a man named Ginzburg.

"What's Mario doing with that Ginzburg?" he asked my mother.

My mother had taken it upon herself, for some time, to learn Russian in order "not to be bored." She and Frances took lessons from Ginzburg's sister.

"He is someone," my mother said, "who is very sophisticated, intelligent, translates from Russian, and does beautiful translations."

"But," my father said, "he is very ugly. Jews are notoriously ugly."

"And you?" said my mother. "You're not Jewish?"

"I am, in fact, ugly too," my father said.

Alberto and Mario's relationship had always been very cold. They no longer fell into those savage and violent wrestling matches of old. Still, they never exchanged a word and when they met in the hall they didn't greet each other. Whenever Alberto's name was mentioned Mario's lip curled with disdain. Mario, however, also knew Alberto's friend Vittorio, and when Mario and Alberto happened to run into each other on the Corso with Ginzburg and Vittorio, who also knew each other well, Mario took the opportunity to invite both Ginzburg and Vittorio home for a cup of tea.

My mother was very happy that day they all came home for a cup of tea because she saw Alberto and Mario together, saw that they shared the same friends, and to her it felt like they'd returned to the era of via Pastrengo when Gino's friends used to come over and the apartment was always full of people.

In addition to her Russian lessons, my mother also took piano lessons. She took her piano lessons from a teacher recommended by Signora Donati, a woman who had also taken up playing the piano at a mature age. Signora Donati, who had white hair, was tall, robust, and beautiful. Signora Donati also studied painting in Casorati's studio. She liked to paint even more than she liked to play the piano. She idolized painting, Casorati, his studio, Casorati's wife and child, and Casorati's apartment where she was sometimes invited to lunch. She tried to convince my mother to also take painting lessons from Casorati. My mother, however, resisted. Signora Donati called her every day and told her how much fun she'd had painting.

"But you," Signora Donati said to my mother, "do you have a sense of color?"

"Yes," my mother said. "I believe I do have a sense of color."

"And volume?" Signora Donati continued. "Do you have a sense of volume?"

"No, I don't have a sense of volume," my mother responded.

"You don't have a sense of volume?"

"No."

"But color! You have a sense of color!"

Now that there was some money around, my mother had clothes

made for herself. Besides piano and Russian, this was her constant occupation and really just another way for her "to not be bored," because my mother never knew when to wear those clothes she had made for herself since she never wanted to go see anyone other than Frances or Paola Carrara, people whom she could easily visit wearing the clothes she already owned. My mother had her clothes made either "at Signor Belom's," an old tailor who had, when he was young, courted my grandmother in Pisa when she was looking for a husband but hadn't wanted "Virginia's leftovers"; otherwise she had them made at home by a seamstress called Tersilla. Rina didn't come to our apartment anymore having disappeared into the mists of time, but my father, whenever he ran into Tersilla in the hall, became furious just as he had, in the past, become furious with Rina. Tersilla was, however, braver than Rina and she greeted my father as she passed him with her scissors stuck into her belt and a polite smile on her small, flushed, Piedmontese face. My father responded with a cold nod.

"Tersilla's here! What is this? Tersilla is here again today!" he'd shout at my mother.

"She's come," my mother said, "to turn out an old coat of mine. A coat made by Signor Belom."

When my father heard Belom's name he was reassured and stopped his objections because he respected Signor Belom, who had courted his mother. He didn't know, however, that Signor Belom was one of the most expensive tailors in Turin. My mother swung between Signor Belom and Tersilla, sometimes favoring one, sometimes the other. When she had Signor Belom make her a dress and found that it wasn't cut very well because it "fit her badly in the shoulders," she would call Tersilla and have her take it apart and put it back together again.

"I'll never go back to Signor Belom! I'll have everything made by Tersilla from now on!" she declared in front of the mirror while trying on the unsewn and resewn dress.

Some dresses she had made she never liked, ones that had "something not quite right" about them, so she gave them to Natalina.

Natalina by this point also had a lot of clothes. She went out on Sunday with a long black coat with many buttons made by Signor Belom. She went out looking like a parish priest.

Paola also had many dresses made for herself. Between Paola and my mother, there was frequently tension over clothes. Paola said that my mother always had the wrong clothes made for her, that she had too many made that were exactly alike, and that she had a Signor Belom dress copied by Tersilla a hundred times over to the point of making everyone thoroughly sick at the sight of it. But my mother liked it this way. My mother said that when she had small children she always had many identical pinafores made for them and now she wanted, as her children had had, both for summer and for winter, many identical pinafores. Paola did not approve in the slightest of the concept of clothes as pinafores.

If Paola came from Milan wearing a new dress, my mother would kiss her and say, "When my children wear a new outfit I love them even more." But then she was immediately afflicted by the desire to have a new dress made for herself as well—not the same dress because Paola's clothes always seemed too complicated to her. She would have her dress made "more in the pinafore style." The same thing happened with me. When she had a dress made for me, she immediately wanted one made for her too, but she didn't tell me this, nor did she tell Paola because Paola and I used to tell her that she had too many dresses made. She would put away some new fabric, neatly folded, in her dresser. Then one morning not long afterwards we would see that fabric in Tersilla's hands.

She also liked to have Tersilla around the apartment because she loved her company.

"Lidia, Lidia, where are you?" my father thundered as he came home. My mother was usually in the ironing room chatting with Natalina and Tersilla.

"You're always with the servants!" my father shouted. "Tersilla is here again today!"

Every so often my father said, "What is Mario up to always hanging about with that Russian?"

"New star rising," he said after running into Mario with Ginzburg on the Corso. But he was no longer suspicious of Ginzburg, seeing him in a new light after having come across him once in Paola Carrara's living room along with Salvatorelli. He couldn't understand, however, what it was he and Mario had in common. "What is he doing with that Ginzburg?" he would say. "What the hell do they talk about?"

"He's ugly," he'd say to my mother, meaning Ginzburg, "because he's a Sephardic Jew. I'm an Ashkenazi Jew and so not as ugly."

My father always spoke relatively favorably about Ashkenazi Jews. Adriano, on the other hand, used to speak well of half-bloods saying they were the best people. Among these half-bloods, the ones he liked best were the children of a Jewish father and a Protestant mother, just as he happened to be.

During that period, we played a game at home. The game had been invented by Paola and it was mostly played by her and Mario, but my mother sometimes participated too. The game consisted of dividing up the people they knew into animals, minerals, and vegetables. Adriano was a mineral-vegetable. Paola was an animal-vegetable. Gino was a mineral-vegetable. Rasetti, whom by the way we hadn't seen in many years, was pure mineral and so was Frances.

My father was animal-vegetable and so was my mother.

"Nonsense!" my father said, overhearing a word or two as he passed by. "Always this nonsense of yours!"

As for pure vegetables—the purely imaginative—there were very few of them in the world. Perhaps a handful of great poets were pure vegetables. As hard as we looked, we never found even one pure vegetable among the people we knew.

Paola claimed to have invented the game but someone then told her that a sorting of this nature had already been done by Dante in "De vulgari eloquentia." I don't know if this is true.

Alberto went to Cuneo to do his military service. Vittorio strolled alone on the Corso because he'd already done his military service.

My father came home to find my mother intently dividing Russian words into syllables. "Ugh, this Russian," he said. Even at the dinner table, my mother continued to divide Russian words into syllables and to recite little Russian limericks she'd learned. "Stop it with this Russian!" my father thundered.

"But I like it so much, Beppino!" my mother said. "It's so beautiful! Frances studies it too!"

One Saturday, Mario didn't come home from Ivrea as he usually did, and neither did he show up on Sunday. My mother, however, wasn't worried because there had been other times when he hadn't come home. She thought he'd probably gone to visit his very thin lover in Switzerland.

On Monday morning Gino and Piera came to tell us that Mario and a friend had been arrested on the Swiss border. The place where they'd arrested him was called Ponte Tresa, and that was all they knew. Gino had heard about it from someone who worked for Olivetti in Lugano. My father wasn't in Turin that day. He came home the next morning and my mother barely had time to tell him what had happened before the apartment filled with police agents who'd come to search the place.

They didn't find anything. The day before, with Gino, we'd looked through all of Mario's drawers to see if there was something we should burn, but we didn't find anything other than his many shirts and "his little things," as my aunt Drusilla called them. The police agents left after telling my father he would have to follow them to the police station for questioning. By the evening, when my father still hadn't returned home, we realized he'd been put in prison. Gino, having returned to Ivrea, was arrested there before being transferred to the prison in Turin. Adriano then came to tell us that Mario had been passing through Ponte Tresa in an automobile with a friend when they were stopped by customs officers looking for contraband cigarettes. While searching the automobile they'd found antifascist pamphlets. Mario and his friend were told to get out of the car. The customs officers were accompanying them by the side of the river to the police station when Mario suddenly broke free, threw himself fully dressed into the river, and swam towards the Swiss side. The Swiss guard finally came out in a boat to get him. Mario was now safe in Switzerland.

Adriano wore that same expression he'd had when Turati fled, an expression that revealed both his terror and his excitement in those dangerous times. He placed at my mother's disposition a car and driver but my mother, not knowing where to go, had no idea what to do with them.

My mother was constantly wringing her hands and saying in a tone of combined happiness, pride, and terror, "In the water with his overcoat on!"

The friend with Mario in Ponte Tresa, who was the owner of the automobile—Mario didn't own a car or know how to drive—was named Sion Segre. We had seen him a few times at our apartment with Alberto and Vittorio. He was a young man, blond, slightly hunched, with a mild-mannered, lazy way about him. He was friends with both Vittorio and Alberto but we hadn't known that he and Mario were also friends. Paola, who'd immediately driven home from Milan, told us that actually she'd known all about it. Mario had confided in her that he and Sion Segre had made several of these trips between Italy and Switzerland carrying pamphlets and each one had always come off without a hitch. Mario had become increasingly bold, packing the car with more and more pamphlets and newspapers, throwing caution to the wind. When he tossed himself into the river, a guard had pulled out his pistol, but the other guard had yelled at him not to shoot. Mario owed his life to the guard who had yelled like that. The water in the river was very turbulent, but Mario was a good swimmer and used to icy-cold water because, as my mother recalled, during one of his cruises he'd gone for a swim in the North Sea with the ship's cook, and the other passengers, watching him from the deck, had applauded. And when they'd learned that Mario was Italian, they'd shouted, "Long live Mussolini!" In any case, while swimming in the Tresa River, he'd been running out of strength, weighed down as he was by his clothes and perhaps also by his emotions, when the Swiss guard had sent a boat out to get him.

My mother, wringing her hands, said, "Who knows if that skinny friend of his in Switzerland will give him anything to eat."

Sion Segre was now imprisoned in Turin and they also arrested his brother. They arrested Ginzburg and many other people who had been associated with Mario in Turin. But Vittorio hadn't been arrested and was shocked, his long face with its prominent chin was pale, tense, and perplexed, because, as he told my mother, he hung around all those same people. Alberto came home on leave for a few days and he and Vittorio went up and down the Corso Re Umberto together.

My mother didn't know how to get clean clothes and food to my father in prison and was very anxious to have some news from him. She told me to look in the telephone book for a number for Segre's relatives. But Segre was an orphan and all alone in the world except for a brother who'd also been arrested. My mother knew the Segre boys were Pitigrilli's cousins and she told me to call Pitigrilli and find out what was going on with him and if he'd found a way to take clean clothes and books to his cousins in prison. Pitigrilli said he would come over to our place.

Pitigrilli was a novelist and Alberto was a big fan of his novels. Whenever my father saw one of his novels around the apartment it was as if he'd seen a snake. "Lidia! Put that book away!" he shouted. He was, in fact, very worried that I might read it. Pitigrilli's novels were not at all "suited" for me. Pitigrilli was the founder of a literary magazine called *Literary Lions*, many issues of which could be found in Alberto's room, tied up in great stacks on his shelf along with his medical books.

Pitigrilli came over to our apartment. He was tall, large, and had long salt-and-pepper sideburns. He wore a big light-colored overcoat that he didn't take off, sitting down gravely in the armchair and speaking to my mother in a somber tone tinged with subdued grief. He had been in prison once years ago and he explained everything to us: you were allowed to bring food to prisoners only on certain days of the week and you had to first, at home, remove the shells from all nuts, the peels from apples and oranges, and cut bread into very thin slices because knives weren't permitted in prison. He explained everything to us and then stayed on for a while to chat politely with my mother, his legs crossed, his big coat unbuttoned, his thick eyebrows knitted together across his brow. My mother told him that I wrote short stories and insisted I show him my little notebook in which I'd copied my three or four stories in very neat handwriting. Pitigrilli, in his usual mysterious, lofty, and mournful manner, briefly leafed through it.

Alberto and Vittorio then arrived and my mother introduced them to Pitigrilli. Pitigrilli left with them, going out onto the Corso Re Umberto, with his heavy step, his lofty, mournful manner, his large, long coat draped over his shoulders.

My father remained in jail, I think, fifteen or twenty days; Gino for two months. My mother went to the prison in the mornings with a bundle of clean clothes, and on the days she was allowed to bring food, she brought packages filled with peeled oranges and shelled nuts. She then went to the police station where she would meet either with a man named Finucci or with a man named Lutri. These two characters seemed all-powerful to her as if they had our family's entire fate in their hands.

"Today it was Finucci!" she said, returning home very happy because Finucci had reassured her, telling her that there was no evidence against my father or Gino and they would soon be released.

"Today it was Lutri!" she said, equally happy, because Lutri had a rougher manner but, my mother believed, perhaps a more sincere heart. She was also flattered by the fact that both of those characters called us all by our first names and seemed to know us very well. They said "Gino," "Mario," "Piera," "Paola." They called my father "the professor" and when she explained that he was a man of science and had never been interested in politics, only ever thinking about his tissue cells, they nodded and told her she needn't worry. My mother, however, little by little, began to get scared because my father didn't come home and neither did Gino. And then one day an article appeared in the newspaper with this prominent headline: "Antifascist Group in Cahoots with Paris Exiles Exposed in Turin."

"In cahoots!" my mother repeated in distress. My mother heard all sorts of dark threats resonating in that expression "in cahoots." She cried in the living room, surrounded by her friends Paola Carrara, Frances, Signora Donati, and the other, younger ones whom she protected, helped, and consoled whenever they were out of money or their husbands yelled at them. Now it was they who helped and consoled her. Paola Carrara said that a letter should be sent to the "*Zurnàl de Zenève.*"

"I wrote right away about this to Gina!" she said. "Soon you'll see a protest published in the *Zurnàl de Zenève!*"

"It's like the Dreyfus Affair!" my mother said repeatedly. "It's like the Dreyfus Affair!"

In our apartment there was a great coming and going of people, among them Paola, Adriano, Terni, who'd come from Florence as soon as he'd heard the news, Frances, and Paola Carrara. Piera, who was in mourning for her own father's death and was pregnant, came to live with us. Natalina ran between the kitchen and the living room carrying coffee cups. She was excited and happy as she always was whenever there was any kind of tumult: people in the apartment, noise, dramatic days, incessant ringing of the doorbell, and many beds to make.

Then my mother went to Rome with Adriano because he'd discovered that in Rome Mussolini's personal physician, Dr. Veratti, an antifascist himself, was disposed to helping other antifascists. It was, however, difficult to get into contact with him and Adriano had found two people, Ambrosini and Silvestri, who knew him. It was his hope that Dr. Veratti might be contacted through them.

Piera and I stayed home alone with Natalina. One night we were awakened by the sound of the doorbell and, scared out of our wits, got up to answer the door. Military officers had come looking for Alberto who was registered as a cadet in Cuneo. He hadn't returned to the barracks and no one knew where he was. Piera said he could be tried for desertion. We speculated all night long as to where he might have gone. Piera thought he must have gotten scared and had probably escaped to France. But the following day, Vittorio told us that Alberto had simply gone to meet a girl in the mountains. He'd been happily skiing with her and had forgotten to return to the barracks. By that point, he'd already returned to Cuneo and was under arrest.

My mother returned from Rome more terrified than ever. She'd nevertheless had a good time in Rome because she always liked to travel. She and Adriano had been guests of Signora Bondi, my father's cousin. In addition to Dr. Veratti, they'd tried to contact Margherita. Margherita was one of the many Margheritas and Reginas that comprised a part of my father's ancestry. But this particular Margherita was famous for her close friendship with Mussolini. However, my parents hadn't seen her for many years. In the end, my mother never did see Margherita because she wasn't in Rome at the time. And neither was my mother able to talk to Dr. Veratti. Still, Silvestri and Ambrosini had raised their hopes, and another of Adriano's informers—"one of my informers," he always said—had told him that both my father and Gino would soon be released. Among all those who'd been arrested, it was said that Sion Segre and Ginzburg were the two most seriously in trouble and would certainly be sent to trial.

My mother continued to repeat, "It's like the Dreyfus Affair!"

Then one evening my father came home. He wasn't wearing a tie and he had no shoelaces because in prison they took those things away. Under his arm he had a bundle of dirty laundry wrapped up in a piece of newspaper. His beard was long and he seemed happy to have been to prison.

Gino, however, stayed in prison for another two months. One day my mother and Piera's mother went in a taxi to the prison to bring him clean clothes and some food and the taxi crashed into another car. Neither my mother nor Piera's mother suffered a scratch but they found themselves sitting in a smashed taxi with their bundles on their laps, the taxi driver swearing, a crowd gathering around them, including prison guards. They were just a few meters from the prison and my mother's only worry was that people would think that since they were going to the prison with all those packages, they must be relatives of a murderer. When Adriano heard the story he said that my mother's stars weren't quite aligned at the moment and this was why she was experiencing a period of such dangerous adventures.

Gino was finally set free and my mother said, "Now we shall return to our boring life!"

When he learned that Alberto was under arrest and at risk of having to go before a military tribunal, my father became furious. "Scoundrel!" he said. "While his family was locked up he went off with girls skiing!" He pronounced this last word in the English fashion.

"I'm worried about Alberto!" he said waking up in the night. "It's no joke if he has to go before the military tribunal!"

"I'm very worried about Mario!" he said. "I'm very worried about Mario! What will he do?"

My father was, however, thrilled to have a conspirator for a son. He hadn't expected it. He'd never thought of Mario as an antifascist. Mario used to constantly contradict him in all their arguments and he used to speak badly of the socialists once so beloved by my mother and father. He used to say that Turati was hugely naive and made mistake after mistake. And whenever my father heard him say this, even though he said it himself, he was mortally offended.

"He's a fascist!" my father would say to my mother. "At heart, he's a fascist!"

Now he could no longer say this. Now Mario had become famous for his political exile. Still, my father was unhappy that his arrest and flight had happened while Mario was an employee at Olivetti's factory. My father was afraid that Mario might have compromised the factory, Adriano, and the old engineer.

"I always said he shouldn't work for Olivetti!" he shouted at my mother. "He has now compromised the factory!"

"What a good man Adriano is!" he said. "He's really put himself out for me. He's a very good man! All of the Olivettis are good people!"

Paola received, through I don't know which Olivetti affiliate, a note in Mario's minuscule and nearly illegible handwriting. The note said, "To my friends, both vegetable and mineral, I'm fine and don't need anything."

Sion Segre and Ginzburg were tried by the special tribunal and condemned—one for two years, the other for four—but the sentence was halved due to an amnesty. Ginzburg was sent to the prison in Civitavecchia.

Alberto did not have to go before the war tribunal and returned home from his military service. He once again began strolling up and down the Corso with Vittorio.

"Thug! Delinquent!" my father shouted, out of habit, whenever he heard him come in no matter what time it happened to be.

My mother started her piano lessons again. Her teacher, a man with a black mustache, was terribly afraid of my father and would sneak down the hall on tiptoe with his sheet music.

"I can't stand your piano teacher!" my father shouted. "There's something shady about him."

"But no, Beppino, he's a very good man! He loves his little daughter!" my mother would say. "He loves his little daughter very much and he teaches her Latin! He's poor!"

My mother had given up Russian since she couldn't take lessons from Ginzburg's sister anymore because it would have been compromising. Some new words had entered our family. We'd say, "We can't invite Salvatorelli over! It's compromising!" and "We can't keep this book in the apartment! It could be compromising. They might search the place again!" And Paola said the entrance to our building was "under surveillance," that there was someone always lurking out there wearing a raincoat and that she felt she was being "tailed" whenever she went out.

Our "boring life," however, didn't last long. A year later they came to our apartment to arrest Alberto and we learned they'd also arrested Vittorio and many other people. They came early in the morning—

maybe it was six in the morning. They began their search, Alberto in his pajamas between two agents who were guarding him while the others leafed through his medical books, his issues of *Literary Lions*, and his detective novels. The agents gave me permission to go to school and my mother, on the threshold of the door, slipped into my school bag envelopes containing her bills and receipts because she was afraid that during the search my father might discover them and scream at her for spending too much.

"Alberto! They've locked up Alberto! But Alberto has never had any interest in politics!" my mother said, stunned.

"They've locked him up because he's Mario's brother, because he's my son, not because he's himself!" my father said.

My mother started to take clean clothes to the prison again and there she met Vittorio's parents and other relatives of the inmates.

"Such respectable people!" she said about Vittorio's parents. "Such a respectable family! And they said that Vittorio is such a fine young man. He's just done very well on his law school exams. Alberto has always chosen such respectable friends!"

"Carlo Levi is locked up as well!" my mother said with a mixture of fear, joy, and pride, because she was terrified by the fact that so many were now in prison, and that they were perhaps preparing a major trial, but the idea that so many were locked up also comforted her. She was flattered that Alberto was in the company of so many respectable and famous adults. "Professor Giua has been locked up too!"

"But I don't like Carlo Levi's paintings!" my father said instantly, never missing the opportunity to declare his dislike for Carlo Levi's paintings.

"But no, Beppino! They're beautiful!" my mother said. "His portrait of his mother is beautiful! You haven't seen it!"

"Dribbledrabs!" my father would say. "I can't stand modern painting!

"Ah, but they'll surely let Giua out right away!" my father said. "He hasn't been compromised!"

My father never understood who were the real conspirators.

After a few days we heard that in Giua's place they'd found letters written in invisible ink and it turned out Giua was, of all of them, the one who was most in danger.

"Invisible ink!" my father said. "Of course, he's a chemist, he'd know how to make invisible ink!"

My father was profoundly shocked, and perhaps even a little envious, because Giua, whom he used to see at Paola Carrara's, had always appeared to him to be poised, calm, and thoughtful. Now Giua had suddenly moved to the center of that political affair. They said that Vittorio also was in an extremely dangerous position.

"Rumors!" my father said. "All rumors! No one knows anything!"

Giulio Einaudi and Pavese were also arrested. My father knew them either slightly or only by name. He, like my mother, however, felt proud that Alberto was among them because by being mixed up with that group—publishers of a journal called *La Cultura*—it appeared that Alberto had suddenly joined company with a more dignified crowd.

"They've locked him up with the people from *La Cultura*! And he's the one who only reads *Le Grandi Firme*!" my father said.

"He was supposed to take the comparative biology exam! Now he'll never take it. He'll never get his degree!" he told my mother in the middle of the night.

Alberto, Vittorio, and the others were then sent to Rome in handcuffs on a troop train. They were taken to the Regina Coeli prison. My mother had started to go again to the police station to see Finucci and Lutri. But Finucci and Lutri said that now the matter was in the hands of the police in Rome, and they knew nothing about it.

Adriano had found out from his informer that all of Alberto's and Vittorio's telephone calls had been taped, each and every one. Vittorio and Alberto did, in fact, call each other constantly during the rare times they weren't together strolling up and down the Corso.

"Those stupid telephone calls!" my mother said. "Taping each one!"

My mother had no idea what they talked about during those telephone calls because Alberto whispered whenever he spoke on the phone. Nevertheless, my mother was convinced, as was my father, that he only talked about useless things.

"Alberto is such a useless fellow!" my father said. "They've imprisoned uselessness itself."

They began to speak again about Dr. Veratti and Margherita. My father, however, didn't want to hear Margherita's name mentioned.

"There's no way I'm going to see Margherita! I'm not going. I wouldn't dream of it!"

This Margherita had written, years ago, a biography of Mussolini. The fact that one of his cousins was Mussolini's biographer was inconceivable.

"Perhaps she wouldn't even see me! There's no way I'm going to Margherita to beg for favors!"

My father went to the police headquarters in Rome to try to get some news. Since he completely lacked any sense of diplomacy and thundered at everyone in his strong, deep voice, I don't believe he was very successful at gaining either information or meetings. He did meet with a man called De Stefani, and my father, who always got people's names wrong, later told my mother this man's name was Di Stefano. He described this "Di Stefano" to her.

My mother said, "But that's not De Stefani, Beppino! That's Anchise! I was there too last year!"

"What do you mean Anchise! He told me his name was Di Stefano! He couldn't have given me false information!"

Whenever Di Stefano and Anchise came up my mother and father would argue and my father would continue to call him Di Stefano even though my mother was certain beyond all doubt that he was Anchise.

Alberto wrote from Rome saying he was disappointed not to be able to see the city. In fact, he had seen the city for half an hour when he was three years old. Once he wrote that he had washed his hair with milk and that afterwards his hair stank and the whole cell stank. The prison director detained that letter and informed Alberto that his letters shouldn't contain so much twaddle. Alberto was exiled to a small town called Ferrandina in Lucania. As for Giua and Vittorio, they were tried and sentenced to fifteen years each.

My father said, "If Mario returns to Italy, he'll get fifteen years! Twenty!"

From Paris, Mario wrote brief, concise letters in his minuscule and illegible handwriting that my parents had to try to decipher. They went to visit him. In Paris, Mario lived in an attic room. He still wore the clothes—now ratty and faded—he'd been wearing when he threw himself into the water in Ponte Tresa. My mother wished he would buy himself a suit but he refused to give up those faded old clothes. He immediately asked for news of Sion Segre and Ginzburg, who were still in prison. He spoke about Ginzburg respectfully but distantly, as someone who, though he remained in his thoughts and affections, was no longer central to them. And as for his own adventure and escape, he seemed to have entirely forgotten about it.

He did his own laundry; he had only two threadbare shirts and he washed them with great care, with the same meticulous attention he'd once devoted to folding his silk undergarments and placing them in drawers. He swept his attic room with similar meticulous attention. He was always well washed, clean shaven, and neat even in his threadbare clothes. My mother said he looked more Chinese than ever.

He had a cat. In a corner of his attic room was a litter box with sawdust. It was a very clean cat, Mario said, and never went poo on the floor. My father said he was obsessed with the cat. He woke up early in the morning in order to go buy milk for the cat. My father, like my grandmother, couldn't stand cats, and even my mother didn't love cats, much preferring dogs.

My mother said, "Why don't you get a dog instead?"

"What do you mean, a dog!" my father shouted. "Taking care of a dog right now is the last thing he needs!"

In Paris, Mario had stopped having anything to do with the Justice and Liberty movement. He had gone to their meetings for a while and had contributed to their newspaper, but then he'd discovered that he didn't like them very much. Mario was the one who, when he was little, had written the poem about the Tosi boys, the ones he didn't like to play with:

> And then the Tosi boys came,
> All nasty, boring, and lame.

The Justice and Liberty movement was now the equivalent of the Tosi boys. All that they said, thought, and wrote irritated him. All he could do was criticize them. And he said,

> ... Among bitter rowans
> It behooves not the sweet fig to ripen.

The sweet fig was him and the bitter rowans were the Justice and Liberty people.

"It's really true!" he said. "It's exactly like that!"

> ... Among the bitter rowans
> It behooves not the sweet fig to ripen.

He said this while laughing and stroking his jaw, just as he had once done while saying "The Brot shot in the pot." He'd taken up reading Dante, having discovered how great he was. He'd also started to study Greek and was reading Herodotus and Homer. On the other hand, he couldn't stand Pascoli or Carducci. Carducci actually sent him into a rage.

"He was a monarchist!" Mario said. "At first he was a republican, and then he became a monarchist because he fell in love with that idiot Queen Margherita. And to think he was of the same era, the same century as Baudelaire! Leopardi, yes, he was a great poet. The only modern poets are Leopardi and Baudelaire! It's ridiculous that in Italian schools we still study Carducci!"

They went, my mother and my father, to the Louvre. Mario asked if they'd seen Poussin. They had not seen Poussin. They'd seen many other things.

"What do you mean?" Mario said. "How could you not have seen Poussin! In that case it was useless for you to have gone to the Louvre. The only reason to go to the Louvre is to see Poussin!"

"It's the first time I've ever heard anyone mention this Poussin," my mother said.

In Paris, Mario had become friends with a fellow named Cafi and could talk about nothing else.

"New star rising," said my father.

Cafi was half Russian and half Italian. He'd emigrated to Paris years ago and was very poor and quite sick. He'd filled up reams of paper that he gave to his friends to read but never bothered to publish. He said that when someone had written something there was no need to publish it. To have written it and to read it to your friends was enough. There was no need for it to be preserved for posterity, because posterity didn't matter at all. What was actually written on those pages, Mario couldn't explain very well. Everything was written there, everything.

Cafi didn't eat. He lived on nothing, he lived on a tangerine, and his clothes were in rags, his shoes full of holes. If he ever had a little money, he bought delicacies and champagne.

"How intolerant that Mario is!" my mother and father said later. "He criticizes everyone, no one is good enough for him! Only this Cafi!"

"He thinks he's the first one to discover that Carducci is boring. I've known that for quite a while," my mother said.

My father and mother were also offended that Mario didn't seem to miss Italy in the slightest. He was in love with France and with Paris. He continually mixed French words into his speech. He spoke of Italy only with his lip curled in deep disdain.

My father and mother were never nationalists. In fact, they loathed nationalism in all its manifestations. But Mario's disdain for Italy seemed to include them, and all of us, and our way of life, our entire lives.

My father was also unhappy that Mario had broken all ties with the Justice and Liberty movement. The leader of the Justice and Liberty movement was Carlo Rosselli, and when Mario had arrived in Paris, Rosselli had given him money and put him up. My father and mother had known the Rossellis for many years and were friends with his mother, Signora Amelia, who lived in Florence.

"There will be hell to pay if you're rude to Rosselli!" my father told Mario.

Besides Cafi, Mario had two other friends. One was Renzo Giua, the son of Professor Giua who was in prison. He was a pale youth with bright eyes and a lock of hair that fell over his forehead. He'd fled Italy, crossing the mountains alone. The other friend was Chiaromonte, whom my mother had met years ago one summer while at Paola's house in Forte dei Marmi. Chiaromonte was big and burly with curly black hair. Both of these friends of Mario's had broken off with Justice and Liberty, and both were friends of Cafi, and they spent their days listening to him when he read those pages written in pencil that would never become books because he disdained published books.

Chiaromonte had a wife who was very sick and he was very poor. Nevertheless, he helped Cafi whenever he could. Mario also helped him. They lived like this, close friends, dividing up whatever they had, without depending on any group, without making plans for the future, because no future was possible. War would probably break out and the idiots would win, because the idiots, Mario said, always win.

"That Cafi," my father said to my mother, "must be an anarchist! Mario is an anarchist too! At heart, he always was an anarchist!"

After Paris, my father and mother went to Brussels where there was a biology conference. They met up with Terni and other friends of my father's as well as his students and assistants, and my father felt relieved because being around Mario exhausted him.

"He thinks everyone is wrong!" he said about Mario. "As soon as I open my mouth he tells me I've said something wrong!"

My father loved to go on those trips whenever there were conferences. He loved meeting up with biologists and having discussions while he scratched his head and his back. He loved dragging my mother along, always being in a hurry, and never letting her stop and see the galleries and museums. He also liked to stay in hotels; except for the fact that he got up very early in the morning and was always starving. Until he'd had his breakfast, he was in a ferocious mood. He roamed around the room looking out the window trying to discern dawn's first light. When five o'clock finally arrived he picked up the telephone and shouted out his breakfast order: "*Deux thés! Deux thés complet! Avec de l'eau chaude!*" The waiters, being at that hour still half asleep, generally didn't remember to bring him the "*eau chaude*" or the jam. Finally, when he had gotten everything he wanted, he devoured his breakfast of croissants and jam, and then woke my mother. "Lidia, let's go, it's late. Let's go see the city."

"What a jackass that Mario is!" he said every once in a while. "He's always been a jackass. He's always been intolerant! I'll be very angry if he's rude to Rosselli!"

"Always with that Cafì! Cafì! Cafì!" my mother said when they were home again and she was telling me and Paola about Mario. She said "with Cafì" in the same way she'd once said "with Pajetta" when complaining about Alberto. And she asked Paola about Poussin, "Is this Poussin really that great?"

Paola also went to visit Mario. They fought and didn't like each other anymore. They no longer played the mineral and vegetable game together. They didn't agree on anything anymore. They had differing opinions about everything. In Paris, Paola bought herself a dress. Mario had always thought she was elegant, he'd always praised her clothes, her taste, and between the two of them it had generally been Paola who made judgments and Mario who agreed with them. Mario did not like the dress that Paola bought in Paris. He said that the dress made her look like "a prefect's wife." Paola was deeply offended. She no longer even liked Chiaromonte, whom she used to get together with at the seaside in Forte Dei Marmi. She no longer recognized Chiaromonte in his new guise of penniless political exile with a very sick wife, and Cafi's good friend, as the guy who used to come visit her at the seaside, who rowed and swam, flirted with her friends, made fun of everything, and went dancing in the evenings at the Capannina.

Mario told her she was bourgeois.

"Yes, I'm bourgeois," Paola said, "and I don't care in the least."

She went to see Proust's grave. Mario had never been. "He doesn't care a thing about Proust!" Paola told my mother when she came home. "He remembers nothing about him. He doesn't like him anymore. He only likes Herodotus!"

Seeing that he didn't have one, she bought him a beautiful raincoat. Mario immediately gave it to Cafi because he said that Cafi shouldn't get wet when it rained since he had a bad heart.

"Cafi! Cafi! Cafi!" Paola also said, disgusted, and she agreed with my father that Mario had made a grave mistake by distancing himself from Rosselli's group, and she said that Mario and Chiaromonte were two lonely men in Paris who had lost their grip on reality.

Alberto had returned from exile, finished his degree, and gotten married. Contrary to all of my father's predictions, he became a doctor and started to treat people. He now had a consulting room. He got angry with his wife, Miranda, if the consulting room wasn't neat and if newspapers were left strewn about. He got angry if there weren't any ashtrays because he chain-smoked and couldn't throw the butts on the ground anymore.

Patients came and he examined them and they told him things about themselves. He listened because he loved to hear things about people's lives. Then, in his white coat with his stethoscope dangling around his neck, he would go into the next room where Miranda was stretched out in an armchair, wrapped in a blanket with a hot-water bottle because she was always cold and lazy. He made her make him some coffee. He was always agitated, just as he'd been as a kid, and he drank coffee continually. He smoked continually without inhaling, taking sips off his cigarette as if he were drinking it.

His friends came to see him and he took their blood pressure and gave them free medicine samples. He found something wrong with everyone. Only with his wife could he find nothing wrong.

She would say to him, "Give me a tonic! I must be ill! I always have a headache. I feel so tired!"

And he would respond, "There's nothing wrong with you. You're just made of second-rate material."

Miranda was small, thin, blond, and blue-eyed. She would stay at home for hours on end, never going out, wearing one of Alberto's bathrobes and wrapped in a blanket.

She'd say, "I think I might go to visit Elena in Ospedaletti!"

She was always dreaming of going to Ospedaletti where her sister, Elena, spent the winter months. Her sister, blond and petite like her but with a little more energy, was at the time in Ospedaletti on a deck chair in the sun wearing dark glasses with a blanket wrapped around her legs. Or perhaps she was playing bridge. Miranda and her sister were excellent bridge players. They had won tournaments. Miranda's home was full of ashtrays she'd won at those tournaments. Whenever she played bridge, Miranda emerged from her torpor. Her expression became lively and devilish, and her eyes shone as she leaned her curved little nose over her cards. Still, rarely was she able to separate herself from her armchair and her blanket. Towards evening she would get up, go into the kitchen, and peer into a pot where a chicken was cooking.

Alberto said, "Why in this family do we only ever eat boiled chicken?"

Alberto also played bridge, only he always lost.

Miranda knew everything about the stock market since her father was a stockbroker. She said to my mother, "You know I'm thinking of selling my Incet stock." And then she added, "You should sell your property shares. Why wait to sell them?"

My mother went to my father and said, "We must sell our property shares! Miranda said so!"

My father said, "Miranda! What does Miranda know about anything!"

But then when he next saw Miranda, he said, "You understand the stock market. Do you really think that I should sell my property shares?"

He then said to my mother, "What a lummox that Miranda is! She always has a headache. But she understands the stock market. She has a great business sense!"

When Alberto announced that he was getting married my father flew into one of his rages. He then resigned himself to it. But waking up in the middle of the night, he said, "What will they do? Neither of them has a penny. And Miranda is such a lummox."

They didn't, in fact, have much money but Alberto soon began to earn some. Well-to-do ladies of a certain age came to be examined and told him all their worries. He listened to them with rapt attention. He was blessed with curiosity and patience. And what he loved most about people was their worries and their diseases.

He no longer read anything but medical journals. He didn't read Pitigrilli's novels anymore. He'd already read all of them and Pitigrilli hadn't written any new ones since he'd disappeared, no one knowing where he'd gone. Alberto no longer strolled up and down the Corso Re Umberto. His friend Vittorio was in prison and only very rarely did he hear from him, like the time when Vittorio's parents had bronchitis and asked him to telephone for them.

Alberto had his clothes made by a tailor called Vittorio Foa. While he was being measured for a suit, Alberto said, "I come to you because of your name." The tailor was pleased and thanked him. Vittorio's name was in fact Foa, just like the tailor's.

Alberto said to Miranda, "It's always bronchitis! Always stupid illnesses! I never get the chance to treat some wonderful and strange disease that's a bit complicated, a bit strange. I'm bored! I'm profoundly bored! I don't have any fun!" Actually, he was having a lot of fun being a doctor but didn't want to admit it.

My mother said, "Alberto has a great passion for medicine!"

She said, "I want to go to be examined by Alberto. Today I have a bit of a stomach ache."

And my father said, "Sure! Do you think that klutz Alberto knows anything? You have a stomach ache because yesterday you ate too much! Take a pill! I'll give you a pill!"

Alberto lived near my parents and every day my mother went by to see him. She found Miranda sitting in her armchair as usual. Alberto came out of his consulting room for a minute in his white coat with his stethoscope dangling against his chest and warmed himself by the radiator. He and my mother had the same habit of always warming themselves by radiators. Miranda was wrapped up in her blanket. My mother said, "Get up! Wash your face in cold water! Let's go out. I'll take you to the cinema!"

Miranda said, "I can't. I have to stay home. I'm waiting for my cousin. And I have too much of a headache anyway."

Alberto said, "Miranda is bloodless. She's lazy. She's made of second-rate material."

Miranda was always waiting for her cousins. She had a lot of cousins.

Alberto said, "I'm sick of treating your cousins!" And he said, "What a boring city Turin is! How bored we are here! Nothing ever happens! At least they used to arrest us! Now they don't arrest us anymore. They've forgotten about us. I feel forgotten, abandoned in the shadows!"

Paola came back to live in Turin. She lived in a big white house in the hills with a circular terrace overlooking the Po. Paola loved the Po, the streets and the hills of Turin, and the paths in Parco del Valentino where she used to go on walks with her small young man. She had always missed these things a great deal. But even to her, Turin now seemed more gray, boring, and sad than ever. So many people, so many friends were either far away or in prison. Paola no longer recognized the streets of her youth when she had only a few dresses and read Proust.

Now she had many dresses. She had them made for her by tailors in their shops but she also had Tersilla come to her house. Paola and my mother fought over her. Paola said Tersilla gave her a sense of security, a sense of life's continuity. Sometimes Paola invited Alberto and Miranda to lunch along with Sion Segre who had returned from prison. Sion Segre had a sister, Ilda, who normally lived with her husband and children in Palestine but came to Turin every so often. Paola and Ilda had become friends. Ilda was beautiful, tall, and blond, and she and Paola would go out for long walks around the town. Ilda's children were named Ben and Ariel and they went to school in Jerusalem. In Jerusalem, Ilda led an austere life and discussed only Jewish problems, but when she came to Turin to stay for a while with her brother, she also liked to talk about clothes and to walk around the town.

My mother was always a little jealous of Paola's friends and whenever Paola had a new friend my mother, feeling neglected, would become glum. She would get up in the morning, her face wan, her eyelids puffy, and say, "I have the mulligrubs." The combination of gloom and a sense of solitude usually compounded by indigestion was called "the mulligrubs" by my mother. Whenever she had "the mulligrubs" she holed herself up in the living room and, feeling cold, wrapped herself in woolen shawls, thinking Paola no longer loved her, never came to see her, was going about the city with her friends instead of her.

"I'm bored!" my mother said. "I have no fun! I'm bored! There's nothing worse than being bored! If only I would come down with some nice illness!"

Sometimes she got the flu. She was happy then because the flu seemed to her to be a nobler illness than her usual indigestion. She would take her temperature—99.3°F.

"Do you realize I'm sick?" she contentedly told my father. "I have a temperature of ninety-nine point three."

"Ninety-nine point three? That's hardly anything!" my father said. "I still go to the laboratory even when I have a fever of one hundred and two."

My mother said, "Let's hope it goes that high by tonight!" But she didn't wait for the evening. She took her temperature every minute. "It's still only ninety-nine point three! And yet I feel ill!"

For her part, Paola was also jealous of my mother's friends. Not of Frances or Paola Carrara. She was jealous of my mother's young friends, the ones she protected and helped, and whom she took with her on walks around the city and to the cinema. Paola came over to see my mother and was frequently told that she was out with one of her young friends. Paola got angry. "She's always out and about! She's never at home!"

Paola also got mad when my mother sent Tersilla to one of her young friends. "You shouldn't lend Tersilla like that!" she said. "I needed her to alter the children's coats!"

"Our mother is too young!" Paola sometimes complained to me. "I would like an old, fat mother with white hair. One who's always at home embroidering tablecloths, like Adriano's mother. It would make me feel so secure to have a mother who was very old and calm, a mother who wasn't so jealous of my friends. I would come to see her and she would always be there, serenely embroidering, dressed all in black, and she would give me good advice!"

She would say to my mother, "If you're so bored why don't you learn embroidery? My mother-in-law embroiders! She spends entire days embroidering!"

My mother would say, "But your mother-in-law is deaf! I can't help it if I'm not deaf like your mother-in-law! I would be very bored always staying at home! I like to go out and about!"

She said, "There's no way I'm learning to embroider! I'm no good at that kind of thing! I can't stitch a thing! When I try to darn your father's socks, I make a mess of it and Natalina has to pull out the stitching!"

She had taken up Russian again, teaching it to herself this time, and she sat on the couch dividing Russian words into syllables. And when Paola came over to see her, my mother would read out sentences from the grammar book, syllable by syllable.

Paola said, "Ugh! What a bore Mama is with this Russian!"

Paola was also jealous of Miranda. She said, "You're always going to Miranda's! You never come to my house!"

Miranda had given birth to a baby boy and they'd named him Vittorio. At about the same time, Paola had given birth to a baby girl. Paola said that Miranda's baby was ugly. "He has ugly, brutish features," she said. "He looks like the son of a railwayman!"

Whenever my mother went to see Miranda's baby she would say, "I'm off to see how the railwayman is doing!"

My mother adored all little babies. She also adored their nannies. Nannies reminded her of the time when her children were small. She'd had a whole collection of nannies, wet nurses, and dry nurses, and they'd taught her songs. She would go about the apartment singing those songs and say, "This one's from Mario's nurse! And this one's from Gino's!"

Gino's son, Arturo, born the year my father was arrested, used to come with us during the summer holidays along with his nanny. Whenever Arturo's nanny was around my mother was always chatting with her.

My father said, "You're always with the servants! You say you're looking after the children but really you're just chatting away with the servants!"

"But she's such a nice woman, Beppino! She's an antifascist! She thinks like we do!"

"I forbid you to discuss politics with the servants!"

Roberto was the only one of all his grandchildren whom my father liked. Whenever he was introduced to a new grandchild, he said, "Roberto, however, is more beautiful!"

Since Roberto was his first grandchild it might have been the case that he was the only one my father had ever cared to look at closely.

When the summer holidays came around, my father always rented the same house. For years now he hadn't wanted to make a change. It was a big, gray stone house looking out onto a pasture. It was near Gressoney, in the hamlet of Perlotoa. Paola's children came with us and Gino's boy too, but Alberto's boy, the railwayman, was taken to Bardonecchia because Elena, Miranda's sister, had a house there.

I'm not sure why, but my mother and father had a very low opinion of Bardonecchia. They said that it was a horrible place where the sun never shone. To hear them talk about it, one would think it was a cesspool.

My father said, "That Miranda is a colossal nitwit! She could have come here. The boy would be much better off here than in Bardonecchia, that's for sure."

And my mother said, "Poor railwayman!"

When the child came back from Bardonecchia he was obviously thriving. He was a beautiful child, blond and rosy-cheeked. He didn't look at all like a railwayman.

My father said, "He's in pretty good shape though it's odd Bardonecchia didn't ruin him."

For a few years we'd spent the summer holidays at Forte dei Marmi because Roberto needed sea air. My father went very reluctantly to the seaside. He would sit under a beach umbrella, dressed for the city, angry because he disliked seeing people in bathing suits. My mother, she would go into the water, but she'd stay very close to the shore since she didn't know how to swim. While she was in the water she enjoyed herself, rolling in the waves, but when she returned to sit next to my father, she also sulked. She was jealous of Paola who would go far out to sea in a pedal boat and not come back in for ages.

In the evenings, Paola went dancing at the Capannina. And my father said, "She goes dancing every single night? What a jackass!"

Instead, when we went to the house in the mountains in Perlotoa my father was always happy and so, therefore, was my mother. Neither Paola or Piera would come, or if they did they stayed a short time. Only the little children came. My mother was very happy when she was with the little children, Natalina, and the nannies. I was there too, bored to death during those vacations. And Lucio and Frances were in the house next to ours. Dressed all in white, they went to the village to play tennis.

Adele Rasetti was also there staying at a hotel in the village. She looked exactly the same: small and thin with a pointy nose and a drawn, greenish face and pinhead eyes. She looked exactly like her son. She gathered insects in her handkerchief and put them, along with a clump of moss, on her windowsill.

My mother said, "How much I like Adele!"

Her son now worked in Rome with Fermi and was a famous physicist.

My father said, "I always said Rasetti was very intelligent. But he's aloof! Very aloof!"

Frances came to sit in the pasture on a bench next to my mother, her hair pulled back by a white headband, her racket still in its cover. She was talking about her sister-in-law who was in Argentina, Uncle Mauro's wife, mimicking the way she spoke Spanish, "*Commo* no!"

My father said to her, "Do you remember when we were young and we went hiking with Paola Carrara, and Paola Carrara would call the crevasses 'those holes you fall into'?"

And my mother said, "And do you remember when Lucio was little and we explained to him that on a hike you should never say you were thirsty and he'd say, 'I'm thirsty but I'm not saying so'?"

And Frances said, "*Commo* no!"

"Lidia, stop picking at your cuticles!" my father thundered every so often. "It's so crass!"

"Between Frances and Adele Rasetti," my mother said, "the days fly by!"

When Paola came to see her children, however, my mother immediately became agitated and unhappy. She followed Paola everywhere and watched as she unpacked her pots of skin cream. My mother also had many skin creams, the same ones even, but she never remembered to use them.

"Your skin is all cracked," Paola said to her. "You should take care of your skin. Every night you should apply a good, nourishing cream."

My mother brought with her to the mountains thick wool skirts and Paola said to her, "You dress like the Swiss!"

"How depressing these mountains are!" Paola said. "I can't stand them!"

"Everyone is mineral!" she said to me, recalling the game we used to play with Mario. "Adele Rasetti is truly pure mineral. I can't stand to be around such mineral people anymore!"

She left after a few days and my father said to her, "Why don't you stay a little longer? What a jackass you are!"

In the autumn, I went with my mother to visit Mario, who was now living in a small town near Clermont-Ferrand. He was teaching in a boarding school. He had become great friends with the school's headmaster and his wife. He said that they were extraordinary people, very sophisticated and honest, the kind of people you could only find in France. In his small room he had a coal stove. From his window you could see the countryside covered in snow. Mario wrote long letters to Chiaromonte and Cafi in Paris. He translated Herodotus and fiddled with the stove. Under his jacket, he wore a dark turtleneck sweater that the headmaster's wife had made for him. To thank her, he'd given her a sewing basket. Everyone in the town knew him. He stopped and chatted with everyone and he was asked by all to come home with them and drink "*le vin blanc.*"

My mother said, "How French he's become!"

In the evenings, he played cards with the headmaster and his wife. He listened to their conversations and discussed educational methods with them. They also spoke a long time about whether or not there had been enough onion in the *soupe* served at dinner.

"How patient he's become!" my mother said. "How patient he is with these people. With us he never had any patience. Whenever he was home, he thought we were all so boring. These people seem even more boring than we are!"

And she said, "He's patient with them only because they're French!"

When winter was over, Leone Ginzburg returned to Turin from the Civitavecchia penitentiary where he'd served his time. His coat was too small and his tattered hat sat slightly askew on top of his black hair. He walked slowly with his hands in his pockets, his lips drawn, his brow knit, his dark tortoiseshell glasses resting halfway down his large nose, while he scrutinized everything around him with his black, penetrating eyes.

He went to stay with his sister and mother in an apartment near the Corso Francia. He was under special surveillance, which meant he had to be back home by sundown and policemen would come check up on him. He spent his evenings with Pavese. They'd been friends for many years. Pavese had also just returned from exile and was, at the time, very depressed after having suffered an amorous rejection. He went to Leone's every evening, hung up his lilac-colored scarf and his half-belted overcoat on the coatrack, and sat down at the table. Leone sat on the couch, leaning his elbow against the wall.

Pavese explained that he came over to Leone's not because he was brave—he had no courage—and not because he was any kind of martyr. He came because he didn't know how else to spend his evenings and couldn't stand to be by himself. He also explained that he didn't come in order to listen to political discussions because he "didn't give a damn" about politics. Sometimes he sat silently smoking his pipe for the entire evening. Sometimes, twirling his hair around his finger, he talked about his problems. Leone's capacity for listening was inestimable and inexhaustible. He knew how to devote his attention completely to another's problems even when he was deeply preoccupied with his own. Leone's sister would bring them tea. She and her mother had taught Pavese to say in Russian, "I love tea with sugar and lemon." At midnight, Pavese grabbed his scarf from the coatrack and flung it around his neck, then grabbed his coat. He went down the Corso Francia, tall, pale, his stride broad and swift, his shoulders hunched, his collar turned up, his extinguished pipe gripped between his strong white teeth. Leone stayed up a while longer perusing his bookshelf, pulling out a book and glancing at it, sometimes reading it, as if randomly, for a long time, his eyebrows knitted together. He stayed like this, reading as if randomly, until three in the morning.

Leone began to work with a friend who was a publisher. There was only him, the publisher, a warehouseman, and a typist named Signorina Coppa. The publisher was young, ruddy-cheeked, shy, and often blushed. When he called for the typist, however, he had a savage yell: "Coppaaa!" They tried to get Pavese to work with them. Pavese balked. He said, "I don't give a damn." He said, "I don't need a salary. I don't need to support anyone. All I need for myself is a bowl of soup and some tobacco." He was a substitute teacher in a high school. He made very little money but it was enough for him.

He also did translations from English. He'd translated *Moby-Dick*. He translated it, he said, purely for his own pleasure. They'd paid him to do it, sure, but he would have done it for free. Actually, he even would have paid for the opportunity to translate it.

He wrote poetry. His poetry had a long, drawn-out, lazy pace, with a kind of cant to it. The world of his poetry was Turin, the Po, the hills, the fog, and the taverns of Barriera di Milano. In the end, he was persuaded to join Leone working for that small publisher. He became a conscientious and meticulous worker who scolded the others for arriving late and for going to lunch, say, at three o'clock in the afternoon. He urged them to adopt a schedule like his: he would come to work early and leave for lunch punctually at one o'clock because at one o'clock his sister, the one he lived with, would put the soup on the table.

Every so often, Leone and the publisher fought. They wouldn't speak afterwards for a few days. Then they would write long letters to each other and, in this manner, would be reconciled. Pavese, instead, "didn't give a damn." Leone's true passion was politics. But besides this essential calling, he had other passions—poetry, philology, history. Having come to Italy as a child, he spoke Italian as well as he spoke Russian. He still spoke Russian at home with his sister and mother, who went out very little and never saw anyone. Leone would describe for them in great detail everything he did and everyone he met.

Before he went to prison, he'd liked attending the salons. He was a brilliant conversationalist even though he spoke with a slight stammer. And though he was always deeply absorbed in thinking about and doing serious things, he was nevertheless open to engaging with people in the most frivolous gossip, especially since he was curious about people and was blessed with a huge memory that retained even the most superficial details.

But when he came back from prison, he was no longer invited to the salons and, in fact, people avoided him because he was by then notorious throughout Turin as a dangerous conspirator. He didn't care at all and seemed to have forgotten about those salons.

We got married, Leone and I, and we went to live in the apartment on via Pallamaglio.

When my mother told my father that Leone wanted to marry me, he flew into his usual rage that occurred whenever any of us intended to get married. This time he didn't say that Leone was ugly. He said, "But he doesn't have a secure position in life!"

Leone, in fact, didn't have a secure position in life. Indeed, his situation was more precarious than ever. They could arrest him and put him in jail again. They could, under any pretext, send him into exile. If, however, fascism were to end, my mother said, Leone would become a great political figure. Furthermore, the small publisher he worked for was, even if small and poor, bursting with promise and potential.

My mother said, "They even publish books by Salvatorelli!"

Salvatorelli's name contained magical powers for my father and mother. At the mention of his name my father became kind and gentle.

I got married. And right after I got married my father would say about me when talking to strangers, "My daughter Ginzburg." My father was always ready to point out changes in any situation, and he would immediately assign husbands' surnames to the women they married. He had two assistants, a man and a woman: he was called Olivo and she, Porta. Olivo and Porta eventually got married. We continued to call them "Olivo and Porta." Every time he heard us say their names, my father got angry. "She's not Porta anymore! Call her Signora Olivo!"

He died while fighting in Spain, Giua's son, that pale youth with bright eyes who was always with Mario in Paris. His father, in prison in Civitavecchia, had contracted trachoma and was at risk of losing his eyesight. Signora Giua often came over to see my mother. They'd met at Paola Carrara's place and had become friends. They spoke informally, addressing each other with the informal pronoun *tu*, but my mother continued to call her, as she always had, Signora Giua. She would say to her, "*Tu, Signora Giua*," because she'd always called her that and found it hard to change.

Signora Giua came over with her daughter, Lisetta, who was about seven years younger than I. Lisetta looked just like her brother, Renzo: tall, thin, pale, upright, with bright eyes and short hair, a tuft of it falling across her forehead. We rode bicycles together and she told me that she sometimes saw an old schoolmate of her brother's at D'Azeglio high school, who was very intelligent. He'd sought her out and loaned her books by Croce. This was how I first heard of Balbo. He was a count, Lisetta told me. She pointed him out to me once on the Corso Re Umberto—a small man with a red nose. Balbo, many years later, would become my best friend, but at the time I certainly had no idea of this and looked upon him, that little count who loaned Croce's books to Lisetta, with complete disinterest.

On the Corso Re Umberto, I sometimes saw a young woman pass by whom I deemed both detestable and beautiful. She had a face that looked as if it had been sculpted in bronze, a small aquiline nose that sliced through the air, half-closed eyes, her stride slow and disdainful. I asked Lisetta if she knew her.

"That," Lisetta said to me, "is a D'Azeglio girl. She's a good mountaineer and has a high opinion of herself. She's detestable."

I said, "She's detestable and very beautiful."

The detestable girl lived on the ground floor of a building on one
of the streets off the Corso. I sometimes saw her in the summer at
her window, her brown hair in a pageboy cut framing her bronzed
cheeks. She watched me with her half-closed eyes, her mouth disdainful and disgusted, her expression bored and mysterious.

I said to Lisetta, "She's got a face asking to be slapped!"

For many years, whenever I was far away from Turin, I carried
with me an image of that "face asking to be slapped." And later
when they told me that the "face asking to be slapped" was employed
by the publishing house and working with Pavese and the publisher,
I was shocked that a girl who was so superb and contemptuous
deigned to mingle with people who were so lowly and close to me. I
was even more shocked when I heard she'd been arrested with a
group of conspirators. But several more years had to pass before she
and I met up again and before she, the "face asking to be slapped,"
became my dearest friend.

When she wasn't reading books by Croce, Lisetta read Salgari's
novels. At the time, she was about fourteen years old, an age at which
one is perpetually slipping back and forth between adulthood and
childhood. I had read Salgari's novels and forgotten them. Resting
our bicycles on the grass in the countryside, we sat down for a rest
and Lisetta told me their plots. Her daydreams and conversations
were a jumble of Indian maharajas, poisoned arrows, fascists, and
that little count named Balbo who came to visit her on Sundays
bringing her books by Croce. Sometimes I found her stories amus-
ing, at other times distracting. As for me, the only thing I'd read by
Croce was his *La letteratura della nuova Italia* or, to be more precise,
in his *La letteratura della nuova Italia*. I'd read novel excerpts and
synopses. Nevertheless, when I was thirteen I'd written a letter to
Croce enclosing a few of my poems and he'd written back, politely
and with great kindness, explaining that my poems weren't very
good.

I didn't dare confess to Lisetta that I hadn't read Croce's books because, since she held me in such high esteem, I didn't want to disillusion her. I was comforted by the thought that even if I hadn't read Croce, Leone would certainly have read all of his books from beginning to end.

Fascism didn't appear to be ending anytime soon. Indeed, it appeared to be here to stay indefinitely.

The Rosselli brothers had been killed at Bagnoles-de-l'Orne.

For years now, Turin was full of German Jews who'd fled Germany. Some of them were even assistants in my father's laboratory. They were people without a country. Maybe, soon, we too would be without a country, forced to move from one country to another, from one police station to the next, without work or roots or family or homes.

Alberto asked me after I'd been married for a while, "Do you feel richer or poorer now that you're married?"

"Richer," I said.

"Me too! And to think that we're actually much poorer!"

I bought food and found that it cost very little. I was surprised because I'd always heard that the prices were high. Sometimes, however, just before the end of the month I was penniless having spent everything I had, thirty centimes at a time.

I was happy, now, whenever anyone invited us to lunch, even if they were people I didn't like. I was happy to be able to occasionally eat food that was both unexpected and free, and that I didn't have to think about, buy, or watch cook.

I had a maid called Martina. I liked her a lot. However, I wondered, "Who knows if she cleans well? Who knows if she's a good duster?"

Given my total lack of experience, I had no idea if my home was clean or not.

When I went to see Paola or my mother, in their homes I saw clothes hanging in the ironing room ready to be brushed or to have their stains removed with gasoline. I immediately became worried and wondered, "Who knows if Martina ever brushes our clothes or gets rid of the stains?" In our kitchen, yes, we did have a clothes brush and there was also a small bottle of gasoline plugged with a rag, but that little bottle was always full and I never saw Martina use it. Sometimes I wanted to tell Martina to do a deep cleaning of the apartment as I'd seen done in my mother's place when Natalina, her head wrapped up in a turban like a pirate, overturned the furniture and whacked it with a carpet beater. But I never found the right moment to give Martina orders. I was shy with Martina, who was, for her part, very shy and meek herself.

Whenever we passed each other in the hall, we exchanged long and affectionate smiles. But I put off from one day to the next the prospect of suggesting a deep clean to her. I didn't dare give her any instructions even though as a girl in my mother's home I gave orders indiscriminately and expressed my desires at every instant. I remember when we were on holiday in the mountains, I insisted that every day great jugs and pails full of hot water be brought to my room since there was no bath in the house. I then washed myself in my room in a kind of sitz bath. My father preached at us that we should wash with cold water but none of us, with the exception of my mother, was in the habit of washing ourselves with cold water. Indeed, all of us children from our earliest days and in the spirit of rebellion had a hatred of cold water. I was now amazed that I had been able to make Natalina heat water on the wood stove and then carry those huge pails up the stairs to me. With Martina, I wouldn't even have dared to ask her to bring me a glass of water. Once married, I suddenly discovered what it meant to be exhausted and what it meant to work. I was seized by a laziness that weakened my will and paralyzed, in my imagination, the people around me and made me believe that I was enveloped in total inertia. I purposefully asked Martina to prepare, for lunch, dishes that could be cooked quickly and dirtied as few pans as possible. I had also discovered money. I hadn't become stingy—as with my mother money tended to slip through my fingers like water—but I'd come to realize that lurking behind all things in the form of a tiresome and tortuous conundrum was the presence of money, and that on the wake of thirty centimes you could ride to who knows where, to some unknown destination. This discovery also introduced me to and filled me with a sense of exhaustion, laziness, and languor. Still, whenever I had money in my hands I spent it right away, regretting it immediately.

During my adolescence, I had three friends. In my family my friends were called "the tootsies." "Tootsies" meant, in my mother's language, coquettes who dressed in frippery. Those friends of mine didn't seem to me to be very coquettish, nor did they dress in frippery, but my mother called them this because she was thinking back to my childhood, and to some coquettish little girls dressed in frippery with whom I might once have played.

"Where is Natalia?"

"She's with the tootsies!"

This was often said in my family.

During high school, those girls were my friends and before I got married I used to spend my days with them. They were poor. In fact, maybe one of the things that I liked about them was precisely their poverty. It was something I was unfamiliar with but which I found highly compelling and wanted to know more about. After I got married, I continued to see those three young women but a little less often, and then days and days would go by without my getting in touch with them, something they would scold me for while also understanding that it was inevitable. Seeing them every once in a while, however, lifted my spirits and momentarily restored to me my adolescence, which I felt was fast slipping away.

All three of my friends, for various reasons, lived in open dissension with society. Society, in their eyes, consisted of an easy, organized, middle-class life, with a set schedule, regular health care, and habitual studies that one's family kept an eye on. Before getting married, I had this kind of easy life and enjoyed its many privileges, but I didn't like it and my ambition was to get out of it. I combed the city, along with those friends, for the most melancholy places—the most desolate parks, the most squalid milk bars, the filthiest cinemas, the loneliest and bleakest cafés—for us to hang out. And while immersed in these squalid, shadowy places, or sitting on those cold park benches, we felt as if we were on a ship, its moorings broken, adrift.

Two of the tootsies were sisters and they lived alone with their old father who had once been very rich but had been ruined and was always meeting with lawyers about a lawsuit. He was so preoccupied with writing long memos, or shuttling back and forth between Turin and Sassi where he still owned a small property, or cooking complicated Jewish meals that his daughters didn't like, that this old father hadn't the slightest idea of what his daughters were up to. They weren't, in fact, up to anything too outlandish, having created for themselves a code of living in which paternal authority, consisting of an occasional screech or grievance, held not the slightest weight. They were both tall, pretty, brunette, healthy, and thriving. One of them was lazy and always stretched out on the bed, the other was energetic and determined. The lazy one treated her father with good-natured impatience; the other one treated him with curt and contemptuous impatience.

The lazy one had the almond-shaped eyes of an Arab, soft black curls, a tendency towards plumpness, and a great fondness for pendants and earrings. And though she claimed to abhor her plumpness, she did nothing about it and was, in her plumpness, profoundly contented and serene. And she used to say about herself, with a smile that revealed her big, white, protruding teeth, "*Nigra sum, sed formosa.*"

The other one was thin and expressed a wish to be even thinner whenever she looked in the mirror at her legs which were strong as columns. Losing weight through sheer force of will, she had vanquished her large hips and solid, overbearing bone structure. If she had a rendezvous with a boy on whom she had a crush, she fasted at lunch, or ate only an apple, because she made her own clothes and she made them so that they fit her snugly, and she was afraid she'd burst her seams if she ate an entire meal. She sewed her clothes with a dedicated, meticulous, almost neurotic care, with her brow furrowed and her mouth full of pins. She wanted her clothes to be as simple and plain as possible since she despised both her sister's plumpness and her penchant for dressing in gaudy silks.

Every time he went out, their father would leave on the kitchen table long letters of complaint, written in a handwriting that was pointed and slanting like a notary public's, either against the servant who'd "received her boyfriend into our home bestowing on him a gift of half a melon which, I have verified this evening, has disappeared," or against a peasant woman from Sassi who had, due to negligence, let some of his "sweet little" rabbits die, or against a neighbor who'd offended him by borrowing a blanket and then returning it with the wool singed: "When reprimanded, she'd had nothing to say in her own defense."

The girls were friends with some German Jewish refugees with whom they shared some of those obscure meals their father would cook for them and leave in large black pots in the kitchen. At their place, I sometimes met those students who lived day to day not knowing what they would be doing the following month, if they would succeed in leaving for Palestine, or if they would be able to reach some unknown cousin in America. I was always profoundly fascinated by that place with its doors open to all, its narrow, dark hallway where you would stumble over the father's bicycle, the small living room full of once lavish, now worn-out furniture, Jewish lamps, and small red apples from the property in Sassi spread across threadbare carpets on the floor. Sometimes I ran into the old father on the stairs or in the hallway. He was perpetually preoccupied with his dealings with lawyers and his legal documents, always busy carrying up and down the stairs baskets full of apples and peppers. In his Piedmontese dialect, he would tell us about his lawsuit while stroking his unkempt gray beard, or while wiping the sweat off his noble, ancient-prophet brow beneath his cap, his impatient daughters telling him to go to his room.

In that place there was a constant coming and going of servant women who were skittish and feebleminded. They were never allowed to cook because the father wanted exclusive reign over his provender. And since they weren't even allowed to dust in the living room because they might break those Jewish lamps or steal the apples, it wasn't clear what they actually did. Inevitably, each one was fired after a few weeks and replaced by another, no less skittish or feebleminded.

Their apartment building was in via Governolo. It was destroyed during the war and I went to see it when I came back to Turin after the war. All that was left was a pile of rubble in the old courtyard, and only the railing was left of the gutted stairs the old father used to go up and down with his bicycle or baskets. The old father had died sometime early in the war before the German occupation. He'd become ill and was taken to the Israelite hospital, bringing with him a live chicken he hoped they would let him cook. He died alone because one of his daughters was in Africa where she'd gotten married and the other, the determined one, was in Rome studying law.

My other friend was called Marisa and she lived on the Corso Re Umberto, but at the end of it, at the tram's terminus, where the Corso opened up into a grassy field and all the boulevards ended. She was small and pretty and did nothing but smoke and knit herself beautiful berets which she then wore at an appealing angle over her curly red hair. She also made sweaters.

"I'll make mythelf a nith thweta," she'd say, lisping, and she had a great selection of these "nith thwetas" that had turtlenecks and roll-necks and which she wore under a camel-hair coat. She'd had a wealthy childhood, staying in health spas and luxury hotels, and dancing, even though she was still just a girl, at the clubs in seaside resorts. Her family then had an economic crisis. Her memories of her former but not so distant life were fond and lighthearted and in no way tinged with bitterness or regret. Hers was a lazy, trusting, and serene nature.

During the German occupation Marisa was a partisan and demonstrated extraordinary bravery that no one ever suspected was within the lazy, delicate girl she'd always been before. She then became an official in the Communist Party and devoted her life to the party, but she never became a prominent figure within it because she was modest, humble, generous, and without the slightest ambition. She could talk only about party issues, and she said "potty" with her lisp, and she said it in the same serene and trusting manner she'd once said, "I'll make mythelf a nith thweta." She never wanted to get married because any man she met never seemed to live up to the ideal man she'd constructed for herself over time, a man she didn't know how to describe but whose characteristics were, in her imagination, unmistakable.

Those three friends of mine were Jewish. In Italy, the racial campaign had begun, but by having known those foreign Jews they'd unconsciously prepared themselves for an uncertain future. Furthermore, they were carefree enough to accept the situation without a trace of panic. We still went, they and I, to our classes at the university but, aside from the determined, energetic one, we approached our studies haphazardly and without much dedication.

As for the old father of my two friends who lived in via Governolo, at the beginning of the racial campaign he received a questionnaire on which it was written: "Indicate honors and special merits." He responded: "In 1911, I was a member of the *rari nantes* swimming club and I dove into the Po in the middle of winter. And on the occasion of some renovations done in my home, I was appointed foreman by the engineer Casella."

My mother wasn't jealous of my friends in the way she was always jealous of Paola's friends. When I got married, my mother didn't suffer like she'd suffered and cried when Paola got married. My mother never had a relationship of equals with me but was, instead, maternal and protective. And she didn't miss me when I left home, partly because, as she always said, I didn't "lend my gear," and partly because, being older, she had resigned herself to the emptiness she felt when her children left home, and had by then defended and cushioned her life in such a way as to not feel the impact of separation.

It seemed the only optimists left in the world were Adriano and my mother. Sulking in her small living room, Paola Carrara still invited

Salvatorelli over in the evenings hoping, in vain, that he would offer encouraging words. But Salvatorelli would arrive in a dark mood; everyone was increasingly dark and gloomy, devoid of comforting words, enveloped by an oblique terror.

From "one of his informers," however, Adriano had learned that fascism's days were numbered. Listening to him, my mother cheered up, clapping her hands, but sometimes she suspected that Adriano's celebrated informer was, in reality, a fortune-teller. Adriano regularly consulted fortune-tellers and knew one in every city he went to; he said some of them were excellent and had revealed things about his past, others had even been able to "read his mind." Adriano considered it normal for someone to "mind read." When asked how his father had learned certain things about someone, Adriano would respond matter-of-factly, "He read his mind." My mother always welcomed Adriano with the utmost delight, both because she loved him and because she could always count on him to feed her own optimism with his good news. Indeed, Adriano used to predict the grandest and most auspicious destinies for each of us. Leone would become, he said, a very great politician.

"How wonderful!" my mother would say, clapping her hands as if it were already a fact. "He'll become prime minister! And what about Mario?" she'd ask. "What will Mario become?"

Adriano had more modest plans for Mario, whom he didn't much like. He said Mario's spirit was too critical and he was also of the opinion that Mario had made a mistake by detaching himself from Rosselli's group. Perhaps, unconsciously, Adriano also held a grudge against Mario for being arrested and fleeing the country many years ago soon after joining the Olivetti company as an employee.

"And Gino? And Alberto?" my mother persisted, and Adriano would patiently make his predictions.

My mother didn't believe in fortune-tellers but every morning while still in her bathrobe, drinking coffee in the dining room, she'd play several games of solitaire. She'd say, "Let's see if Leone will become a great politician. Let's see if Alberto will become a great doctor. Let's see if someone will give me a lovely cottage." It wasn't exactly clear who was supposed to give her this lovely cottage. Certainly not my father, who was increasingly worried about money and seemed to have none again now that there was the racial campaign.

"Let's see if fascism will last for a while," my mother said, shuffling the cards while pouring herself more coffee and tussling her gray hair, which was always drenched in the mornings.

Early in the racial campaign, the Lopezes left for Argentina. All the Jews we knew had left or were preparing to leave. Nicola, Leone's brother, had emigrated to America with his wife. They had an uncle there, Uncle Kahn, an old uncle whom they had never actually met because he'd left Russia as a teenager. Leone and I sometimes spoke about also going "to America, to Uncle Kahn's place." But our passports had been taken away. Leone had lost his Italian citizenship and was stateless.

"If only we had Nansen passports!" I said frequently. "If only we had Nansen passports!"

A Nansen passport was a special passport given to certain important stateless people. Leone had once mentioned it to me. To have a Nansen passport seemed to me to be the most wonderful thing in the world, even though deep down neither of us would have wanted to leave Italy. When it had still been possible for Leone to leave, he'd been offered a job in Paris in the group Rosselli had been in. He turned it down. He didn't want to become an émigré, an exile.

We nevertheless thought of the Parisian exiles as wonderful, miraculous beings, and it seemed to us an extraordinary fact that in Paris you could run into them on the street, touch them, shake their hands. I hadn't seen Mario, who was also part of that marvelous crowd, for years and I didn't know when I would see him again. And then there was Garosci, Lussu, Chiaromonte, Cafi. Except for Chiaromonte, whom I'd met at Paola's house at the seaside, I'd never seen the others. "What's Garosci like?" I asked Leone. While walking along the Corso Francia, I thought Paris wasn't very far away, perhaps right at the end of the Corso Francia, just over the mountains, in that veil of azure mists. Any yet we were separated from Paris by an abyss.

Just as unreachable and miraculous were those in prison: Bauer, Rossi, Vinciguerra, Vittorio. They seemed ever-more distant from us. They seemed to be sinking farther and farther into a distant darkness that resembled the remoteness of the dead. Was it possible that in a not so distant past Vittorio, with his jutting chin, had strolled up and down the Corso Re Umberto? Was it possible that we'd played the vegetable and mineral game with him and Mario?

My father, like others, lost his position at the university. He was offered a position at an institute in Liège and my mother went with him. My mother stayed in Belgium for a few months. She was, however, very depressed and wrote desperate letters home. In Liège it rained all the time. "What an accursed place Liège is!" my mother said. "Accursed Belgium!"

Mario wrote to her from Paris saying that Baudelaire couldn't stand Belgium either. My mother didn't much like Baudelaire—her favorite poet was Paul Verlaine—but suddenly she was a great fan of Baudelaire. My father, however, liked his job in Liège and he'd even taken on a student there, a young man named Chèvremont.

"Besides Chèvremont and our landlord, I don't like the Belgians," my mother said when she returned to Italy.

She resumed her usual life; she came over to visit me, went to see Miranda and Paola Carrara, and went to the cinema. Paola, my sister, had taken an apartment in Paris and was spending the winter there.

"Now that Beppino isn't here and I'm alone, I'll economize," my mother, feeling herself poor, declared around-the-clock. "I'll eat very little. A soup, a chop, one piece of fruit."

Every day she recited this menu. I think she liked to say "one piece of fruit" because it gave her a sense of frugality. As for fruit, she used to always buy a certain kind of apple, which in Turin was called *carpandue*. She'd say, "They're *carpandues*!" just as she said, "It's from Neuberg's!" when speaking about a sweater, and "It's made by Signor Belom!" when speaking about a coat. Whenever my father would complain that the apples brought to the table were bad, my mother, shocked, would say, "Bad? They're *carpandues*!"

"Who knows why I like to spend money so much," my mother said occasionally with a sigh. In fact, she never was able to stick to the austerity regime she'd imposed on herself. In the morning, in the dining room, after her games of solitaire, she'd go over the accounts with Natalina. And they fought, Natalina and my mother, because Natalina also liked to spend money, money also slipped through her fingers. Whenever Natalina cooked, she cooked enough, my mother said, for all the poor of the entire parish.

"Yesterday, you made a meat dish and there was enough for all the poor of the parish!" she said to her.

"If I make too little he yells at me, if I make too much he screams at me, yesterday he said that Tersilla was coming too," Natalina said, moving her thick lips and gesticulating excitedly.

"Stay still! Don't wring your hands! You have a dirty apron. Why don't you change it? I've bought you so many aprons, by now you have enough for all the poor of the entire parish."

"Oh, poor Lidia," my mother said, sighing, while shuffling the cards and pouring herself more coffee. "This is dishwater not coffee. Couldn't you make it a little stronger?"

"It's the coffee maker that's no good. If he would buy me a better coffee maker, I've told him a hundred thousand times, this one has holes in the filter that are too big, the water passes through too quickly, instead she should go slowly. Coffee, she is very delicate."

"How I'd like to be a boy king," my mother said with a sigh and a smile, because the things she found most seductive in the world were childhood and power. She loved the combination of the two, as if the charm of the former would mitigate the latter, and the autonomy and prestige of the latter would enrich the former.

"Will you look at what an ugly hag I've become!" she'd say, putting on a hat in front of the mirror. She was putting on the hat simply because she'd bought it and it had cost a lot, but she would take it off before she reached the end of the block. "To think how much I liked being young! Today, I feel forty!" she said to Natalina at the door.

"He is older than forty, he is almost sixty, because he is six years older than I am," Natalina said, brandishing the broom threateningly. She always spoke in an excited tone and with a threatening expression on her face.

"With that kerchief around your head," my mother said to her, "you don't look like Louis XI, you look like Marat," and she left the apartment.

She went by Miranda's. Miranda was wandering about the apartment, tired, pale, with her blond hair drooping over her cheeks. She looked as if she'd escaped from a sinking ship.

"Wash your face with cold water! Come out with me!" my mother said to her.

For my mother, cold water was the surest remedy for laziness, depression, and bad moods. She herself washed her face "with cold water" several times a day.

"I spend very little. Natalina and I, all alone, we spend very little. A broth, a chop, one piece of fruit," my mother recited.

"Sure! You hardly spend a thing! You, the great spendthrift!" Miranda said. And then she said, "Today I've bought a chicken. I find chicken easy." Miranda said "chicken" with an odd intonation, a nasally, singsong drawl that she put on whenever her household habits were compared to ours, and whenever she felt a sense of superiority over us.

"It's something to be alone as you are, it's another thing to have Alberto who's never satisfied," Miranda went on. Whenever comparing two situations, she always said "It's something" when she meant "It's one thing."

My father stayed in Belgium for two years. Many things happened during those two years. My mother, as a matter of principle, went to visit him every so often, but aside from the fact that Belgium made her depressed, she was also afraid that international events would "cut her off" from Italy and from me. My mother felt a sense of protectiveness over me that she didn't feel for her other children, perhaps because I was the youngest. And when my children were born, she extended this sense of protection over them as well. Besides, she always seemed to think that I was in danger because Leone was arrested now and again. They arrested him as a precautionary measure every time some notable politician or the king visited Turin. They kept him in jail for three or four days, letting him go as soon as the political figure had left. Leone would then come home, a black beard covering his cheeks and a bundle of laundry under his arm.

"Accursed king! If only he'd stay at home!" my mother said.

She didn't dislike the king and he often made her smile. She liked it that he had those short, crooked legs and that he was so irritable. But it annoyed her that they were always arresting Leone "because of that nitwit." As for Queen Elena, she couldn't stand her. "A great beauty," she'd say, using what was for her a disparaging expression. "A peasant! An idiot!"

During the time my father was in Belgium, my first two children were born a year apart. My mother left her place to come stay with me and brought Natalina along.

"I'm back living on via Pallamaglio!" my mother said. "But it now seems a little less ugly, perhaps because I'm comparing it with Belgium! Liège is worse than via Pallamaglio!"

She liked my two children a lot. "I like them both so much I wouldn't know which to choose," she said, as if she'd been forced to make a choice between the two. "Today, he's gorgeous!" she'd say and I'd ask her, "Which one?"

"Which one? Mine!" my mother would say and I still wouldn't know which one she was talking about because she changed her preference continually. As for Natalina, whenever she spoke about either of the children she referred to them as "she" since they were both male.

She'd say, "You mustn't wake her up. She'll be fussy if you wake her up and she'll have to be taken for a two-hour walk because she's fussy."

Because I was exhausted by those two small children, and Natalina was too distracted and agitated to look after them, my mother suggested I hire a nanny. She wrote to some of her former nannies in Tuscany with whom she'd stayed in touch. The nanny arrived just as the Germans invaded Belgium. We were all so upset that we had little patience with the nanny's demands for embroidered aprons and bell-shaped skirts. Nevertheless, my mother, even though very worried about my father from whom she hadn't heard a word, found a way to buy her the aprons and was cheered at the sight of the robust Tuscan nanny wearing a wide, rustling skirt as she bustled about the apartment. I, on the other hand, felt profoundly uncomfortable with that nanny and missed old Martina who'd gone home to her village in Liguria because she couldn't get along with Natalina. I felt uncomfortable because I was constantly afraid of losing that nanny, afraid of her judging us unworthy of her because of our simple ways. Furthermore, that nanny, a large woman, with her embroidered aprons and her puffed sleeves, reminded me of the precariousness of my situation, that I was poor, and that without the help of my mother I never would have been able to have a nanny. I felt as if I were Nancy in *The Devourers* when she looks out of the window at her little girl walking hand in hand down the boulevard with her magnificent nanny, knowing that all their money had been lost at the casino.

The invasion of Belgium terrified us but we were still sure that the German advance would stop. In the evenings, we listened to the French radio in hopes of hearing some reassuring news. Our anguish grew as the Germans continued their advance. In the evenings, Pavese and Rognetta, a friend of ours in those days whom we saw a lot of, came over to our place. Rognetta was a tall, ruddy-faced young man who spoke with the soft *r*. He worked for I don't know what industry and traveled often between Turin and Romania. We, who led a cloistered and sedentary life, admired the way he always seemed on the verge of jumping on a train or to have just leapt off of one. And whenever around us he, perhaps conscious of our admiration, emphasized this way of his and played up his importance as a businessman and world-class traveler. During his travels, Rognetta heard news. Up until the invasion of Belgium, the news he heard was always optimistic. After the invasion the news was tainted with a pessimism as black as ink.

Rognetta said that Germany would soon be invading not only France and certainly Italy but the entire world and there wouldn't be a foot of ground left to survive on. Before he went on his way, he would ask after the children, and I would tell him they were fine. Once my mother said to him, "What does it matter how they are if Hitler will soon be killing off everyone?" Rognetta was always very polite and used to kiss my mother's hand before leaving. That evening, as he kissed her hand he said to her that it was, perhaps, still possible to go to Madagascar.

"Why Madagascar of all places?" my mother asked.

Rognetta replied that he would have to tell her another time because just then he had to catch a train. And my mother—who had great faith in him, and who, in that period when she was particularly anxious, hung on every word others said—that evening and the entire next day, repeated over and over again, "Who knows why Madagascar of all places!"

Rognetta never did have the time to explain to us why. I wouldn't see him again until many years later and I don't think Leone ever saw him again. As we'd been expecting for several days, Mussolini declared war. That same evening the nanny left, and I watched with great relief as her ample backside, no longer dressed in her nanny's uniform but in black percale, disappeared down the stairs. Pavese came to see us. We said goodbye to him believing that we wouldn't see him again for a while. Pavese hated goodbyes and when he left he said goodbye as he usually did, grumpily holding out only two of his fingers.

That spring Pavese often arrived at our place eating cherries. He loved the first cherries, the ones that were small and watery, and he'd say they "tasted like heaven." From the window, we'd see him appear at the end of the street, tall, with his swift stride, eating cherries and spitting the pits against the walls, his shots lightning-fast and exact.

For me, the fall of France would forever be associated with those cherries which, when Pavese arrived, he made us all try, pulling them one by one from his pocket with his parsimonious and grumpy hand.

We thought the war would immediately turn everyone's lives upside down. Instead, for years many people remained at home, unaffected, continuing to do what they'd always done. Then, just when everyone thought that they'd managed to survive with what little there was to go around, that there weren't going to be all sorts of upheavals, that homes wouldn't be destroyed and people wouldn't have to flee or be persecuted, bombs and mines suddenly exploded everywhere, buildings collapsed, and the streets were full of rubble, soldiers, and refugees. Soon no one was left who could pretend it wasn't happening, who could close their eyes, plug their ears, and hide their heads under a pillow; those people were all gone. This is what the war was like in Italy.

Mario returned to Italy in '45. He may have been upset and depressed, but he didn't show it. His jaw and furrowed brow set in a wry expression, he leaned towards my mother for her to kiss his tanned face. By now he was entirely bald, his head, as if made of bronze, naked and shiny. He wore a tunic of sorts, clean but shabby, that appeared to be made from gray silk lining and resembled something you'd see in the movies worn by a Chinese shopkeeper.

Whenever Mario wanted to show his approval of things he took seriously or his appreciation for new novelists and poets, he wrinkled his face into an expression of gravitas. He would say about a novel, "It's good! Not bad at all. It's really rather good!" (He always spoke as if he were translating what he was saying from the French.) He'd given up on Herodotus and the Greek classics, or in any case, he never mentioned them anymore. The novels he liked most were, in general, novels about the French Resistance. It seemed he'd become more restrained in his judgments, or at least more restrained about what he liked, and was no longer subject to sudden infatuations. He hadn't, however, become more restrained in his tendency to disparage and condemn things, the hatred he'd always harbored was still conveyed by a reckless violence.

He didn't like Italy. Almost everything in Italy seemed to him to be ridiculous, fatuous, badly conceived, and badly built. "Education in Italy is pitiful! It's much better in France! It's not perfect in France, but it's much better! Italy is notorious for having too many priests. Everything here is in the hands of the priests!"

"There are so many priests here!" he said, every time he went out. "You have so many priests in Italy! In France we can go kilometers without seeing a priest!"

My mother told him about something that had happened to the son of a friend of hers many years earlier, before the war and before the racial campaign. The boy was Jewish and his parents had put him in a state school but had asked his teacher to excuse him from religious instruction. One day his teacher was absent and there was a substitute teacher who hadn't been told about the boy's exemption and when the time for religion class came around, the teacher was surprised to see the child put away his notebook and prepare to leave the room.

"You, why are you leaving?" she asked.

"I'm leaving," the boy answered, "because I always go home during religion class."

"And why is that?" asked the substitute teacher.

"Because I," the child responded, "don't love the Madonna."

"You don't love the Madonna!" the scandalized teacher yelled. "Did you all hear that children? He doesn't love the Madonna!"

The entire class joined in, yelling, "You don't love the Madonna! You don't love the Madonna!"

His parents had no choice but to take him out of the school.

Mario liked this story immensely. He couldn't stop raving about it and asked if it was really true. "Unbelievable!" he said, slapping his knee. "It's just unbelievable!"

My mother was happy that her story pleased him so much, but she soon tired of hearing him repeat that teachers like the one in her story not only didn't exist in France but weren't even imaginable. She was fed up with hearing him say, "Back home in France, we...." And she was fed up with hearing him speak disparagingly of the priests.

"Better a government of priests than fascists," my mother said.

"It's the same thing! Don't you understand, it's the same thing! The exact same thing!" he said.

During the war years when we didn't see him, Mario had gotten married. The news of his marriage had reached my parents just a little before the end of the war; he'd married, someone told them, the daughter of the painter Amedeo Modigliani. For the first time, my father, upon hearing about one of us getting married, remained calm; this seemed to my mother and me very strange, inexplicable, and remains a mystery. Perhaps my father had been so afraid for Mario during those years, thinking he'd wind up a prisoner of the Germans, or dead, that his having simply gotten married was a minor mishap. My mother was very happy, and used to go into reveries about the marriage, and about Jeanne, whom she'd never met, but about whom it was said resembled one of Modigliani's paintings, her hairstyle the same as the hairstyles on the women in his paintings. My father's only observation was that Modigliani's paintings were a horror: "Dribbledrabs! Doodledums!" And he said nothing else. But the way I saw it, he regarded that marriage with vague approval.

When the war was over, a letter from Mario arrived containing a few short lines. He said he'd gotten married for reasons regarding his residency in France and was already divorced.

"What a shame!" my mother said. "How sorry I am!"

My father said nothing.

When I saw him again, Mario did not seem disposed to talking about his marriage and divorce. He let it be understood that marriage and divorce had all been part of the plan from the beginning, and his whole attitude towards the subject indicated that he thought marriage and divorce the simplest, most natural things in the world. Moreover, he didn't seem much disposed towards talking about anything that had happened to him during those years. If he'd experienced deprivation or terror, disappointment or mortification, he never said so. But sometimes when he was resting, as he used to do with his hands clasped between his knees, his bronzed head leaning against the back of the couch, his lips would curl into a ribbon of disappointment and a kind of embittered but good-natured smile would spread across that hardened face of his with its melancholic wrinkles.

"You're not going to visit Sion Segre?" my father asked him. He expected Mario would immediately go in search of Sion Segre, his partner in their original misadventure.

"I'm not going to see him. We have nothing to say to each other anymore," Mario said.

Nor did he want to go visit any of his siblings in their respective cities, even though he hadn't seen them for years. He repeated what he'd said about Sion Segre: "By now we wouldn't know what to say to each other!"

Nevertheless, he seemed happy to see Alberto who had returned to Turin after the war. He no longer despised him. "He must be a good doctor!" he said. "Not bad, as a doctor, he must be not at all bad!"

He asked Alberto about Cafi's illness, describing his symptoms and telling him what the doctors who were treating him said. Cafi lived in Bordeaux and at this point was bedridden, had lost all his strength, and could barely talk anymore.

How Mario had coped during those years we came to know piecemeal, in brief snatches, from the terse and impatient things he occasionally dropped into the conversation, grumbling and shrugging his shoulders, almost irritated that we didn't already know what he was talking about. He was in Paris during the German advance, having left that boarding school in the countryside where he'd been teaching and returned, with his cat, to live in the attic room. Every day the Germans advanced farther and Mario said to Cafi that they should get out of Paris, but Cafi had a bad foot and didn't want to move. Chiaromonte, his wife having died in the hospital just a few days before, decided to go to America. He embarked from Marseille on the last civilian ship still sailing.

Mario finally persuaded Cafi to leave Paris. With the Germans by now only a kilometer away, it was impossible to find any means of transportation so they set off on foot. Cafi limped along leaning on Mario and they made their way with an exasperating slowness. Every so often Cafi sat down to rest by the side of the road and Mario redid his bandage. They then started walking again and Cafi, wearing a slipper and a thick sock darned with red wool, dragged his painful foot through the dust.

They ended up in a village near Bordeaux. Mario was interned in a camp for foreign refugees. When he was let out, he joined the Maquis. At the end of the war he was in Marseille and part of the Purge Commission. Chiaromonte returned to Paris from America and he, Mario, and Cafi resumed their friendship. It didn't even occur to Mario to return to Italy to live. In fact, he'd requested French citizenship.

He secured a position as the financial adviser to a French industrialist and with this Frenchman drove to Italy, where Mario showed the industrialist around the museums and factories. The Frenchman, however, actually drove the car because Mario still hadn't learned to drive. My father and mother anxiously wondered if this new job had any future or if it was temporary and precarious.

"I'm afraid he's wound up doing some silly little job!" my mother said. "It's such a shame! He's so intelligent!"

"But who is that Frenchman?" my father said. "He seems shady to me!"

Mario didn't stay in Italy more than a week. He left with the Frenchman and we didn't see him again for a long time.

The once small publishing house had become big and important. Many people worked there now. It had moved to a new location in the Corso Re Umberto, the old office having been destroyed during an air raid. Pavese had an office to himself with "Editorial Director" written on a sign on the door. He sat at his desk smoking his pipe while reviewing page proofs at lightning speed. Whenever he took a break from work, he read the *Iliad* out loud in Greek, chanting the verses in his sad, singsong voice. Or he worked on his novels, writing rapidly and violently crossing things out as he went along. He'd become a famous writer.

The publisher—handsome, with a ruddy complexion, a long neck, and hair slightly graying at his temples like the wings of a dove—was in the office next to Pavese's. On his desk, he now had many telephones with bells and buzzers and he no longer yelled, "Coppaaa!" In any case, Signorina Coppa didn't work there anymore. The old warehouseman was also gone. Now when the publisher wanted to call someone, he pushed a button and talked on an internal telephone with the floor below where there were many typists and warehousemen. Every so often, the publisher walked up and down the hallway with his hands clasped behind his back, his head tilted towards his shoulder, peering into the offices of his employees and, in his nasal voice, telling them something. The publisher was not shy anymore, or rather, he became shy only when he had to have meetings with people he didn't know, and even then it didn't seem like timidity overcame him but rather a cold, silent mysteriousness. This shyness of his intimidated outsiders who, caught in his icy, luminous, blue-eyed gaze, felt they were being sized up and scrutinized as they sat on the opposite side of his glass-top desk at an icy and luminous distance. That shyness of his had become a great business tool, a powerful force against which outsiders, like dazzled moths flying into a light, collided. And if they had arrived confidently, their briefcases filled with projects and proposals, by the end of the meeting they would find themselves strangely exhausted and disconcerted by the unpleasant suspicion that they might have been a bit stupid and unsophisticated as they pitched superficial projects to a cold interrogator who had silently scrutinized and dissected them.

Pavese rarely agreed to see outsiders. He said, "I'm busy! I don't want to see anyone! Let them hang themselves! I don't give a damn!"

The new young employees, on the other hand, liked to meet with outsiders. Outsiders could bring in ideas.

Pavese said, "We don't need ideas! We have too many ideas as it is!"

The internal phone on his desk rang and from the receiver came that notorious nasal voice saying, "So-and-so is downstairs. Have him come up and see you. He might have a proposal or two."

Pavese would say, "Who needs proposals? We're up to our ears in proposals! I don't give a damn about proposals! I don't want ideas!"

"Get Balbo to do it then," the voice said.

Balbo accommodated everyone. He never refused to meet someone new. Balbo had nothing against proposals and ideas. He liked all proposals and ideas, felt stimulated by them, and when they excited him, he brought them to Pavese. Balbo—a small, serious man with a red nose—became even more serious whenever he had a proposal to show Pavese, whenever he believed he'd landed on a new human experience, awed as he was always awed before every new human innovation that appeared on his horizon, always disposed to see the intelligence in all things, to see it teeming in all the nooks and crannies his penetrating and innocent, gullible and intense, small blue eyes gazed upon. Balbo would talk and talk and Pavese would smoke his pipe, twisting his hair around his finger.

Pavese would say, "It's an idiotic proposal! Beware of idiots!"

And Balbo would respond that, yes, it was partially an idiotic proposal but that it was also not that idiotic, that it had a very good, lively, and fertile kernel at its core, and Balbo would go on and on because he was always talking, never quiet. When he had finished talking with Pavese, the small, serious man with the little red nose went into the publisher's office and spoke to him, and the publisher would rock back and forth in his chair, his legs crossed, an unlit cigarette dangling from his lips, and every so often he would look up from the piece of paper on which he was doodling geometric shapes and flash one of those clear, cold looks of his.

Balbo never corrected page proofs. He said, "I'm not capable of correcting page proofs! I'm too slow. It's not my fault!"

He never read a whole book. He read a few sentences here and there, then got up to go speak to someone about what he'd read because everything sparked his interest, everything got him excited and set him off on a train of thought that chugged on and on, and by nine o'clock at night he was still there, speaking among the desks, because he had no schedule, never remembered to go have a meal. Only when all the desks were empty and the office was deserted would he look at his watch with a start, put on his coat, and pull his green hat firmly down over his forehead. He walked down the Corso Re Umberto, that erect little man carrying his briefcase under his arm, and he would stop to look at the parked motorcycles and scooters because he was greatly intrigued by all machines and had a special fondness for motorcycles.

Pavese would say to him, "Must you always talk while everyone else is working?"

And the publisher would say, "Leave him alone!"

On the wall in his office the publisher had hung a portrait of Leone: his hat slightly at an angle, his eyeglasses low on his nose, his thick black hair, his deeply dimpled cheeks, his feminine hands. Leone had died in prison, in the German section of the Regina Coeli prison one icy February in Rome during the German occupation.

I never saw the three of them—Leone and Pavese and the publisher—together again after that spring when the Germans took France, except for once when Leone and I came back from exile where we'd been sent soon after Italy entered the war. We'd been given a permit to return home for just a few days, and while we were there we often had dinner with Pavese and the publisher, and others who were becoming important at the publishing house, others who had come from Rome and Milan with projects and ideas. Balbo wasn't there though because at the time he had gone to war and was fighting on the Albanian front.

Pavese almost never mentioned Leone. He didn't like to speak of those absent or dead. He said so himself: "When someone goes away, or dies, I try not to think about him because I don't like to suffer."

Still, perhaps he suffered from time to time over Leone's loss. They'd been best friends. Perhaps his loss numbered among the things that tormented Pavese. He certainly wasn't able to spare himself the suffering he endured every time he fell in love; his suffering at those times was most bitter and cruel. Love came over him like a bout of fever. It lasted a year or two and then he recovered from it, but he was dazed and exhausted like someone after a grave illness.

That spring, the last spring in which Leone worked regularly at the publishing house, when the Germans took France and Italy awaited war, that spring seemed to become ever-more distant, in the past. Even the war, little by little, receded into the distant past. For a long time at the publishing house there were brick stoves used when the heating didn't work because of the war. The boilers for the radiators were then fixed but those stoves stayed around for a long time. Then the publisher had them taken away. Manuscripts were scattered in messy piles throughout the offices since there weren't enough bookcases. Finally, Swedish bookcases that reached all the way to the ceiling were built with removable shelves. At the end of the hallway, a wall was painted black and prints and reproductions of paintings were tacked up on it. Then the tacks were removed and real paintings in glistening frames were hung on the wall.

He was in Belgium during the German invasion. He'd stayed in Liège right until the last minute, working at his institute, unable to believe that the Germans would arrive so soon, remembering the other war when they'd stopped outside the gates of Liège for fifteen days. Now, though, with the Germans on the verge of entering the city, he finally decided to close the by then deserted institute and to get out of there; he went to Ostend. He arrived there on foot, hitching a ride whenever possible as he made his way along the crowded roads. At Ostend, he was recognized by someone in a Red Cross ambulance and given a lift. He was made to wear a white coat and the ambulance got as far as Boulogne where it was commandeered by the Germans. My father was brought before the Germans and told to state his name. Even though it was obviously a Jewish name, they said nothing about it, asking him what his plans were. He told them he intended to return to Liège, and they took him there.

He stayed in Liège another year. He was alone that year, since no one else was at the institute anymore, not even his student and friend Chèvremont. He was then advised to return to Italy, and so he came back to my mother in Turin. My father and mother stayed in Turin until their place was damaged during an air raid. During the bombings, my father never wanted to go down into the cellar. Every time there was an air raid my mother had to beg him to go down into the cellar with her, telling him that if he didn't go down she wouldn't go either.

"Nitwitteries!" he would say on the stairs. "If the building collapses, the cellar will certainly collapse too! The cellar is hardly safe! This is an utter nitwittery!"

They then took refuge in Ivrea. When the armistice was announced, my mother happened to be in Florence and my father sent word for her to stay put. In Ivrea, he was staying at the house of one of Piera's aunts who'd fled elsewhere. He was advised to hide because the Germans were searching for and deporting Jews. He hid in the countryside in an empty house loaned to him by friends, and he finally agreed to get falsified identification papers—his new name was Giuseppe Lovisatto. When he went to visit friends, and the woman who answered the door asked who she should say was calling, he always gave his real name. "Levi. No, I mean, Lovisatto," he'd say. He was then warned that he'd been recognized and left for Florence.

They stayed in Florence, my father and mother, until the north was liberated. There was little to eat in Florence and my mother would say, as she gave each of my children an apple at the end of a meal, "An apple for the little ones and a devil to peel them for the big ones." And she told them about Signora Grassi who every evening during the other war would divide a walnut into four pieces. "A walnut, Lidia!" And she gave her four children—Erika, Dina, Clara, and Franz—a piece each.

When Leone and I lived in the Abruzzi in exile, my mother liked very much to come visit us. She also went to visit Alberto who wasn't very far away in Rocca di Mezzo. She compared one village to the other and announced that they both made her think of *The Daughter of Iorio*. Since there was nowhere for her to sleep at our place, she stayed in a hotel. The only hotel in the village had a few rooms clustered around a kitchen with an arbor, a vegetable garden, and a terrace. Behind it were fields and then, in the distance, low, bare, windswept hills. We had become friendly with the hotel owners, a mother and daughter, and we used to spend our days with them, whether my mother was staying there or not, in that kitchen and on that terrace. We discussed, in that kitchen during winter evenings and on that terrace in the summer, everyone in the village including the internees who had, like us, come with the war and blended into village life, sharing its fortunes and woes. Like us, my mother learned the nicknames that had been given by the town to internees and villagers alike. There were many internees, both rich and very poor. The rich ate better, buying flour and bread on the black market, but aside from the food, they led the same life as the poor, sitting sometimes in the hotel kitchen or on the terrace, or sometimes in Ciancaglini's haberdashery shop.

There were the Amodajes, wealthy hosiery merchants from Belgrade; a cobbler from Fiume; a priest from Zara; a dentist; two German-Jewish brothers named Bernardo and Villi, one a dance instructor and the other a stamp collector; a crazy old Dutch woman known in the village as "Skinny Shins" because she had thin ankles; and many more.

Before the war, Skinny Shins had published volumes of poetry in praise of Mussolini. "I wrote poems for Mussolini! What a mistake!" she said to my mother when she met her on the street, raising her long hands to the heavens. She wore white musketeer gloves that had been given to her by I don't know which society for Jewish refugees. Skinny Shins spent her entire day going up and down the street, as if in a daze, stopping to talk with people to whom she told her troubles while raising her gloved hands to the heavens. All the internees walked up and down the street like this, going to and fro a hundred times a day over the same stretch of road because it was forbidden for us to venture into the countryside.

"Do you remember Skinny Shins? Whatever happened to her?" my mother said to me many years later.

My mother, when she came to visit us in the Abruzzi, always brought a small tub with her because bathtubs didn't exist there and she was constantly preoccupied with being able to find a way to wash in the morning. She also brought one for us and had me bathe the children many times a day because in every letter my father wrote he recommended that they be washed frequently since we were in a primitive village lacking any standards in hygiene. A servant we had at the time used to say, with an expression of repugnance, whenever she saw us washing the children, "They're cleaned so often they shine like gold."

This servant was large, around fifty, and always dressed in black. Her father and mother were still alive and she called them "the old man" and "the old woman." In the evening, before she went home, she gathered packets of sugar and coffee up into a bundle and tucked a bottle of wine under her arm, saying, "May I? I want to bring something to the old woman! I want to bring a little wine to the old man. He really enjoys it!"

Alberto was transferred farther north. This transfer north was seen as a good thing. Whoever was transferred north had a greater probability of being set free sooner. Every so often, we too requested to be transferred north, but we would have been sad to leave the Abruzzi, just as Miranda and Alberto had regretted it, finding their new place of exile in Canavese dull. In any case, our transfer requests were ignored.

My father, he too came to visit us sometimes. He found the village dirty. It reminded him of India. "It's like India!" he said. "The filth in India is unimaginable! The filth I saw in Calcutta! In Bombay!" Talking about India made him very happy. He became animated with pleasure whenever he mentioned Calcutta.

When my daughter, Alessandra, was born, my mother stayed with us for a long while. She didn't want to leave. It was the summer of '43. We all hoped the war would end soon. It was a calm period and these were the last months we would spend together, Leone and I. My mother finally left and I accompanied her to L'Aquila. While we were waiting for the bus in the square, I had the feeling that I should prepare myself for a long separation. Actually, I had the disorienting feeling that I would never see her again.

Then July 25 arrived and Leone left for Rome. I stayed on in the village. There was a field that my mother called "the field of the dead horse," because one morning we'd found a dead horse there. I would go to that field every day with the children. I missed Leone and my mother, and I was overwhelmed with sorrow by that field where I'd been so many times with them. My heart was heavy with the saddest premonitions. Along the dusty road, surrounded by hills burned by the summer sun, Skinny Shins, in her rapid, awkward gait, walked up and down, up and down, wearing a straw hat. And so did the brothers Bernardo and Villi, dressed in long half-belted coats, given to them by that Jewish society, which they wore even at the height of summer since their clothes were torn. Except for Leone, the internees had all remained in the village because they didn't know where to go.

The armistice came, the brief and delirious exultation of the armistice. Then, two days later, the Germans. German trucks ran up and down the road; the hills and village were crawling with soldiers. There were soldiers in the hotel, on the terrace, under the arbor, and in the kitchen. The village was paralyzed with fear. I kept on taking the children to the field of the dead horse, and whenever the airplanes passed over we threw ourselves down into the grass. When I ran into other internees on the street we looked at each other questioningly, silently asking each other where we should go and what we should do.

I received a letter from my mother. She, too, was frightened and didn't know how to help me. For the first time in my life I realized that there was no one who could protect me and that I'd have to manage on my own. I now understood that bound up with my love for my mother was the belief that she would protect and defend me from tragedy. Now all that remained was my love for her, my expectation of protection no longer part of my love. In fact, it was likely that from then on I would be the one to protect and defend my mother because by then she had become quite old, despondent, and helpless.

I left the village on the first of November. I'd received a letter from Leone, brought to me by hand by someone who came from Rome. In it, he told me to leave the village immediately because it was difficult to hide there and the Germans would identify and deport us. The other internees were by now hiding in places scattered about the countryside or in nearby towns.

The people of the village came to my rescue. They all coordinated among themselves and helped me. The owner of the hotel, who had the Germans occupying her few rooms, Germans sitting in the kitchen around the fire where so often we'd sat quietly, she told those soldiers that I was a relative of hers, a refugee from Naples, that I had lost my papers during the air raids, and that I had to get to Rome. German trucks went to Rome every day, so one morning I climbed onto one of those trucks and the villagers came to kiss my children, whom they'd watched grow up, goodbye.

Arriving in Rome, I breathed a sigh of relief believing that a happy period was about to begin for us. I didn't have any good reason to believe this, but I did. We had a place to stay near the Piazza Bologna. Leone was the editor of a clandestine newspaper and was never home. They arrested him twenty days after our arrival and I never saw him again.

I found myself back with my mother in Florence. Tragedy always made her feel terribly cold and she'd wrapped herself up in her shawl. We didn't talk much about Leone's death. She'd loved him very much but didn't like to talk of the dead. Her constant preoccupation was washing the children, brushing their hair, and keeping them warm.

"Do you remember Skinny Shins? Villi?" she said. "I wonder what happened to them."

Skinny Shins, we later learned, died of pneumonia in a peasants' farmstead. The Amodajes, Bernardo, and Villi had hidden in L'Aquila. But other internees had been arrested, handcuffed, and put on a truck, disappearing into the dust on the road.

By the end of the war, my father and mother had both aged considerably. The terror and tragedy caused my mother to age suddenly, overnight. In those days she always wore a violet angora wool shawl that she'd bought from Parisini and she wrapped herself up in it. She was always cold because of her fears and sorrows, and she became pale with large dark circles under her eyes. Tragedy had beaten her down and made her despondent, made her walk slowly, mortifying her once triumphant step, and carved two deep hollows into her cheeks.

They went back to Turin, to the apartment on via Pallamaglio, now called via Morgari. The paint factory on the square had burned down during an air raid and so had the public baths. But the church had only been slightly damaged and was still there, supported now by iron scaffolding.

"What a shame!" my mother said. "It should have collapsed. It's so ugly! But no, by God, it's still standing!"

Our apartment was repaired and put in order. Broken glass had been replaced by boards and my father had stoves put in the rooms because the radiators didn't work. My mother immediately called Tersilla and once Tersilla was installed in the ironing room in front of the sewing machine, my mother breathed a sigh of relief and felt that life could go on as it once had. She bought floral fabric to re-cover the armchairs that had been stored in the cellar and were stained here and there with mold. Finally, the portrait of Aunt Regina was re-hung over the couch in the dining room and once again she looked down at us from on high with her limpid round eyes, her gloves, her double chin, and her fan.

"An apple for the little ones and a devil to peel them for the big ones," my mother continued to say at the end of a meal. But then she stopped saying this because there were, once again, apples for every-one. "These apples have no taste!" my father said. And my mother said, "But Beppino, they're *carpandues*!"

My father informed Chèvremont that he intended to donate to the University of Liège his library, which had remained there, in grati-tude because they had hosted him during the racial campaign in It-aly. He'd stayed very much in touch with Chèvremont. They wrote regularly to each other and Chèvremont sent him copies of his pub-lications.

My mother thought of places only in regard to the people she knew who lived there. For her, in all of Belgium only Chèvremont existed. Whenever anything happened in Belgium—floods or a change in government—my mother would say, "I wonder what Chèvremont thinks!"

Before Mario went to France, the only person who existed there for her was a man called Signor Polikar, whom my father and she had met at a conference. She'd always say, "I wonder how Polikar is!"

In Spain, she knew someone named Di Castro. If she read about thunderstorms or sea squalls in Spain, she'd say, "I wonder how Di Castro is!"

During one of his visits to Turin, this Di Castro fell ill and it wasn't clear what was the matter with him. My father checked him into a clinic and called in a posse of doctors to examine him. Some-one said it was possibly heart disease. Di Castro had a high fever, was delirious, and didn't recognize a soul. His wife, who'd come from Madrid, kept repeating, "It's not his *corazon*! It's his *cabezza*!"

Once cured, Di Castro returned to Spain, then came Franco's government and the world war, and we didn't hear anything more from him.

My mother, however, evoking Spain and Signora Di Castro, con-tinued to say, "It's not his *corazon*! It's his *cabezza*!" The war also swallowed up Signor Polikar. Nor did we have any news about Si-gnora Grassi who lived in Freiburg, Germany. My mother mentioned her often. She'd say, "Who knows what Signora Grassi is doing right now?" Or she'd sometimes say, "She's dead! Oh, I have the feeling Signora Grassi might be dead!"

After the war, my mother's geography was all mixed up. She could no longer speak of Signora Grassi or Signor Polikar without becoming agitated. They'd once been able to transform distant and unknown countries into something domestic, familiar, and happy for my mother. They transformed the world into a neighborhood or a street that she could, in her mind, swiftly roam along, as if in the shoes of those few familiar and reassuring names.

By contrast, after the war the world seemed enormous, unknowable, and without end. Nevertheless, my mother tried to live in it again as best she could. She inhabited the world again with joy because her temperament was joyful. Her spirit was incapable of growing old and she never understood old people who retreated from life, bemoaning the desolation of the past. My mother looked dry-eyed upon the past's desolation and didn't mourn for it. Besides, she didn't much like mourning clothes. She was in Palermo when her mother died in Florence, suddenly and alone. She went to Florence and it was very painful to see her mother dead. She then went out to buy herself a mourning outfit, but instead of buying a black dress, as she was supposed to, she bought herself a red dress and went back to Palermo with that red dress in her suitcase. She said to Paola, "What should I have done? My mother couldn't stand black clothes and she would have been so happy if she could have seen me in this beautiful red dress!"

> One day Cía's foot began to hurt,
> In the evening, puss oozed from it,
> So the Health Service sent her to Vercelli.

Young poets wrote, and submitted to the publishing house, verse of this sort. This particular tercet about Cía was part of a long poem describing the women who worked in the rice fields. The postwar period was a time when everyone believed himself to be a poet and a politician. Everyone thought he could, or rather should, write poetry about any and all subjects since for so many years the world had been silenced and paralyzed, reality being something stuck behind glass—vitreous, crystalline, mute, and immobile. Novelists and poets had been starved of words during the fascist years. So many had been forbidden to use words, and the few who'd been able to use them were forced to choose them very carefully from the slim pickings that remained. During fascism, poets found themselves expressing only an arid, shut-off, cryptic dream world. Now, once more, many words were in circulation and reality appeared to be at everyone's fingertips. So those who had been starved dedicated themselves to harvesting the words with delight. And the harvest was ubiquitous because everyone wanted to take part in it. The result was a confused mixing up of the languages of poetry and politics. Reality revealed itself to be complex and enigmatic, as indecipherable and obscure as the world of dreams. And it revealed itself to still be behind glass—the illusion that the glass had been broken, ephemeral. Dejected and disheartened, many soon retreated, sank back into a bitter starvation and profound silence. The postwar period, then, was very sad and full of dejection after the joyful harvest of its early days. Many pulled away and isolated themselves again, either within their dream worlds or in whatever random job they'd taken in a hurry in order to earn a living, jobs that seemed insignificant and dreary after so much hullabaloo. In any case, everyone soon forgot that brief, illusory moment of shared existence. Certainly, for many years, no one worked at the job he'd planned on and trained for, everyone believing that they could and must do a thousand jobs all at once. And much time passed before everyone took back upon his shoulders his profession and accepted the burden, the exhaustion, and the loneliness of the daily grind, which is the only way we have of participating in each other's lives, each of us lost and trapped in our own parallel solitude.

As for the poem about Cía of the injured foot, at the time we didn't think it was very good; in fact, it seemed very bad to us. Today, however, it seems poignant, whispered to us in the language of the era. At the time, there were two ways to write: one was a simple listing of facts outlining a dreary, foul, base reality seen through a lens that peered out over a bleak and mortified landscape; the other was a mixing of facts with violence and a delirium of tears, sobs, and sighs. In neither case did one choose his own words because in one case the words were inextricable from the dreariness, and in the other the words got lost among the groans and sighs. But the common error was to still believe that everything could be transformed into poetry and words. This resulted in a loathing for poetry and for words, which was so powerful it extended to true poetry and true words. In the end everyone kept quiet, paralyzed by boredom and nausea. It was necessary for writers to go back and choose their words, scrutinize them to see if they were false or real, if they had actual origins in our experience, or if instead they only had the ephemeral origins of a shared illusion. It was necessary, if one was a writer, to go back and find your true calling that had been forgotten in the general intoxication. What had followed was like a hangover: nausea, lethargy, tedium. In one way or another, everyone felt deceived and betrayed, both those who lived in reality and those who possessed or thought they possessed a means of describing it. And so everyone went their own way again, alone and dissatisfied.

Adriano occasionally stopped by the publishing house. He liked publishing houses and wanted to own one himself. But the publishing house he had in mind wouldn't publish poetry or novels. In his youth, he had liked only one novel: *Dreamers of the Ghetto* by Israel Zangwill. All of the novels he'd read subsequently hadn't moved him in the slightest. He had enormous respect for novelists and poets, but he didn't read them. Urban planning, psychoanalysis, philosophy, and religion were the only subjects he had any interest in.

By then Adriano had become a great and famous industrialist, but he'd maintained something of the tramp about him and he moved in the shuffling, lonely gait of a vagabond as he had in his youth when he was a soldier. He was still shy and had no idea how to take advantage of his shyness, how to make it a strength the way the publisher did, so he tried to suppress it whenever he met someone for the first time, whether they were political figures or poor young men who'd come to the factory looking for a job. He would throw back his shoulders and stand tall, his eyes lit by a frozen glare, cold and pure.

I met him on the street in Rome one day during the German occupation. He was on foot, alone, moving along in his tramp-like gait, his eyes veiled in the blue mists of his perennial daydreaming. He was dressed like everyone else in the crowd but to me he looked like both a beggar and a king: a king in exile, he seemed.

Leone was arrested in a clandestine printer's shop. We were living in the apartment near the Piazza Bologna and I was home alone with my children. I waited, and as the hours went by and he failed to come home, I slowly realized that he must have been arrested. The day passed, then the night, and the next morning Adriano came over and told me to leave the place immediately because Leone had, in fact, been arrested and the police might show up at any moment. He helped me pack the suitcases and dress the children and we hurried out of there. He took me to friends who'd agreed to put me up.

For the rest of my life, I will never forget the immense solace I took in seeing Adriano's very familiar figure, one I'd known since childhood, appear before me that morning after so many hours of being alone and afraid, hours in which I thought about my parents far away in the north and wondered if I'd ever see them again. I will always remember Adriano hunched over as he went from room to room, leaning down to pick up clothes and the children's shoes, his movements full of kindness, compassion, humility, and patience. And when we fled from that place, he wore on his face the expression that he'd had when he came to our apartment for Turati; it was that breathless, terrified, excited expression he wore whenever he was helping someone to safety.

When Adriano came to the publishing house, he'd always spend time talking with Balbo because Balbo was a philosopher and Adriano was fascinated by philosophers. Balbo, for his part, was fascinated by industrialists, engineers, factories, and all questions related to factories, machines, and engines. He boasted about this fascination, this passion of his to us, to Pavese and me, saying that we were intellectuals but that he was not; he said we didn't understand a thing about factories or machines. It was a fascination and a passion that culminated in the contemplation, on his way home at night, of parked motorcycles.

Adriano and Paola divorced after the war. She lived near Florence in the hills of Fiesole and he in Ivrea. Even so, he and Gino remained friends and saw each other often despite the fact that Gino, after the war, had left Ivrea and the factory to work in Milan. In fact, Gino was, perhaps, one of Adriano's few friends because he was loyal to the friends he'd known in his youth and the things he'd discovered then, just as he'd remained loyal in the depths of his soul to the novelist Israel Zangwill. His loyalty was, however, purely emotional and didn't extend to the practical world where he was always ready to dismantle whatever he'd accomplished, always seeking new and more modern methods and techniques, those he'd just invented already obsolete in his view. In this way, he was much like the publisher who was also always ready to throw out whatever he'd chosen to work on the day before. Adriano was always anxious and restless in his quest to discover the new, a quest he deemed more important than everything else, and he would stop at nothing to achieve it: not at the notion that he owed his fortune to his previous inventions nor at the confusion and protests of those around him who'd become wedded to the old inventions and couldn't understand why they should be tossed aside.

By then, I was also working at the publishing house. My father looked upon the publishing house—and the fact that I worked there—with kindness and approval, my mother with suspicion and skepticism. My mother, in fact, believed that the atmosphere there was too left-wing because after the war she'd become afraid of communism, something she hadn't really given any thought to before. She didn't even like Nenni's socialism, which she considered too similar to communism. She preferred Saragat's followers, but she wasn't thrilled with them either, and Saragat's face seemed to her to be "far too insipid."

"Turati, Bissolati!" she'd say. "Kuliscioff! They were good people. I don't like politics today!"

She went to visit Paola Carrara, who was still in her small, dark living room packed with artificial little birds, postcards, and dolls. Paola was also glum because she didn't like the communists either and was afraid they'd take over Italy. Her sister and her brother-in-law had died and she no longer had any reason to go to Geneva or to read the "*Zurnàl de Zenève.*" Nor did she have to wait any longer for the end of fascism or the death of Mussolini, both having disappeared some time ago. She therefore cultivated an active dislike for communism and a regret that the work of Guglielmo Ferrero, her brother-in-law, hadn't been appreciated in Italy to the degree it deserved after the end of fascism and the death of Mussolini. She no longer invited people over in the evenings to her small living room. Those who used to frequent her small living room, the antifascists of the day, had gone to live in Rome after having been given jobs in the government. Only my parents and a few others stayed behind and occasionally she invited them over in the evening, but without the same enthusiasm she'd once had. She found everyone "too far to the left," with the exception of my mother, and so she wound up in a sulk, falling asleep in her gray silk dress, her hands enfolded in her crocheted gray shawl.

"You let Paola Carrara turn you against the communists!" my father said to my mother.

"I don't like the communists!" my mother said. "Paola Carrara has nothing to do with it. I don't like them! I love freedom! In Russia there is no freedom!"

My father admitted that in Russia there wasn't, perhaps, much freedom. He was, however, attracted by the left wing. Olivo, his longtime assistant, who now had a position in Modena, was a left-winger.

"Even Olivo is a left-winger!" my father said to my mother.

And my mother said, "You see, you're the one who's under Olivo's influence!"

My father and mother had returned, after the war, to the apartment in via Pallamaglio, now called via Morgari. My children and I lived with them. Natalina wasn't with us any longer because right after the war she'd set herself up in an attic room with some furniture my mother had given her and now worked by the hour.

"I don't want to be a slave any longer," Natalina had said. "I want my freedom!"

"What an idiot you are!" my mother told her. "Imagine me keeping a slave! You have more freedom than I do!"

"I'm a slave. I'm a slave!" Natalina said, in her threatening and excited tone, brandishing the broom.

As my mother left the apartment, she said, "I'm going out because I can't bear to look at you! You've become very unpleasant!"

And she went to blow off steam at the greengrocer's and the butcher's. "At my place she's always warm and has everything she could possibly want!" she explained. "She's really an idiot."

She went to visit Alberto and Miranda who lived nearby on the Corso Valentino and blew off steam with them as well. "Doesn't she have all the freedom she could possibly want? I'd never enslave anyone!" she said.

And she said, "But how will I ever cope without Natalina?"

Natalina had moved into her attic room but she always came over to visit my mother, who in the beginning hoped Natalina would regret her decision and return to live with her. Eventually my mother resigned herself to the situation and got a new maid.

"Goodbye, Louis XI," she said to Natalina, who left to go back to the attic room she described as "splendid" and where she invited Tersilla and her husband over in the evening for coffee.

"Goodbye, Louis XI! Goodbye, Marat!"

Many of my father's and mother's friends were dead. Paola Carrara's husband had already died before the war. Carrara had been a tall, thin man with a white toothbrush mustache who always rode his bicycle around, his black cape flapping about him. My mother thought him very respectable. "Respectable like Carrara," she'd say whenever she wanted to suggest the pinnacle of rectitude. She continued to say so even after he was dead. Adriano's parents, the old engineer Olivetti and his wife, were both dead too. They died—first he and then she a little while later—during the months after the armistice in the countryside near Ivrea where they'd been in hiding. Lopez returned from Argentina at the end of the war and died soon after. And even Terni had died in Florence. My father kept in touch with his wife, Mary, but he hadn't seen her for several years.

"Have you written to Mary?" he'd say to my mother. "You must write to Mary! Remember to write to Mary!"

"Have you been to visit Frances?" he'd say. "Go visit Frances! Today you must go visit Frances!"

"Write to Mario!" he'd say to her. "God help you if you don't write to Mario today!"

Mario no longer worked with the Frenchman. He now had a job on the radio. He'd remarried and obtained French citizenship. When he'd let it be known that he'd married again, this time my father became angry. But not too angry. He and my mother went to Paris to meet his new wife. Mario lived in an apartment near the Seine. It was rather dark and my father wasn't able to see Mario's wife too well. He only saw that she was tiny and had bangs over her eyes. During a moment when she wasn't there, he asked Mario, "Why did you marry a woman so much older than you?"

Actually, Mario's wife wasn't even twenty years old and by then Mario was forty.

They had a baby. My father and mother went back to Paris for the birth of the little girl. Mario went crazy for his daughter and would walk around with her cradled in his arms from room to room. "*Elle pleure, il faut lui donner sa tétée!*" he'd say excitedly to his wife.

And my mother would say, "How French he's become!"

During this visit my father became furious one day when he discovered Mario's other wife, Jeanne, whom he'd divorced and with whom he was still friends, in the apartment with Mario and his baby daughter. My father didn't like that apartment on the Seine. It was dark, he said, and must be humid. As for Mario's wife, she seemed too small to him.

"She's too small!" he would repeat.

My mother said, "She's small but elegant! Her feet are a bit too small. I don't like tiny feet."

My father didn't agree. His mother's feet had been small. "You're wrong! Small feet on a woman are extremely beautiful! My mother, poor thing, always boasted about her small feet!"

"They talk about eating too much!" my father said about Mario and his wife. "Their place is too humid! Tell them they should move!"

"But you're crazy, Beppino! They really like living there!" my mother said. "This job at the radio, though, I'm afraid it's not serious."

And my father said, "What a shame! With his intelligence! He could have had a wonderful career!"

Cafi had died in Bordeaux. Mario and Chiaromonte had collected all of his disparate papers, written in pencil, and tried to decipher them. While Chiaromonte had been in America he'd remarried. He left Paris and came back to live in Italy with his wife. Mario thought this was stupid, that he couldn't do a stupider thing. They nevertheless stayed close friends and met up every summer in Bocca di Magra. They played chess. Mario by then had two children and worked at UNESCO. My father wrote to Chiaromonte to ask him what kind of job Mario had and if it was financially secure.

"Perhaps this one isn't some meaningless little job! Perhaps it's a good job!" my mother said.

Even though he'd received reassuring tidings from Chiaromonte, my father shook his head in disappointment. He was very stubborn and incapable of budging from his first impressions. He remained convinced that Mario had missed out on a brilliant and prosperous career.

He was still very proud of having in Mario a conspirator for a son who'd crossed the border many times carrying clandestine pamphlets, and he was proud Mario had been arrested and then made a dramatic escape, but he also held on to his regret that Mario had put the Olivettis at risk and compromised the factory. So when Adriano died a few years later and Mario sent a telegram from Paris to my father saying, "Tell me if my presence at Adriano's funeral is appropriate," my father responded right away with an equally terse telegram: "Your presence inappropriate at funeral."

My father was, after all, perpetually quite anxious about each one of his sons. He woke up in the middle of the night and ruminated over Gino. Having left Olivetti, Gino went to Milan where he'd become a manager and consultant for large companies.

"The last time he came home he seemed depressed," my father said of Gino. "I hope there's nothing wrong! You know he's got significant responsibilities!"

Of all of us, Gino was the most faithful to our old family customs. He continued to go every Sunday to the mountains in both winter and summer. He still went sometimes with Franco Rasetti who lived in America now but occasionally showed up in Italy.

"Gino is such an excellent mountaineer!" my father said. "He does extraordinarily well on hikes! And he's a great skier too!"

"No," Gino said, "I'm actually a terrible skier. I ski in the old way. The younger generation now skis much better!"

"You're always modest!" my father said, and after Gino left he'd repeat, "How modest Gino is!"

"How intolerant Mario is!" he said every time Mario visited from Paris. "He never likes anyone! He only likes Chiaromonte!"

"I hope they don't fire him from UNESCO," he'd say. "The political situation in France is hardly stable! I'm very worried! What an idiot he was to get French citizenship! Chiaromonte didn't get it! Mario was a real idiot!"

Nevertheless, my mother was touched by Mario's children whenever he brought them to see her. "How sweet Mario is with his children," she'd say. "How much he loves them!"

"*Sa tétée! Il faut lui donner sa tétée!*" she'd say. "They're so French!"

"The little girl is gorgeous," she'd say, "but out of control! She really is a little devil!"

"They don't know how to raise them," my father said. "They're too spoiled."

"Why have kids if you can't spoil them?" my mother said.

"He told me I was bourgeois!" my mother said when Mario had left. "I seem bourgeois to him because I keep the closets neat. Their place is a huge mess. And Mario was so meticulous, so precise! He was the one like Silvio! Now he's entirely different. But he's happy!"

"Idiot! He told me I was too right-wing! He treated me as if I were a Christian Democrat!"

"But it's true you're right-wing," my father said. "You're afraid of communism. You let yourself be influenced by Paola Carrara!"

"I don't like the communists," my mother said. "I used to like the socialists, the old ones. Turati! Bissolati! How nice Bissolati was! I went to listen to him with my father on Sundays. Maybe this Saragat isn't so bad. It's a shame he has such a dull face!" my mother said.

And my father thundered, "Don't say such nitwitteries! You don't really think Saragat is a socialist! Saragat is a right-winger! The true socialism is Nenni's, not Saragat's!"

"I don't like Nenni! Nenni might as well be a communist! He always thinks Togliatti is right. I can't stand that Togliatti!"

"Because you're right-wing!"

"I'm not right-wing or left-wing! I'm for peace!" And she'd go out, her stride once again young, smooth, and glorious, her hat in hand, her by now white hair blowing in the wind.

She always stopped by Miranda's apartment for a little while in the mornings when she went shopping or in the afternoons on her way to the cinema.

"You're afraid of communists," Miranda told her, "because you're afraid they'll take away your maid."

"It's true. If Stalin came to take away my maid, I'd kill him," my mother said. "What would I do without my maid? I, who don't know how to do a thing?"

Miranda was always there, leaning back in her armchair with her blanket and her hot-water bottle, her blond hair drooping over her cheeks, speaking in her high-pitched, singsong, childish voice. Her parents had been taken by the Germans. They'd been taken like so many unfortunate Jews who didn't believe the persecution would really happen. They found they were too cold in Turin so they moved to Bordighera in order to be a little warmer. Bordighera was a small place and everyone knew them. Someone denounced them to the Germans and the Germans took them away.

When Miranda heard that they'd decided to move to Bordighera, she wrote begging them not to go because everyone there would know who they were. Big cities were safer. But they'd written back telling her not to be so silly. "We're peaceful people! Nothing happens to peaceful people!"

They wouldn't hear of false names, false papers. It seemed rude to them. They said, "Who will bother us? We're peaceful people!"

So the candid, cheerful little mother with heart trouble and the big, heavy, peaceful father were taken away by the Germans. Miranda heard that they were in prison in Milan so she and Alberto went there bringing letters, clothes, and food. They didn't manage to talk to anyone inside the prison and later learned that all the Jews from San Vittore Prison had been forced to leave for unknown destinations.

Miranda, Alberto, and their son went to Florence under false names. They had two rooms near the Campo di Marte. The boy came down with typhoid and during an air raid they had to carry him with a high fever wrapped in a blanket to a shelter.

After the war, they came back to Turin. Alberto reopened his doctor's office. In his waiting room there were always many sick people, and he, in his white coat, his stethoscope dangling over his chest, escaped occasionally to his living room to warm himself against the radiator or to drink a cup of coffee.

He'd gained weight and was almost totally bald but still had a bit of soft, blond, disheveled plumage on the crown of his head. Every so often, he decided to lose weight. He went on a diet taking special diet pills that he'd been given as samples. But during the night he got hungry and went to the kitchen to forage in the refrigerator for leftovers.

They had a gorgeous big refrigerator that Adriano had given them one time after Alberto had cured him from an illness. And Miranda, who was always complaining, also complained about that gift. "It's too big!" she said. "What will I put in it? I only buy a stick of butter at a time."

They were always reminiscing about the years they spent in exile in the Abruzzi. They were always pining for those years.

"How happy we were in exile in Rocca di Mezzo!" Alberto would say.

"We really were happy! I wasn't lazy. I went skiing," Miranda said, pronouncing the word "ski" in the English way like my father. "I took my little boy skiing. I got out of bed early in the morning and lit the stove. I never had a headache. Now I'm always tired again!"

"You didn't get up early," Alberto said. "Let's not romanticize! You didn't light the stove. The maid came in and did it!"

"What maid? How could she do it if we didn't have a maid!"

The boy, the old railwayman, was by now a teenager. He often played soccer with my children in Parco del Valentino. He was big and blond, and had a deep voice. In that deep voice, however, was the echo of his mother's singsong voice.

"Mama," he'd say, "can I go to the park with my cousins?"

"Don't get hurt!" my mother would tell him.

Miranda would say, "Don't worry. They're as cunning as serpents!"

"He's quite well-behaved," Alberto and Miranda would say about their son. "Who knows who brought him up to be so well-behaved. Certainly not us! He must have taught himself!"

"Perhaps I'll go to the mountains on Sunday," Alberto said, rubbing his hands together.

Alberto, like Gino, continued to go to the mountains but he didn't go in the same manner as Gino, the way my father had taught us. Gino went to the mountains by himself, or occasionally with his friend Rasetti. What he liked about going to the mountains was the cold, the wind, the fatigue, the discomfort, sleeping little and badly, eating little and in a hurry. Instead, Alberto went with a group of friends. He got out of bed late and stayed for hours in the hotel lounge, chatting and smoking. He had delicious warm meals in warm restaurants, lounged about for a while in his slippers, then finally went skiing. When he skied, he flung himself furiously into the sport just as he'd learned to do as a child. Not knowing how to pace himself or to judge his own stamina, he came home to Turin exhausted and jittery, with dark circles under his eyes.

Miranda wanted nothing to do with the mountains because she despised the cold and snow, with the exception of the nostalgia-tinged snow of Rocca di Mezzo on which she claimed to have skied so happily and which she missed so terribly.

"What an idiot Alberto is!" she'd say. "He always goes to the mountains hoping to have fun, and instead he never has fun, he just gets tired. What kind of fun is that? And why does he want to have fun now! When we were young we had fun going skiing or doing anything! We're not so young now and we don't have fun anymore!"

"It's something to do activities when you're young, it's another thing to do them now!"

"How depressing Miranda is!" Alberto said. "You depress me! You're a killjoy!"

Vittorio sometimes went over to their place in the evening when he was passing through Turin. Vittorio had been released from prison under Badoglio's government, then became one of the leaders of the Resistance in Piedmont. He was a member of the Action Party. He'd married Lisetta, Giua's daughter. After the demise of the Action Party, he became a socialist. He'd been elected to the Chamber of Deputies. He lived in Rome.

Lisetta hadn't changed much from the time years ago when we used to ride our bikes and she'd tell me the plots of Salgari's novels. She was still thin and pale, and stood tall with bright eyes and a tuft of hair that fell across her forehead. At fourteen, she'd dreamed of having adventurous escapades and she'd had a taste of what she'd dreamed of during the Resistance. She'd been arrested in Milan and imprisoned at the Villa Triste. She'd been interrogated by Ferida. Friends disguised as nurses helped her escape. She then bleached her hair so she wouldn't be recognized. Between her escapes and disguises, she had a baby girl. For a long time after the war, her short brown hair was streaked with blond.

As for her father, he'd also become a member of parliament and commuted between Rome and Turin. Her mother, Signora Giua, still came to visit my mother but they fought because my mother thought her too left-wing. They argued over where the borders were in Asia, and Signora Giua brought over her De Agostini mini-atlas in order to prove with documentary evidence that my mother was wrong. Signora Giua took care of Lisetta's little girl because Lisetta, who was still very young, didn't much want to be a mother to that child who was born almost without her noticing it. Lisetta had been thrust from a life still full of childish fantasies into the life of an adult without having had a moment to stop and think.

Lisetta was a communist and she saw in everyone and everything the dangerous remnants of the Action Party, which no longer existed. She called it the "AP" and saw its influence in the shadows of every corner. "You belong to the AP! You have the incurable mentality of the AP!" she'd say to Alberto and Miranda. Her husband, Vittorio, would look at her as if she were a kitten playing with a ball of string and laugh, his arrogant chin jutting out and his large shoulders shaking.

"It's impossible to live in Turin anymore! It's such a boring city!" Lisetta would say. "It's such an AP city! I can't live here anymore!"

"You're absolutely right!" Alberto said. "Everyone's bored to death here! Always the same faces!"

"What an idiot this Lisetta is!" Miranda said. "As if there were a place where anyone could have fun anymore! No one has fun anymore!"

"Let's go eat snails!" Alberto said, rubbing his hands together. And they would go out, crossing the Piazza Carlo Felice, the arcades dimly lit and nearly deserted at ten o'clock in the evening. They went into a nearly empty restaurant. There were no snails. Alberto ordered a plate of pasta.

"Weren't you on a diet?" Miranda said, and Alberto responded, "Shut up. You're such a killjoy!"

"What a pain Alberto is!" Miranda would complain to my mother in the mornings. "He's always restless, he always wants to do something! He always wants to eat something or drink something or go somewhere! He's always hoping to have fun!"

"He's like me," my mother said. "I always want to have fun too! I'd like to go on a beautiful trip somewhere!"

"Whatever for!" Miranda said. "We're so comfortable at home! Maybe I'll go visit Elena in San Remo for Christmas. But what'll I do when I actually get there? I might as well stay here!"

"Did you know I gambled at the San Remo casino?" she told my mother when she returned from her visit. "I lost! And that idiot Alberto lost too! We lost ten thousand lire!"

"Miranda," my mother told my father, "gambled at the San Remo casino. They lost ten thousand lire."

"Ten thousand lire!" my father thundered. "See what complete imbeciles they are! Tell them not to gamble ever again! Tell them I absolutely forbid it!"

He wrote to Gino: "That idiot Alberto lost a large sum at the San Remo casino."

My father's ideas about money became even more cloudy and confused after the war. Once, during the war, he asked Alberto to buy him ten cases of condensed milk. Alberto got them on the black market, paying more than a hundred lire each. My father asked him how much he owed.

"Nothing," Alberto said, "don't worry about it."

My father put forty lire into his hand and said, "Keep the change."

"You know my Incet stock has plummeted," Miranda told my mother. "Maybe I'll sell!" And she smiled the way she did whenever she spoke of money, won or lost—a joyful, shrewd, and mischievous smile.

"Did you know that Miranda is going to sell her Incet stock?" my mother told my father. "And she said we'd also do well to sell our property shares!"

"What do you think that nitwit Miranda knows about anything!" my father shouted.

Nevertheless, he thought it over. He asked Gino, "Do you think I should sell the property shares? Miranda said we should. You know Miranda understands the stock market. She's got great instincts. Her father, poor man, was a broker."

Gino said, "I don't understand a thing about the stock market!"

"That's right, of course, you wouldn't understand a thing about it! In our family we have no instinct for business matters!"

"When it comes to money, all we're good at is spending it," my mother said.

"That's certainly true for you," my father said. "But I wouldn't say that I spend too much! I've been wearing this same suit for seven years."

"In fact, it shows, Beppino!" my mother said. "It's all worn out and threadbare! You should get another one made!"

"I wouldn't dream of it! Not a chance. This is still a very good suit. How dare you tell me to get a new one!"

"Gino too," my father said, "he's not remotely a spendthrift. He's very moderate! He has moderate habits! Paola spends too much. All of you let money slip through your fingers, except Gino! The rest of you are megalomaniacs!"

"Gino," he said, "is very generous with others but with himself he's moderate. Gino, he's better than the lot of you!"

Occasionally Paola came from Florence to visit. She came alone by car.

"You came alone? By car?" my father said to her. "You shouldn't have. It's dangerous. What would you do if you had a flat tire? You should have come with Roberto! Roberto knows a lot about cars. He's been obsessed with cars since he was little. I remember he could talk about nothing else!"

He then said, "Tell me about Roberto!"

By now Roberto was grown up and going to university.

"I like Roberto very much. He's so good-natured!" my father said, then added, "But he likes women too much. Make sure he doesn't get married! Make sure he doesn't get it into his head to marry anyone!"

Roberto had a motorboat and he used to ride around in it during the summer with his friend Pier Mario. Once the motor broke down and the sea was very rough and things hadn't looked so good.

"Don't allow him to go in the motorboat alone with Pier Mario! It's dangerous!" my father said to Paola. "You must put your foot down! You have no authority!"

"Paola doesn't know how to bring up her children," my father said to my mother in the middle of the night. "She spoils them too much and they do whatever they like! They spend too much money! They're megalomaniacs!"

"Tersilla is here!" Paola said, entering the ironing room. "How marvelous to see Tersilla!"

Tersilla stood up, her smile revealing her gums, and asked Paola about her children: Lidia, Anna, and Roberto. Tersilla was making trousers for my children. My mother was always afraid that they would run out of trousers. "If they don't have trousers, they'll have nothing to cover their bottoms!" she said. She was so afraid that they would have "nothing to cover their bottoms" that she had five or six pairs made for them at a time. My mother and I fought over this issue of the trousers. "It's useless to make them so many pairs!" I'd say.

And she'd say, "All right, I understand you're a Soviet! You're for austerity! But I want to see the children properly dressed! I don't want them going around with nothing to cover their bottoms!"

Whenever Paola came to Turin my mother went out with her, arm in arm, strolling along the arcades, chatting, and window-shopping. She complained to Paola about me. "She never lends me her gear!" she'd say. "She doesn't talk. And then she's too much of a communist! She's a true Soviet! Luckily, I have my children!" she'd say, meaning my children. "They're so adorable! How I love them! I love all three of them and I wouldn't know which one to choose!"

"Luckily, I have my children so I don't get too bored. If it were left to Natalia, she'd send them out without covering their bottoms, but I wouldn't do that, I dress them properly! I have Tersilla come!"

The old tailor Belom had died some time ago. Now my mother had her clothes made in one of the arcade shops called Maria Cristina. For sweaters and blouses she went to Parisini.

"It's a Parisini!" she'd say, showing Paola the blouse she'd just bought. She spoke of it in the same way she spoke of the apples when they came to the table: "They're *carpandues*!"

"Come," she said to Paola, "let's go to Maria Cristina's! I want to have her make me a beautiful tailleur!"

"Don't get another tailleur made," Paola said, "you already have so many. Don't dress so much like the Swiss! Have her make you an elegant black coat instead, something distinguished that you can wear in the evenings when you go to visit Frances!"

My mother ordered the black coat. She then found that it didn't fit her very well in the shoulders. She had Tersilla adjust it for her at home, but still she never wore it. "It's too grande dame!" she said. "Perhaps I'll give it to Natalina!"

As soon as Paola had gone, my mother ordered her tailleur. She showed up at Miranda's one morning wearing her new tailleur.

"What's this," Miranda said, "you've had yourself another tailleur made!"

And my mother said, "Many clothes, much honor!"

Paola still had friends in Turin and sometimes she met up with them. And my mother was always a little jealous.

"How come you're not with Paola," Miranda would ask her, seeing her come in.

And my mother would say, "Today she went out with Ilda. I don't like that Ilda very much. She's not very pretty. She's too tall! I don't like women who are too tall. And she talks too much about Palestine."

Ilda had left Palestine by then but went on talking about it all the same. Her brother, Sion Segre, had a pharmaceutical company. He and Alberto were still friends.

Alberto said to Paola, "Shall we go eat snails with Ilda and Sion tonight?"

"I don't like snails," my mother said. And she stayed home to watch television. My father despised television saying it was nitwittery. At the same time he approved of my mother watching it because it had been a present from Gino. In fact, if she didn't turn it on in the evening and instead sat in an armchair reading a book, my father would say, "How come you don't turn on the television? Turn it on! Otherwise it's useless to have one! Gino gave it to you and you don't watch it! Since you've caused him to throw away his money, the least you could do is watch the thing!"

During the evenings my father read in his study. My mother watched television with the maid. After Natalina, my mother's maids always came from the Veneto. She got them from a town called Motta di Livenza. One of her maids started spitting up blood one evening. Everyone was terrified and we called Alberto to make an emergency visit. He told us to take her for an X-ray the following day. The woman was sobbing desperately. He said he didn't think the blood was coming from her lungs but from a scratch in her throat. In fact, the X-ray showed nothing. It was a scratch in her throat. The woman nevertheless continued to cry desperately. And my father said, "These proletarians, they have such a fear of dying!"

Before Paola's departure, my mother would hug her and cry, "How sad I am that you're leaving! Just when I'd gotten used to having you here!"

And Paola would say, "Why don't you come visit me for a while in Florence?"

"I can't," my mother said, "Papa won't let me. And besides Natalia goes off to that office of hers so I must look after my children."

Whenever Paola heard her say "my children," she became a bit jealous and irritated. "They're not your children! They're your grandchildren! And my children are your grandchildren! Come be with my children for a while!"

Sometimes my mother did go. "See Mary, too," my father said to her. "Make sure you go right away to see Mary!"

"Of course, I'll go," my mother said. "I very much want to see Mary! I like Mary!"

"How nice Mary is," she'd say when she came back. "She's such a good person! I've never known anyone as good as Mary! I had a great time in Florence. I like Florence. And Paola has that beautiful house!"

"I, on the other hand, can't stand Florence. I can't stand Tuscany," my father said. During the war when olive oil was hard to come by, Paola sent him some because there were olive trees on her property in Fiesole, and my father got angry. "I don't want olive oil. I can't stand olive oil. I can't stand the Tuscans! I don't want any kindnesses!"

"Paola didn't act like a jackass with you did she?" my father asked my mother.

"No! Poor Paola! She had breakfast brought to me in bed. I had a delicious breakfast while staying all warm in bed! I was very well taken care of!"

"That's good to hear! Because Paola can be a jackass!"

"And who keeps you from having breakfast in bed here at home?" Miranda asked my mother.

"Here, no, here I get up! I immediately take a nice cold shower. Then I wrap myself up well and play solitaire while I slowly warm up!"

She was playing solitaire in the dining room when Alessandra, my daughter, came in. Alessandra was in a foul, belligerent mood because she didn't want to get out of bed in the morning, nor did she want to go to school. And my mother said to her, "Look, here comes Hurricane Maria!"

"Let's see if I'll soon be going on a nice trip somewhere. Let's see if someone is going to give me a lovely cottage. Let's see if Gino will become famous. Let's see if instead of that job at UNESCO Gino will get a better and more distinguished job."

"Nonsense!" my father said, passing by. "Always this eternal nonsense!"

He put on his raincoat to go to the laboratory. He never went to the laboratory before dawn anymore as he used to. Now he went at eight o'clock in the morning. At the door, he shrugged his shoulders and said, "Who's going to give you a cottage? You're such a nitwit!"

I spent all my evenings at the Balbos' place. Sometimes Lisetta was there, but not Vittorio because he rarely came to Turin, and when he did he preferred to see his old friend Alberto in the evening. Lisetta and Balbo's wife were friends. Lola, Balbo's wife, was that beautiful but detestable girl I once used to see out my window or walking down the Corso Re Umberto, her stride slow and disdainful. Lola and Lisetta had become friends during the years I was in exile. I don't know at what point Lola had stopped being detestable. When she and I became friends, she explained to me that she was well aware that back in those days she'd been detestable and had, in fact, tried to seem as detestable as possible because deep down she was paralyzed by timidity, insecurity, and boredom. Throughout our friendship I would look back with sheer astonishment at the old image of her as arrogant and detestable—so detestable that under her gaze I'd felt like a worm and had despised her and myself because of it. I looked back upon that image and compared it to the effortless and sisterly one I had of my friend today, for me one of the most effortless and sisterly in all the world.

While I was in exile, Lola had worked briefly as a secretary at the publishing house. She proved to be, however, a very absentminded and dreadful secretary. She was then arrested by the fascists and put in prison for two months. During the German occupation, between her escapes and disguises, she married Balbo. She was still very beautiful but she no longer had the neat, compact pageboy haircut that made her look as if she were wearing an iron helmet. Now she had disheveled hair that drooped over her cheeks; it was American Indian hair though not the hair of a squaw but the beaten-by-the-sun-and-the-rain hair of a chief. And her profile, once sharp and static, had transformed into a face that was anxious and lined, raw and weathered by the sun and the rain. Every so often for a moment or two, however, that old sharpened and disdainful profile of hers would reappear, as would her swaying and disdainful stride.

Whenever someone mentioned her, my father would immediately rejoin with how beautiful she was: "She's so beautiful that Lola Balbo! Ah, she is beautiful!"

And he'd say, "I understand the Balbos are very good mountaineers. I understand they're friends with Mottura."

Mottura was a biologist, whom my father respected. The fact that Balbo and Mottura were friends made him feel better about my evenings spent over there. Every time I went out in the evening, he'd say to my mother, "Where is she going. Is she going to Balbo's place? The Balbos are very good friends with Mottura!"

And he'd say, "How come they're such good friends with Mottura? How do they know each other?"

My father was always curious to know why someone was friends with someone else. "How does he know him? How did they meet?" he'd ask, insistently. "Ah, maybe they met in the mountains! Surely they met in the mountains!" And once the origin of the relationship between the two people was established he would relax, and if he respected either one of them, he was happy to give the other his kindly approval.

"Is Lisetta also going to the Balbos' place? How do they know Lisetta?"

The Balbos lived on the Corso Re Umberto. They had a ground-floor apartment and the door was always open. People came and went continually: friends of Balbo's who accompanied him to the publishing house followed him to the Café Platti where he always ordered a cappuccino, followed him home in the evening and talked with him there late into the night. If his friends came to the apartment and found he wasn't there, they sat down in the living room anyway and spoke amongst themselves, or walked up and down the halls, or perched on the desk in his study, having learned from him to never keep a schedule, nor to remember a mealtime, and to argue incessantly.

Lola was totally fed up with having so many people hanging around her place. All the same, she got on with whatever it was she had to do. She looked after her child with a mixture of apprehension and annoyance because, like Lisetta, she didn't really know how to be a mother, her transition from the fog of adolescence to tempestuous adulthood having been abrupt and lacking in any sense of continuity.

Occasionally she left her son with her mother or mother-in-law and enjoyed dressing up very elegantly, putting on pearls and jewels, and going out for a walk on the Corso Re Umberto, as she had long ago, her stride slow, her eyes half closed, her aquiline profile slicing the air. When she came home and found everyone just as she'd left them, sitting around arguing on the box seat in the front hall or perched on tables, she let out a long, guttural cry of exasperation to which no one paid any attention.

Whenever her husband was away she used endearing nicknames for him and lamented his temporary absence with a long, guttural but affectionate cry, like a dove calling to its mate. But then as soon as she saw him again she immediately reproached him, either because he always arrived late to lunch or because he'd left her without a penny for food or because of that door that was always open and those people who were always coming and going. So they fought, he armed with his fine-tuned quibbling, she with nothing but her fury; and the rights and wrongs committed by each became hopelessly entangled. Moreover, they were never alone, not even when they fought, and she would randomly insult any friend who happened to be nearby, yelling at him to get out. But the friend would never dream of doing so, and would wait, calm and amused, until the storm had passed.

Balbo always ate the same thing at lunch: rice with butter, a steak, a potato, an apple. Ever since he'd had parasites during the war, this was all he'd been able to eat. "Is there any steak?" he'd ask anxiously, sitting down at the table. As soon as he was reassured on this front, he ate distractedly as he continued to talk with his friends who were always there even during his meals, and to fight with his wife, his arguments rife with his fine-tuned quibbles.

"He's boring!" Lola would say to his friends. "I find him so boring! Yes, there's steak. How boring he is always carrying on about his steak! If only for once he'd eat a fried egg!" And she would recall the time in Rome during the Resistance when they were in hiding and penniless and she'd run all over the city trying to buy butter, steak, and rice on the black market. Balbo paused to explain that he couldn't eat fried eggs because they made him sick, then solemnly and distractedly went on eating, indifferent to what kind of steak he was consuming just as long as it was a bona fide grilled steak.

"I don't like these friends of yours!" Lola complained. "They don't have any kind of private life. They don't have wives or children, or if they do, they neglect them! They're always here!"

On Saturday and Sunday the place became deserted. Lola left her child with her mother-in-law and they went, she and her husband, skiing.

"How sweet he was yesterday," Lola would say about her husband to the friends who were once again in her place on Monday morning. "He was so sweet, if only you could have seen him. He knows how to ski like an instructor! He looks like ballet dancer! He wasn't at all boring anymore. We had so much fun! But now he's become boring again!"

Sometimes they went, she and her husband, to a nightclub to dance. They danced, the two of them, until late into the night. "We had so much fun!" Lola would say afterwards. "He is so good at waltzing! He's got such a light step!" And as she hung up her evening gown in the closet she would aim that guttural and affectionate dove cry of hers in the direction of her husband who was just then at the office.

Every so often Balbo would say to his wife, "Buy yourself a new evening gown. It would please me."

To please him, she bought a dress and then was unhappy, realizing the dress was ridiculous and she'd never wear it. "That idiot!" she'd say. "To please him, I bought a dress that makes no sense!"

Lola never worked again after her brief stint as a secretary at the publishing house. She and her husband were in agreement over the fact that she had been a dreadful secretary. But they both also agreed that the right job for her did exist, though precisely what job had yet to be discovered. Balbo even asked me to search among the thousands of jobs that existed on the planet for one that truly suited Lola.

Lola used to remember with great longing the time she spent in prison. "When I was in jail," she'd often say. She would recount how in jail she finally felt tremendously at ease, finally at home and at peace with herself, finally free of her complexes and inhibitions. She'd made friends there with some young women from Yugoslavia who'd been arrested for political reasons and she also made friends with some of the ordinary prisoners. She knew how to talk to them, how to earn their trust, and was often surrounded by other prisoners seeking her help and advice. The conversations that Balbo and his wife had about a possible job for her always wound up back "in jail" and they both concluded that they should find a job for her in which she felt, as she had in jail, entirely at ease, free, without any inhibitions, and fully in control of her powers. Such a job, however, was not so easy to find. She then got sick and had to stay for a short time in the hospital, and in the hospital among the sick young women she rediscovered some of her leadership powers; evidently they came alive in dramatic situations involving extreme tension, risk, and urgency.

In Rome, Lisetta found a job as an employee of the Italy-USSR Association. She'd learned to speak Russian. She began to study it right after the war with Lola and me. She, however, had gone on to learn the language properly while we'd stopped somewhere along the way. So Lisetta went to the office every day and somehow managed to run her household and bring up her children, though she pretended not to bother much about the children, pretended that even though they were very small, they were entirely independent. She still came to Turin for holidays and brought the children with her. Whenever we asked her where the children were she became distracted and vague and said she couldn't remember exactly where she'd left them. She liked to give off the idea that she'd sent them alone to play in the street. Her children would actually be in the park, looked after by their grandmother and their nanny, and she'd go get them as soon as it got dark, bringing their scarves and hats; without noticing, and without admitting it to herself or to anyone else, she'd become an affectionate, scrupulous, and anxious mother.

She also frequently pretended to be in a fight with her husband over politics. In truth, she was, when it came to her husband, meek as a lamb and fundamentally incapable of having an opinion at odds with his. Besides, there was no real difference between them in terms of their political beliefs. The Action Party, the AP, had by now been lost to the mists of time and no traces of it were left anywhere. But Lisetta often declared that she saw its ghost appearing everywhere and especially within the walls of her own home. As soon as her children could think for themselves, she began to argue with them, above all with her eldest daughter, who was sententious and sarcastic and always ready with a barbed response. So mother and daughter would argue at length, a plate of meat in front of them, trotting out the poor and the rich, the left and the right, Stalin, the priests, and Jesus Christ, while eating their plate of meat.

"Stop acting like such a countess!" Lisetta would say to her friend Lola whenever Lisetta saw Lola bedecking herself with jewels and painting her face in front of the mirror. Eventually Lisetta too would put on just a touch of black eyeliner and they would go out onto the Corso Re Umberto and walk along the boulevards: Lisetta wearing sandals over her childish bare feet, her raincoat open, Lola in her form-fitting black coat with large buttons, a brooch on the lapel, her prominent aquiline nose slicing through the air as she took up her old swaying and disdainful stride.

They went to the publishing house where they found Balbo chatting in the hallway either with some priest or with Mottura or with one of his friends who'd followed him there from home.

"He hangs around priests too much," Lisetta said of Balbo. "He's with them too often!" She never described him as having "an AP mentality"; in fact, he was one of the few people she didn't describe this way. Balbo, though, sometimes accused her of being "a little AP" and accused her of perhaps being the last AP still in existence. She, on the other hand, accused him of being too Catholic, but she was disposed to forgive him for it, even though this was something for which she wouldn't forgive anyone else in the world. But she still remembered how, in her younger days, his eloquence had fascinated her whenever he came on Sundays to bring her books by Croce.

"A count! At heart he is a count! At heart they are a count and a countess!" Lisetta would say whenever she thought of the Balbos when she was far away in Rome. She saw other friends in Rome but she didn't like them as much. She agreed with these friends on most things but they didn't share memory's firm bonds so she was actually quite bored with them, though she'd never admit it to herself. The fact that Balbo was Catholic and came from a noble family seemed to her, especially from afar, to weaken all the arguments he'd made to her when they were together. Every time she came back to Turin, however, the Balbos' home was an irresistible draw. Yet she could never admit the truth to herself and say, "They're my friends and I love them and I don't care a fig if their opinions are right or wrong, I don't care a fig if he likes priests so much." Because in her childish, affectionate, and naive nature her opinions and ideas, as well as those of others, took root and branched out like large leafy trees that obscured from her own eyes the clear reflection of her soul.

Mottura chatted with Balbo so often and at such length that a new verb was coined at the publishing house: "to motturize." "What's Balbo doing? He's motturizing! Of course, he's motturizing!" we'd say. Balbo, after having had a conversation with Mottura, went to the publisher to pass on his friend's suggestions regarding a series of science books Balbo had nothing to do with, but he liked to poke his nose into what was happening with the various series and to offer his two cents. Balbo had no scientific expertise even if, during his youthful confusion, before going to law school he'd spent two years in medical school. But he didn't remember a thing from those two years. Mottura was the only scientist he knew aside from my father, who'd taught him in his anatomy course years ago. But Balbo was inspired by his conversations with Mottura to seek out science books that he never read but only dipped his red nose into here and there for a moment or two. After having discussed things with Mottura, Balbo was always very quick to offer his opinions and ideas on the subject. But just as he never had any specific agenda when talking to anybody, with Mottura he conversed for the sheer pleasure of it and was in no way motivated by trying to glean from him his ideas and opinions. And even if initially he may have had such an aim, he almost immediately forgot this intention. His conversations would follow a thread of disinterested inquiry, utterly devoid of purpose. And then, like someone who out of necessity takes a crap in a garden and realizes that in any case he was fertilizing it, Balbo would impart upon the publishing house some of what he'd learned. His concept of work would have been unthinkable, and certainly not tolerated, in any place other than that publishing house. Later on, at another job, he did, in fact, learn how to work differently, but at the time that was how he worked, never acknowledging that he was tired until the evening when he lay down and was overcome by exhaustion. He was also writing a book then, though when he found the time to write it no one could possibly imagine, but somehow he did find the time because at a certain point the book was ready to be published and he begged others to proofread the galleys for him because he didn't know how. He could look at galleys for months and never see an error.

I stayed at the Balbos' home in the evenings until late. Three friends of the Balbos were permanent fixtures: a small man with a mustache, a tall man who had a striking resemblance to Gramsci, and another curly-haired man with a florid complexion who was always smiling. The one who was always smiling came to work at the publishing house on the science-books series, which was very strange since he didn't appear to have had any experience whatsoever in the sciences, but he was evidently successful because he kept his job for years and, in fact, became the director of that series, always wearing his gentle, helpless, sad smile, always opening his arms wide while claiming he knew nothing about science. Eventually he left and opened his own publishing house specializing in scientific books.

Balbo would take a momentary break from his discussions with his friends in order to expound to Pavese and to me on his ideas concerning our writing. Pavese listened to him with a wicked smile while sitting in an armchair beneath a lamp, smoking his pipe; he would reply to everything Balbo said that he was already aware of it and had been for a very long time.

Nevertheless, he listened to Balbo with real pleasure. Pavese's relationship with his friends always included an ironic banter that he called upon whenever he was talking with us or about us or getting to know us. This irony of his was perhaps one of his most wonderful qualities, but he never knew how to bring his sense of irony to bear upon those things most important to him; he didn't bring it to his relationships with the women he fell in love with, nor did he bring it to his writing. He was able to bring it to his friendships because friendship came to him naturally and he was in some ways careless about his friendships in the sense that they were something he didn't give excessive importance to. In love, and in his writing, he threw himself into such a state of feverish calculation that he no longer knew how to laugh or to ever be entirely himself. And sometimes when I think about him now, his sense of irony is the thing I remember best about him and I cry because it no longer exists. There's no trace of it in his books and it's nowhere else to be found except in that flash of his wicked smile.

As for me, I was eager to hear someone talk about my books. Balbo's words sometimes seemed dazzlingly incisive, but I was also well aware that he only ever read a few lines of any book. His days were such that there was neither the time nor the space for reading. But he made up for the lack of time and space with a very astute and sharp intuition that allowed him to form an opinion based on barely a few sentences. When he wasn't around I would decide I hated his way of forming an opinion and accused him of being superficial. But I was wrong because he was anything but generic and superficial. Even from a prolonged and attentive reading he wouldn't have reached a more thorough and profound opinion. What was generic and superficial, however, was the practical advice he gave regarding books or people. He didn't know how to give practical advice to others or to himself. The practical advice he gave to me about my books, or when he saw that I was depressed, was to go more often to the cell and branch meetings of the Communist Party—I was a member then—and to become more involved. He seemed to think that this was the best way to get me back into the real world from which, he said, I'd become detached. During the postwar period, it was a widely held view that writers should, through participating in left-wing parties, come down out of their ivory towers and get a grip on the real world. I wasn't able, at the time, to tell Balbo his advice was wrong, and simply became unhappier and even more confused. Instead of saying something to him about how I felt, I obeyed him and went to those meetings that I found profoundly sad and boring, though I was unable to admit it at the time.

I understood only later that his practical advice shouldn't be followed under any circumstances, that practical suggestions needed to be excised from his talk. When his words were stripped of any practical content they were informative and useful. But at the time I felt compelled to follow his every step and to make every mistake he did. As for Pavese, he didn't make the mistakes we did; he made others of his own. He stumbled down other paths where he walked alone, his attitude contemptuous and stubborn, his gentle heart aching.

Pavese's mistakes were worse than ours. Our mistakes were born of impulsiveness, imprudence, stupidity, and naiveté. Instead, Pavese's mistakes were the result of prudence, guile, calculation, and intelligence. Nothing is more dangerous than this sort of mistake, which can be, as it was for him, fatal. It's difficult to recover from a mistake made through guile. Mistakes made through guile tie us up in tight knots. Guile puts down roots in us that are stronger than those put down by recklessness or imprudence. How does one get rid of those tenacious, firm, profound roots? Prudence, calculation, guile have the face of reason, the bitter face and voice of reason, presenting infallible arguments to which there is no response, nothing to do but submit.

Pavese killed himself one summer in Turin when none of us was there. He had contrived and calculated the circumstances regarding his death in the way he planned a walk or an evening out. On his walks or evenings out, he didn't like to encounter anything unforeseen or surprising. Whenever the Balbos, the publisher, Pavese, and I went for a walk in the hills, he became very irritated if we strayed from the designated path or if someone arrived late to our meeting point, or if we suddenly changed plans, or if someone unexpectedly joined us, or if by some fortuitous circumstance, instead of going to eat in the restaurant he'd chosen, we ate at the home of an acquaintance we unexpectedly ran into along our way. The unforeseen made him anxious. He didn't like to be taken by surprise.

He had talked about killing himself for years. No one ever believed him. When he came over to my and Leone's place eating his cherries while France was falling to the Germans, he was already talking about it—not because of France or the Germans, and not because of the war encroaching upon Italy. He was afraid of the war, but not enough to kill himself. Even so, for quite a while after the war was over, he continued to be afraid of the war, as, in fact, we all were. As soon as the war was over, we were immediately afraid that another war would start and we thought about it obsessively. He was more afraid than any of the rest of us, however, of another war. For him, fear was the vortex of the unknown and the unexpected, and horrendous to his clear thinking: dark poisoned waters swirling against the barren shores of his life.

He didn't have any particular motive for killing himself. However, he'd put together various motives, adding them up with lightning precision, combining them this way and that, proving to himself that from any angle the result was the same and therefore definitive, a decision he confirmed wearing his wicked smile. He also gazed beyond his own life into the future to see how people would behave with respect to his books and his memory. Like those who love life and don't know how to detach themselves from it, he looked beyond death and imagined death to the point where it was no longer death he imagined but life. In any case, he didn't love life, and his gaze beyond his own death was not out of a love of life but was a shrewd calculation of circumstances so that nothing, even after he was dead, could take him by surprise.

Balbo left the publishing house and went to live in Rome. He floundered between crazy projects and erroneous endeavors for years. Finally he got a real job and learned to work like other people, but as he had done at the publishing house, he forgot to go to lunch and to leave the office at the end of the day when everyone else did. Without realizing it, he ended up working harder than any of his colleagues and was astonished by how exhausted he was in the evening.

The Balbos had three children by then and though they tried to become regular parents they were incapable, which made them feel guilty. They would accuse each other daily of this inadequacy. Neither one of them claimed to know how to bring up children, but each asked from the other to be something he or she was not. Balbo did his best to teach his children geography, a subject he knew well, but he couldn't remember a thing about any of the other subjects taught at school even though, according to him, he'd been a stellar student.

He never broached historical subjects with his children; for one thing he knew very little history, but he also was afraid that his own political opinions and judgments would insinuate themselves into any historical discussion he had with his kids and he didn't want them fed already formed opinions. He believed they should make their own judgments and form their own opinions. This seemed strange in someone who for so long had been quite aggressive and intrusive when imparting his judgments and opinions to his friends; he'd also been aggressive and intrusive in terms of appropriating others' opinions and judgments, which he pulled apart, reassembled, then imprinted with the stamp of his own way of thinking. He proved to be unusually reticent when serving the food of his thought to his children.

Lola and her husband, therefore, never discussed politics in the presence of their children—she, because she hated sectarianism; he, because he believed one should abstain from involving children in complex topics. And since both of them feared muddling their children's minds and causing them to be wary and suspicious of established authority, Lola's prison experience was never mentioned.

As for Lola, she created an idealized version of children which clashed considerably with the reality of her children, and she was always comparing the ideal children with her own lazy, messy, and absentminded ones. The result was that all she did was scold them in her gruff and random manner, which didn't frighten them, but the combination of the noise, the chaos, and the dissonance made for a discombobulated atmosphere in their home. She also created an ideal husband and father entirely opposed to the man Balbo was or ever could be. Occasionally she would hurl in the direction of her husband and children a long, guttural, exasperated cry, like the ones she used to hurl at the random people who roamed her apartment.

In their Rome apartment people didn't come and go as they had at their place on the Corso Re Umberto in Turin. In fact, they now had only a few friends who came to visit at reasonable hours. They were people to whom Balbo had nothing particular to say so he would either engage with them in silly banter or remain silent. His former penchant for elevated and aggressive conversation had subsided. Nowadays, he called up his intelligence only for precise goals involving specific people at specific times of the day, after which he would close himself off in silence, as one closes the shutters at the end of the day.

Occasionally, when the children were away on holiday or when Balbo and his wife were traveling alone, they still enjoyed their days and evenings as they once had: sleeping whenever they felt like it, wandering the streets to buy dresses and shoes for her that pleased him, or dancing at nightclubs.

Lola finally got a job. She didn't find it but rather it fell into her lap when she was least expecting it. If she could have chosen any job, it probably wouldn't have been that one, and it didn't remotely resemble her jail experience, which she considered the best and noblest time of her life. Nevertheless, she was good at her job and brought to it a modicum of her intelligence. She also brought to it disorderliness, impatience, anxiety, and her tendency to pick a fight. Her love of a fight revealed itself most often at the post office, where she sometimes went as part of her job to mail brochures and parcels.

She worked for some magistrates. She usually worked from home while shouting out commands to her maid and children, telephoning her mother-in-law and her friends, and being fitted for clothes. Her job added chaos to chaos. She sometimes had to wrap up parcels and would suddenly decide that this was something she could have her children do, suddenly imagining that her children were experts at wrapping parcels. So she would shout "Luucaaa!" and Luca, a large boy, would appear covered in ink stains and lost in a fog of indolence, as idle and indifferent as a prince. She ordered him to wrap up twenty or so parcels immediately, though Luca had never wrapped a parcel in his life. She placed in his hands a sheaf of packing paper and a roll of string. Luca wandered through the apartment holding the roll of string, preoccupied, forgetful, and sluggish, moving slowly and aimlessly until Lola suddenly smothered him in shouts and ripped the string from his hands while he stared out at her from his regal and silent remove through proud and stagnant green eyes.

In the winter the Balbos always took their children skiing in the mountains. They insisted on going to the north since the low, wind-swept, crowded mountains near Rome weren't good enough for them. They went to Sestriere or to Switzerland, and there on the snow-covered slopes Lola was free. She forgot about her magistrates; she forgot about her children's studies; she forgot about her maid who perhaps consumed too much olive oil; she forgot about her bad moods and her eternal resentments. But in order to reach that freedom, she first had to endure several days in Rome of complete and invincible chaos—suitcases were packed and unpacked, sweaters lost and found, errands run breathlessly throughout the city. There was constant shouting, orders given then repealed, telephones ringing, last-minute appointments with the magistrates—all while her bewildered maid and the impenetrable Luca stained with black ink looked on.

In the summers, Lola went to the seaside in Ostia. She went alone because her husband didn't much like the sea and during those years her children would go away to a Boy Scout camp. She usually went with anyone she could find who was willing to drive her there and bring her home. The conversations she had with these acquaintances neither bored nor amused her since there was a worldly part of her nature unaffected by boredom or amusement but rather driven by some immediate interest such as being given a ride somewhere or finding the address of an upholsterer. Her practical life was thus further complicated by her search for an upholsterer on the far side of the city, or an inexpensive carpenter who didn't have a telephone, or a remote fabric shop where, because of some acquaintance, she would be given a small discount. She loved to go to Ostia by herself, taking long swims in the sea, then drying herself in the sun. She became absurdly tan even though her doctor had told her not to get too much sun on account of that illness she'd once had and which she was terrified of having a recurrence, but not terrified enough to keep her away from the sea, the sun, and the sand. She would come home around four o'clock to eat lunch, hurling that tender, guttural cry of hers at her husband and feeling pacified by that morning of freedom and holiday, loving the summer, the heat, that her children were away at camp, and that she could roam around the apartment in her bathing suit and bare feet.

I was still living in Turin but I often went to Rome and was preparing to move there permanently. I had remarried, my husband taught in Rome, and we were looking for an apartment there. Soon the children and I would install ourselves down there for good.

I went to visit the Balbos. We were still friends and we spoke about the old days. I said to Balbo, "Do you remember when we used to do self-criticism?"

During the postwar years, self-criticism was a popular practice. Whenever one of us made a mistake, we would analyze it and pull it apart out loud to the point where the mistake became confused with and inextricable from the self-criticism—a bit like when the music in an opera engulfs the libretto so that the meaning of the words is lost, carried away by the music's glorious rhythm.

I said, "Do you remember when we used to hold those political rallies?"

Lola let out an anguished moan at the recollection of her husband's political rallies, imagining his diminished figure up on the wooden platform among waving banners, picturing him looking out over a square packed with people while he spun out sentences in his indecisive voice, occasionally scratching the crown of his head with his forefinger. The dark, cold night would begin to settle in and he'd still be up there spinning out his sentences, lost in trying to follow his own tortuous and quibbling reasoning, convinced that those listening were following him along the winding, stony, blind path down which he was leading them. The people waited in vain to hear slogans that would resonate and chime clear as bells, the kind they were used to hearing and applauding. But they applauded anyway, perhaps out of sympathy and blind trust, or perhaps they applauded so that he would finally shut up.

My father also once held a political rally during those years. He had been asked to put his name on the list of candidates running for the Popular Front. The Popular Front was the name of the coalition party formed by the communists and the socialists. He accepted. He was told he would have to lead one political rally, only one. They told him he could say whatever he liked. They brought him into a theater, got him onstage, and my father began his rally with these words: "Science is the pursuit of truth."

He spoke exclusively about science for nearly twenty minutes as people silently looked on, stupefied. At a certain point, he said that scientific research was far more advanced in America than in Russia. The people, even more confused, remained silent. He then unexpectedly happened to mention Mussolini and the fact that he usually referred to him as the "Jackass from Predappio." The audience erupted into resounding applause and my father looked around him, now stupefied himself. This was my father's political rally.

Balbo, who had been present at that rally, laughed at the recollection of it. He had liked my father very much and was the only professor Balbo remembered from his two years of medical school. At the start of the scholastic year, the freshmen would form an unruly throng outside the institute entrance and my father, Balbo recounted, threw himself into the middle of that mob with his head down, like a buffalo charging into a herd, in order to clear a path for himself through the crowd.

I remembered my father running like a buffalo with his head down through the streets during the war whenever there was an air raid. My father wouldn't go down into the shelters and whenever the sirens sounded he started to run, not to a shelter but towards home. Under the roar and whistle of planes, he ran hugging the walls with his head down, happy to be in danger because danger was something he loved.

"Nitwitteries!" he'd say afterward. "No way I'd ever go into a shelter! What do I care if I die!"

When I told my mother that I would be leaving Turin and going to live in Rome she was terribly upset.

"You're taking my children away!" she said. "What a shrew you are!"

"She'll let them go around in rags," she told Miranda. "She'll let them go around without buttons! With nothing to cover their bottoms!"

She was remembering when she came to visit me in exile and in the kitchen there was a box full of mending because I never did the mending. I would begin to sew something, then put it down and say, "I can't sew anymore. I lost the needle."

For many years, I hadn't had my own home, or a cupboard for sheets, or a box full of mending. For many years, I'd lived with my father and my mother, and my mother had taken care of everything.

During the summer, it was they, my father and my mother, who organized taking the children to the mountains, usually to Perlotoa where they rented the same house they always rented with the meadow in front of it. I stayed behind alone in the city and only ever left for a few days when the publishing house closed.

"Let's go for a hike!" my father said in the mountains, early in the morning, dressed in his old rust-colored coat, thick socks, and hobnailed boots. "Rise and shine! We're going for a hike! Stop being so lazy! You can't just stay here in the meadow all day! I won't have it!"

They came home in September and my mother called Tersilla in to make trousers, school pinafores, pajamas, and coats.

"I want them tidy. I like to keep children tidy. I like them to have all their little things organized. If I know they're nice and warm I feel very consoled!"

In the evenings my mother read *Nobody's Boy* to them. "How wonderful *Nobody's Boy* is!" she'd say. "It's one of the most beautiful books ever written!

"The Marchesa Colombi's books are very lovely too," she said. "It's too bad you can't find them anymore. You should tell your publisher," she said to me, "to bring the Marchesa Colombi's books back into print. They were so beautiful!"

I had given the children *Misunderstood*. Paola had read it to me when I was a girl. At the time she'd loved stories that were very sad and moving, that made you cry and ended badly. My mother didn't like *Misunderstood*. She thought it was too sad. "*Nobody's Boy* is much better," she said. "There's no comparison. *Misunderstood* is too sentimental. I don't like it very much at all. But *Nobody's Boy*, now that's something else! Capi! Signor Vitalis! The beautiful swaddling clothes lied! Honor your father and mother! The beautiful swaddling clothes told the truth!" And she would go on to list all the characters in *Nobody's Boy*, followed by the chapter titles, which she knew by heart, having read the book innumerable times to her children and now to my children, a chapter a night, always falling under the spell of those exploits that might take a sudden dramatic turn but would never end badly. She also fell under the spell of Capi, the dog, for whom she had a particular liking since she loved dogs. "I would love to have a dog like him! But Papa would never let me have a dog!"

"I would also love to have a beautiful lion! I love lions! I love all ferocious beasts!" she said. And whenever she could, she would run to the circus using the children as her excuse to go. "It's such a shame Turin doesn't have a zoo. I would go every day. I always have a burning desire to see the face of a ferocious beast!"

"*Misunderstood* is not a good book," she said. "Paola liked it when she was a teenager because Paola and Mario, at the time, had an obsession with sad things. Fortunately, they've outgrown that now!"

"Mario and Paola were very close when they were children," my father said. "Do you remember when they used to whisper all the time with poor Terni? They were obsessed with Proust and could talk about nothing else. Now Paola and Mario are so standoffish, they won't even look each other in the eye anymore. He thinks she's bourgeois. What jackasses!"

"When is your translation of Proust coming out?" my mother asked me. "I haven't read Proust in a long time. But I remember reading him. He writes so beautifully! I remember Madame Verdurin! Odette! Swann! Madame Verdurin must have been a bit like Drusilla!"

Sometime after I remarried I moved to Rome and my mother held a grudge against me for a little while. But her grudge never lodged very deeply or bitterly in her heart. At first, I went back and forth between Rome and Turin, preparing myself to leave Turin for good.

I said goodbye in my heart to the publishing house, to the city. I thought about continuing to work for the publishing house in the Rome office, but I thought it would be too different from what I had known. The one I loved was the publishing house that opened onto the Corso Re Umberto only a few meters from the Café Platti, a few meters from where the Balbos used to live when they were still in Turin, and only a few meters from the hotel under the arcades where Pavese had died.

I loved my colleagues at the publishing house, those particular colleagues, not any other ones. I believed I wouldn't know how to work with other people. In fact, when I moved to Rome I did leave the publishing house for good, finding myself incapable of working without the publisher and my old colleagues.

Gabriele, my husband, wrote to me from Rome and told me to hurry up and come down there with the children. He'd become friends with the Balbos and when he was alone he went to see them in the evenings.

"But in Rome you must learn to darn!" my mother said. "Or if you don't, you must find yourself a maid who is good at darning! Find yourself a seamstress who will come to the apartment, a bit like Tersilla. Ask Lola. Lola will get you a seamstress in no time! Or ask Adele Rasetti. Go visit Adele Rasetti. She's so nice! I really like Adele!"

"Write down Adele Rasetti's address," my father said. "I'll write it down for you! Don't lose it! I'll also write down for you the address of my cousin, the son of poor Ettore! He's a very good doctor! You could call him!"

"Make sure you go right away to visit Adele!" my father said. "If you don't go, you'd better watch out! Don't be a jackass with Adele! The whole lot of you are jackasses! With the exception of Gino, the whole lot of you are jackasses towards other people! Mario is a jackass. He must have been a grand jackass with Frances when she went to Paris to visit them! He must not have lent her much gear. And she indicated to me that their apartment was a wreck as usual!"

"To think he was once so neat, Mario!" my mother said. "He was so meticulous, so fussy. He was like Silvio!"

"But now," my father said, "he's changed. Frances let me know the place was a mess. You lot are slobs!"

"Not I. I'm neat," my mother said. "Look in my closets."

"Hardly! You mess everything up! You couldn't find my winter suit!"

"Yes, I did find it! I knew just where it was! But I put it aside to mend because it's old. You can't wear it anymore, Beppino!"

"There's no way I'm getting rid of it. I wouldn't dream of it. I'll be dead before long so I'm hardly going to have a new suit made for me!"

"You had that suit made when you went to Liège! You wore it throughout the war! You've been wearing that suit for nearly ten years now!"

"So what if I've worn it? It's still a very good suit! I don't throw money away like the rest of you. You lot are all megalomaniacs!"

"Even my poor little mother," he said, "always insisted that I get suits made. She didn't want me to look bad when I went to visit La Vendée. My poor cousin Ettorino was very elegant and she didn't want me to make a bad impression when compared to him!"

"At La Vendée's place," he said, "there were lunches to which fifty, sixty people were invited. There was an entire procession of carriages. Bepo, the porter, served at the table. Once he fell down the stairs and broke a large pile of dishes! When my brother, poor Cesare, was weighed after those lunches he'd have gained five or six kilos!"

"My poor brother Cesare was too fat. He ate too much. I wouldn't want Alberto, who also eats a lot, to become fat like poor Cesare!"

"Everyone ate too much. In those days everyone ate too much. I remember my grandmother Dolcetta. How she could eat!

"On the other hand, my mother, poor thing, ate very little. She was thin. Poor thing. My mother was very beautiful when she was young. She had a beautifully shaped head. Everyone said that she had a beautiful head. She also gave lunches for fifty or sixty people. There was hot ice cream and cold ice cream. We ate very well!

"At those lunches my cousin Regina was very elegant. She was beautiful, ah, Regina, she was very beautiful!"

"But no, Beppino," my mother said, "she was a fake beauty!"

"Ah, no, you're wrong. She was very beautiful! I liked her a lot. Poor Cesare, he liked her a lot too. As a young woman, however, she was a bit silly. She was very silly! Even my mother often said it about her. She said, 'Regina is very silly!'"

"My uncle, the Lunatic, sometimes went to those lunches of your mother's," my mother said.

"Sometimes, but not always. The Lunatic put on airs, he found the atmosphere too bourgeois, too reactionary. He put on airs, your uncle."

"He was so nice!" my mother said. "He was such a nice man, the Lunatic! He was so witty! He was like Silvio! Silvio took after him!

"Most eminent Signor Lipmann," my mother said. "Do you remember what he said? He would always say 'Blessed are the orphans!' He said that many crazy people were made crazy by their parents. 'Blessed are the orphans,' he'd always say. He understood psychoanalysis and it hadn't even been invented yet! Most eminent Signor Lipmann," my mother said. "I can still hear him!"

"My mother, the poor thing, had a carriage," my father said. "Every day she went for a ride in her carriage."

"She took Gino and Mario with her in the carriage," my mother said, "and after a little while they started vomiting because the smell of the leather bothered them and they got the whole carriage filthy and she got very angry!"

"Poor thing!" my father said. "She was so upset when she had to give up that carriage!

"Poor thing," my father said. "When I came back from Spitzberg, where I had gone inside a whale's cranium to look for cerebrospinal ganglia, I brought back with me a bag full of my clothes covered in whale blood and she was too disgusted to touch them. I took them up into the attic and they stank beyond belief!"

"I never did find those cerebrospinal ganglia," my father said.

My mother said, "He got all his good clothes dirty for no reason!"

"Maybe you didn't look hard enough, Beppino!" my mother said. "Maybe you should have kept looking!"

"Sure! What a nitwit you are! It wasn't as easy as all that! You're always ready to put me down. What a jackass you are!"

"When I was at boarding school," my mother said, "I also studied whales. They taught natural history very well and I liked it a lot. But at that school we had to go a little too often to mass. We were always having to confess. Sometimes we didn't know what sin to confess and so we'd say, 'I stole the snow!'"

"'I stole the snow!' Ah, how wonderful my boarding school was! How much fun I had!"

"Every Sunday," she said, "I went over to Barbison's place. Barbison's sisters were nicknamed 'the Blesseds' because of their sanctimoniousness. Barbison's real name was Perego. His friends wrote this poem for him:

Night or day there's no grander feller
Than Perego and his wine cellar."

"Let's not begin again with Barbison!" my father said. "How many times have I heard her tell that story!"

NOTES

5   *"negroism"*: According to Shaul Bassi, the director of the Venice Center for International Jewish Studies, in the Judeo-Italian language of the Venetian Jews, in which Ginzburg's father was raised, "negro" meant "foolish, awkward, or stupid," and *"negrigura,"* which I have translated as "negroism," meant "foolish thing." Bassi claims that the words never had overtly racial content. Ginzburg, however, was very aware of the words' racial significance and her deliberate placement of these terms on the opening pages of her novel resonates throughout the book.

9   *the soft* r: In some regions of Italy, notably Piedmont and other parts of the northwest near the French border, *r* is produced as an uvular sound in the back of the mouth. This is known as the *erre moscia* or soft *r* or to linguists as rhotacism. The use of this *r* has been regarded by some Italians as a sign of snobbery or as a speech impediment.

10   *irredentist*: The Irredentist Party was founded in 1878 to advocate for the union and recovery to Italy of all Italian-speaking districts subject to other countries. This included Trieste, Ginzburg's father's native city, which remained under Austrian rule until the end of World War I.

   La Vendée: A staunchly royalist district in France renowned for its revolt against the revolutionary government in 1793.

17   *boarding school:* A *collegio* or boarding school in Italy is understood primarily to be a charitable institution established by religious orders for the education of children from underprivileged families or for children who due to learning disabilities or behavioral problems are unable to succeed at regular public day schools.

18   *Metastasio:* Pietro Metastasio (1698–1782) was an Italian poet and the most celebrated librettist in Europe writing during the eighteenth

century for the "serious opera." The verse here parodied is from part one of his oratorio *Il Guiseppe Rinconosciuto* (1756):

> *Se a ciascun l'interno affano*
> *Si leggesse in front scritto;*
> *Quanti mai, che invidia fanno,*
> *Ci farebbero pietà!*

> If each man's inner stress
> His forehead did express;
> How many who invite our envy,
> Would instead gain our pity!

18 *nicknamed "Barbison":* In Milanese dialect "*il Barbison*" means a man with large whiskers.

19 *Bissolati, Turati, and Kuliscioff:* Leonida Bissolati (1857–1920) was a prominent member of the Italian Socialist Party until he was expelled in 1912. He then co-founded the right-wing Reformist Socialist Party. Filippo Turati (1857–1932) was the founder of the Italian Socialist Party in 1892; when he was expelled in 1921, he founded the United Socialist Party along with Anna Kuliscioff and Giacomo Matteotti in opposition to the emerging fascism. Anna Kuliscioff (1857–1925), born in Russia, was a Jewish Russian revolutionary, a medical doctor, a feminist, and an anarchist who converted to Marxism. She was a close collaborator with Turati and helped him found the Italian Socialist Party.

22 *come to Bergamo on a military campaign:* In 1859, during the Second War of Independence, Giuseppe Garibaldi and his army freed the city of Bergamo from the Austrian Empire to become part of the Kingdom of Italy.

24 *fifty lire:* At the time, the exchange rate was 19 lire to 1 United States dollar.

the Karst Plateau: The Karst is a region in southwest Slovenia and northeastern Italy near Trieste and is the location of the twelve Battles of Isonzo between the Italian and Austrian armies during World War I.

26 The Daughter of Iorio: A poetic play by Gabriel D'Annunzio about the fears and superstitions of peasants from the Abruzzi, which was first performed in 1904.

40 *Andrea Costa:* Originally an anarchist, Costa renounced anarchy to co-found the Partito dei Lavoratori Italiani in 1892. He was married to Kuliscioff and they had a daughter, Andreina. Kuliscioff eventually left him for Turati. Costa remained an active politician throughout his life, serving as the mayor of Imola and a representative in the Italian parliament.

45 *a friend of Father Semeria's:* Father Semeria (1867–1931) was a Barnabite priest renowned throughout Italy for his popular sermons and books on Catholicism.

Adele Rasetti, Galeotti's sister: Adele Galeotti Rasetti was a distinguished painter and student of the artist Giovanni Fattori (1825–1908), the leader of the Macchiaioli group. For more about her see Andrea Baffoni, *Adele Galeotti Rasetti: Vita e opere di un'allieva di Giovanni Fattori* (Perugia: Effe Edizioni, 2011).

51 *the paintings of Casorati:* Felice Casorati (1883–1963) was an Italian painter. Born in Novara he moved to Turin in 1918. He was a leading figure of the Return to Order, a European postwar art movement that rejected cubism, futurism, and the extreme avant-garde and was associated with a revival of classicism and realistic painting. He was briefly arrested in 1923 for antifascist activity. The cover art of the present edition of *Family Lexicon* shows a detail from Casorati's 1925 painting, *Raja*.

53 *Nella Marchesini:* The painter Nella Marchesini (1901–1953) was best known for her portraits and figurative work. She exhibited widely in the 1930s and '40s but is now largely forgotten.

good friends with Petrolini: Ettore Petrolini (1884–1936) was an Italian actor considered to be one of the most influential figures in Italian theatrical comedy. He was famous for his character sketches, parodies, and comic musical monologues. Petrolini was a public supporter of the fascist regime in Italy though he satirized Mussolini in his famous piece *Nerone*.

58 *Debenedetti wrote short stories:* Giacomo Debenedetti (1901–1967) was a writer, journalist, and Italy's foremost critic of twentieth-century literature. He was among the first to grasp the full extent of the genius of Proust. Debenedetti was Jewish and wrote under an assumed name

during the fascist regime. With the Nazi occupation of Italy, he and his family were forced to go into hiding. Among his many works are two extraordinary essays about racial atrocities: "October 16, 1943" is a first-hand account of the roundup in Rome of a thousand Jews who were sent to the gas chambers in Auschwitz; "Eight Jews" was written in response to the Ardeatine Cave massacre on March 24, 1944.

61 *my friend Pajetta's place:* Giancarlo Pajetta (1911–1990) was a prominent member of the Italian Communist Party and a politician. He served in parliament from 1946 until his death in 1990. He fought with the partisan Resistance in the Garibaldi Brigade during World War II.

62 *the Pestelli who writes for* La Stampa. *His mother is Carola Prosperi:* Luigi "Gino" Pestelli (1885–1965) was a journalist for *La Stampa*, one of Italy's best-known and most influential daily newspapers, published in Turin. He worked there for twenty years and was an antifascist who fought for freedom of the press. Carola Prosperi (1883–1981) was a prolific journalist, novelist, and children's book author. During her lifetime she wrote more than two thousand eight hundred short stories and thirty-five novels.

63 *Adriano Olivetti:* Adriano Olivetti was the son of Camillo Olivetti, the founder of Olivetti. In the 1930s Adriano would reorganize and modernize the company to make it a leading Italian manufacturer renowned throughout the world. Olivetti shared with his workers the productivity gains by increasing salaries, fringe benefits, and services. By 1957 Olivetti workers were the best paid of all in the metallurgical industry and showed the highest productivity. Adriano married Paola Levi in 1928. They had three children.

74 *Rosselli and Parri:* Carlo Rosselli (1899–1937) was an Italian political leader, journalist, historian, and the founder of Justice and Liberty (Giustizia e Libertè), an antifascist militant movement. In 1926, he organized, along with Ferruccio Parri (1890–1981, a partisan, politician, and the twenty-ninth prime minister of Italy) and Sandro Pertini (1896–1990, a journalist, socialist politician, and the seventh president of the Italian Republic), Turati's escape to France. Rosselli and Parri were later captured, convicted, and exiled to the Sicilian island of Lipari.

79 *Franz Joseph:* Franz Joseph (1830–1916) was the emperor of Aus-

tria, apostolic king of Hungary, king of Bohemia, king of Croatia, king of Galicia and Lodomeria, and grand duke of Kraków from 1848–1916.

82 *Salvatorelli will be there:* Luigi Salvatorelli (1886–1974) was a historian, political journalist, and author. He was the co-director of *La Stampa* from 1921 to 1925; the director of the weekly magazine *La Nuova Europa* from 1944 to 1946; and a founding member of the Action Party in 1942. He returned to *La Stampa* as an editorialist in 1949.

   Vinciguerra, Bauer, and Rossi: Mario Vinciguerra (1887–1972) was a historian, editor, and author. He was a well-known antifascist activist and a member of the National Alliance for Freedom. Ricardo Bauer (1896–1982) was a historian, politician, and antifascist activist, and a member of the Action Party. Ernesto Rossi (1897–1967) was a politician, journalist, and antifascist activist; a member of the Action Party; and a founder of the Justice and Liberty movement.

83 *Guglielmo Ferrero:* Guglielmo Ferrero (1871–1942) was a historian, journalist, and novelist. His best-known books are *The Young Europe* (1897) and the five-volume *Greatness and Decline of Rome* (1907). When the fascist Blackshirts forced intellectuals to leave Italy in 1925, Ferrero refused and was placed under house arrest. In 1929, he accepted a position at the Graduate Institute of International Studies in Geneva. Ferrero was invited to the White House by Theodore Roosevelt in 1908.

84 *the Justice and Liberty group:* An antifascist Resistance group founded in 1929 in Paris by Italian refugees Carlo Rosselli, Emilio Lussu, Alberto Tarchiani, and Ernesto Rossi. Carlo Levi and Leone Ginzburg were the leaders of the Italian branch based in Turin.

88 *"De vulgari eloquentia":* "On Eloquence in the Vernacular" (ca. 1304) is an essay that was part of an unfinished book by Dante Alighieri on the historical evolution of language, the relationship between Latin and vernacular, his search for illustrious vernacular, and literary genres.

90 *named Sion Segre:* Sion Segre Amar was an antifascist activist and a member of Justice and Liberty in Turin.

91 *They arrested Ginzburg and … Mario in Turin:* This event came to be known as the Ponte Tresa affair. Fifteen young Turinese Jews were arrested in conjunction with Mario's trips carrying antifascist literature over the border from Switzerland.

91   *Pitigrilli's cousins:* Pitigrilli was the pen name for Dino Segre (1893–1975) a popular novelist and journalist. He was later discovered to be a spy for OVRA, the fascist secret police. He had infiltrated the Turin group of Justice and Liberty and betrayed many of its members including Leone Ginzburg, Vittorio Foa, and members of the Levi family.

     a literary magazine called Literary Lions: *Le Grandi Firme* was published in Turin from 1924 to 1938, when it was banned under the Race Laws of the fascist government.

93   *"It's like the Dreyfus Affair!":* The Dreyfus Affair was a famous political scandal that erupted in France in 1894 over the conviction for treason of the young French artillery officer Captain Alfred Dreyfus, who was Jewish. In 1906, after it was proved that the evidence against him had been falsified, he was released from a penal colony in French Guiana, fully exonerated, and reinstated as a major in the French army.

94   *this particular Margherita:* Margherita Sarfatti (1880–1961) was a journalist, art critic, socialite, and propaganda adviser to the National Fascist Party. She was also one of Mussolini's mistresses and the author of the biography *The Life of Benito Mussolini*, originally published in England in 1925 and the following year in Italy under the title *Dux*. It was a huge success, reprinted seventeen times and translated into eighteen languages.

97   *"Carlo Levi is locked up as well!":* Carlo Levi (1902–1975) was a painter, writer, medical doctor, antifascist, and political activist, and a co-founder of the Justice and Liberty movement. As a result of his activism, from 1935 to 1936 Levi was exiled to Aliano, a remote town in an impoverished region of southern Italy. His memoir *Christ Stopped at Eboli* recounts his experiences there.

     "Professor Giua has been locked up too!": Michele Giua (1889–1966) was a chemistry professor at the University of Turin and an active member of Justice and Liberty. From 1948 to 1958 he was a senator for the Italian Socialist Party.

98   *Giulio Einaudi and Pavese:* Giulio Einaudi (1912–1999) founded one of Italy's most prestigious publishing houses in Turin in 1933. Natalia Ginzburg worked as an editor for the publishing house and her books were later published by Einaudi. Cesare Pavese (1908–1950) was a poet,

novelist, literary critic, translator, and antifascist. He worked as an editor and translator for Einaudi's publishing house.

98 *a journal called* La Cultura: *La Cultura* was a literary magazine founded in Rome in 1881. Pavese was the editor in the 1930s, publishing many antifascist articles. The magazine was closed down in 1936.

101 *Pascoli or Carducci:* Giovanni Pascoli (1855–1912) was a tragic poet and classical scholar. His teacher and mentor while studying at the University of Bologna was Giosuè Carducci. Carducci (1835–1907) was a poet, essayist, and translator. He was the first Italian to be awarded the Nobel Prize in Literature (1906).

Leopardi, yes, he was a great poet: Giacomo Leopardi (1798–1837) was a lyric poet, essayist, philosopher, and philologist. One of the nineteenth century's greatest poets, his prose reveals him as one of the era's most radical thinkers.

103 *Renzo Giua:* Renzo Giua (1914–1938) was an antifascist activist, an exile, and for a time a member of Justice and Liberty. He fought to defend the Republicans in the Spanish Civil War and died in battle at Zalamea de la Serena in Estremadura.

The other friend was Chiaromonte: Nicola Chiaromonte (1905–1972) was an antifascist activist and writer. He also fought in the Spanish Civil War against General Francisco Franco's fascist regime, flying in the French novelist André Malraux's squadron. The character Scali in Malraux's novel *Man's Hope* is based on him. He moved to New York in 1941 and wrote anti-Stalinist pieces for *The Nation*, *The New Republic*, and *Partisan Review*. He was a good friend of Mary McCarthy.

107 *Vittorio's name was in fact Foa:* Vittorio Foa (1910–2008) was a politician, trade unionist, journalist, and writer, as well as an antifascist and a leader of the Resistance movement in Italy. For an in-depth profile of him and his family see Alexander Stille, *Benevolence and Betrayal: Five Italian Jewish Families Under Fascism* (New York: Picador, 1991).

109 *Ilda, who normally lived with her husband and children in Palestine:* Palestine at the time was a British protectorate where Jews were beginning to emigrate in significant numbers in hopes of forming the new State of Israel.

113 *Her son now worked in Rome with Fermi and was a famous physicist:* Franco Dino Rasetti (1901–2001), along with Enrico Fermi (1901–1954, the recipient of the 1938 Nobel Prize in Physics), discovered key processes leading to nuclear fission. He refused, on moral grounds, to participate in the Manhattan Project.

116 *Barriera di Milano:* An industrial and working-class neighborhood on the outskirts of Turin.

118 *loaned her books by Croce:* Benedetto Croce (1866–1951) was a philosopher, a philosopher of history, and politician. He initially supported Mussolini and his fascist government that came to power in 1922, but in 1925 Croce composed the "Manifesto of the Anti-Fascist Intellectuals." When the fascist government's anti-Semitic policies were adopted in 1938, Croce was the only non-Jewish intellectual who refused to state any information regarding his "racial background" on an obligatory government questionnaire.

This was how I first heard of Balbo: Felice Balbo (1914–1964) was a writer and philosopher. He was a militant Catholic and communist intellectual and one of the most influential thinkers on Italian culture in the first half of the twentieth century.

119 *Lisetta read Salgari's novels:* Emilio Salgari (1862–1911) was an enormously popular novelist who wrote more than two hundred adventure stories and novels that were set in exotic locations. His heroes were mostly pirates, outlaws, and barbarians who fought against greed, corruption, and the abuse of power. His work was admired by Sergio Leone, Federico Fellini, Umberto Eco, Gabriel García Márquez, Pablo Neruda, Isabelle Allende, Carlos Fuentes, Jorge Luis Borges, and Che Guevara.

La letteratura della nuova Italia: The Literature of the New Italy was a six-volume book of critical essays on Italian literature written during the period from unification (1861) to the First World War. It was published in 1914 by Laterza.

123 *"Nigra sum, sed formosa":* Song of Solomon 1:5: "Dark am I, yet lovely."

126 *the racial campaign had begun:* On November 17, 1938, Mussolini's government introduced the Laws for the Defense of the Race, legislation that excluded Jews from the civil service, the armed forces, and the

National Fascist Party, and restricted Jewish ownership of certain companies and property; intermarriage was also prohibited.

126 *the* rari nantes *swimming club:* "*Apparent rari nantes in gurgite vasto*" ("A few men appear swimming in the immense whirlpool"), from Virgil, *Aeneid* 1.118.

128 *And then there was Garosci, Lussu:* Aldo Garosci (1907–2000) was a politician, historian, antifascist, and co-founder of Justice and Liberty. He fought against Franco's government in the Spanish Civil War and was a member of the Action Party. In government, he was a representative of the Italian Democratic Socialist Party. Emilio Lussu (1890–1975) was an Italian soldier, politician, writer, radical antifascist, and co-founder of Justice and Liberty. He fought in the Spanish Civil War and later worked in the government for various left-wing parties. He was married to Joyce Lussu (1912–1998), a writer, poet, translator, and antifascist.

133 *I felt as if I were Nancy in* The Devourers: *I Divoratori* was a novel by Annie Vivanti (1866–1942) first published in England as *The Devourers* in 1910. Published a year later in Italy, it became a huge best seller. Vivanti was a highly regarded poet, playwright, and novelist who was internationally renowned. Croce included two essays on her work in volumes I and VI of *La letteratura della nuova Italia*.

134 *it was, perhaps, still possible to go to Madagascar:* The Madagascar Plan was a Nazi government proposal to relocate European Jews to Madagascar.

137 *the painter Amedeo Modigliani:* Amedeo Clemente Modigliani (1884–1920) was a renowned painter and sculptor. He was born in Livorno and trained in art schools in Rome, Florence, and Venice. He moved to Paris in 1906 where he lived and worked among the avant-garde until his death.

139 *he joined the Maquis:* The Maquis were French Resistance fighters during the German occupation of France in World War II.

the Purge Commission: Following the liberation of France, the Provisional Government of the French Republic led by Charles de Gaulle established a Purge Commission that resulted in a wave of official trials of traitors and collaborators.

144 *When the armistice was announced:* Following the Allied invasion of Sicily in early July 1943, the Grand Council of Fascism met on July 24 and 25 and passed a vote of no confidence against Mussolini. This led to the change of Italian government and the appointment of Marshal Pietro Badoglio as prime minister. An armistice, agreed to by Marshal Badoglio and General Eisenhower, was announced on September 8.

until the north was liberated: Following the Badoglio-Eisenhower armistice, the Germans almost immediately occupied Rome and the north of Italy. Mussolini became the puppet leader of the Nazi-controlled Italian Social Republic, informally known as the Republic of Salò for the town on Lake Garda where it was based, until April 1945 when Mussolini was shot by partisans.

155 *Nenni's socialism:* Pietro Sandro Nenni (1891–1980) joined the Socialist Party in 1921, when Mussolini left to become a fascist and the wing that would become the Communist Party split off. He was arrested for antifascist activity in 1925 and went into exile in France in 1926 where he became the secretary of the Socialist Party. He was a central figure of the Italian left for the greater part of the twentieth century.

156 *She preferred Saragat's followers:* Guiseppe Saragat (1898–1988) was a reformist socialist who split from the Socialist Party in 1947 because he disapproved of the close alliance with the Communist Party. That year, he founded the Socialist Party of Italian Workers, which would become the Italian Democratic Socialist Party. He was elected the fifth president of the Italian Republic and served from 1964 to 1971.

158 Elle pleure, il faut lui donner sa tétée!: She's crying, we must give her the breast!

161 *"He treated me as if I were a Christian Democrat!":* The Christian Democratic Party, founded in 1943, was a Roman Catholic centrist party that played a dominant role in Italian politics.

"He always thinks Togliatti is right": Palmiro Togliatti (1896–1964) was a founding member and leader of the Italian Communist Party in 1921 with Antonio Gramsci.

164 *He was a member of the Action Party:* The *Partito d'Azione* was a liberal, socialist, anti-Marxist political party founded in 1942 by former members of Justice and Liberty. In January 1943, it began publishing a

clandestine newspaper, *Free Italy*, edited by Leone Ginzburg. The Action Party folded in 1946.

164 *She'd been interrogated by Ferida:* Luisa Ferida (1914–1945) was an actress and a prominent fascist. She belonged to Pietro Koch's band of fascists, renowned for its extreme cruelty and gratuitous violence. Its headquarters was a villa in Milan that came to be known as the Villa Triste (sad house) because of the terrible and tragic practices that went on there. In 1945 in Milan, the Partisans arrested and executed Ferida and her lover, the actor Osvaldo Valenti.

169 *my mother said, "Many clothes, much honor!":* A parody of the fascist slogan "Many Foes, Much Honor."

179 *had a striking resemblance to Gramsci:* Antonio Gramsci (1891–1937) was a highly influential leader of the Italian Communist Party, which he founded in 1921. He was a writer, philosopher, sociologist, and linguist. He was imprisoned by Mussolini's fascist regime in 1926 and released for health reasons in 1934.

189 Nobody's Boy: *Sans Famille*, a children's book written in 1879, by the French author Hector Malo (1830–1907), about an orphan abandoned at birth.

   The Marchesa Colombi's books: Maria Antoinetta Torriani (1840–1920) was a popular novelist, children's writer, and journalist who published under the pen name Marchesa Colombi.

   I had given the children Misunderstood: A children's book written in 1869 by the English writer Florence Montgomery (1843–1923).

190 *Gabriele, my husband:* Gabriele Baldini (1919–1969) was a professor of English literature at the University of Rome. He and Natalia Ginzburg were married in 1950.

AFTERWORD

LEXICON: a dictionary, or, more precisely, an assemblage of words meaningful only to initiates, or a collection of phrases, any one of which, when uttered, no matter when or where, will at once identify the speaker as a member of a particular tribe. "If my siblings and I were to find ourselves in a dark cave or among millions of people," writes Natalia Ginzburg in *Family Lexicon*, "just one of those phrases or words would immediately allow us to recognize each other. Those phrases are our Latin, the dictionary of our past, they're like Egyptian or Assyro-Babylonian hieroglyphics, evidence of a vital core that has ceased to exist but that lives on in its texts, saved from the fury of waters, the corrosion of time." Most of us have such phrases or their equivalents in our repertoire and understand the virtues and satisfactions of membership codes and passwords that confirm belonging, summon the flavor of a shared world.

Ginzburg was born in 1916 in Palermo, but her childhood and early adulthood were spent in the northern industrial city of Turin where her father was a medical researcher and university professor. Her father, Giuseppe Levi, was Jewish; her mother, Lidia Tanzi, was Catholic; but neither parent was religious and the household was fiercely nonsectarian. If there was a religion practiced it was anti-fascism. There was no deity worshipped and the only form of prayer practiced was laughter; indeed, the rich and reliably laughter-inducing compendium of stories and sayings that make up *Family Lexicon* can be said to comprise a kind of prayer missile or psalter for practical, spirit-renewing use.

*

Ginzburg began work on *Family Lexicon* while living in London with her second husband, Gabriele Baldini, in the early 1960s. The book was published in 1963 and awarded the coveted Strega Prize for fiction, though it reads like a memoir and is entirely based on facts. At the time Ginzburg was in her mid-forties and already well-known as the author of five novels, in addition to stories, essays, and plays. It was not until she was living in England, in a city she disliked, among people she regarded as cold and lacking in joie de vivre, that she was moved to write intimately about Italy and her family.

In London, where Baldini was busy with his diplomatic post, Ginzburg spent most of her time at home taking care of her three children from an earlier marriage. She felt isolated and unhappy, and she missed Italy. In an interview in 1990 she told me that she had felt somewhat at sea living among Brits and that when she began writing *Family Lexicon* she was "greatly relieved to be writing as a Torinese." And so it was during this moment of intense longing that Ginzburg set out to write the story of her Torinese childhood and of the years leading into and through World War II, finding in the re-membered anecdotes and phrases that constituted her family lexi-con the Italian companionship she craved. Though the avowed motive informing the work is by no means therapeutic, its very com-position helped Ginzburg get through a difficult period. And in the stories themselves, the alternation of light and dark, terror and relief that characterizes them, there is a discernible will to confront every-thing, past and present, no matter how horrific or disheartening, and to make from each encounter some modest affirmation of life.

"*Si tira avanti*" is the ready answer Italians often give when greeted by the standard "*Come stai?*" (How are you?) Not "Very well, thank you," but rather "One pulls oneself forward." "We will not lie and say, *Bene, benissimo, grazie*," they seem to say with a steady, bemused irony, "We pull ourselves forward, but—*si capisce*—with difficulty." To pull herself forward in monochromatic London, Ginzburg conjured for herself the colorful details of her family history, rich in pleasure as well as in pain. Not for her the programmatic hopelessness that often characterizes narratives set in fascist Italy, in well-known films like *Rome, Open City*; *The Conformist*; or *The Garden of the Finzi-Continis*. Ginzburg's project is not to whitewash the varieties of tragic loss suffered by Italians and others of her generation. Her focus, rather, is the mundane interior landscape of a household, the daily experience of *living* in the haven of family life even as death prevails outside and catastrophes follow catastrophes on every front.

In the mid-1930s, we learn, Natalia's older brother, Mario, escapes arrest for distributing antifascist propaganda and flees to Switzerland. As a consequence, her father, known as "Beppino," is deemed guilty by association with a subversive and jailed. Somehow, though everyone in the Levi household is preoccupied and fearful, comedy prevails: Natalina, the maid, continues to get her pronouns mixed up, referring to all feminine objects and persons as "he," while Lidia, the mother, continues to break involuntarily into song "at the top of her lungs," with lyrics like these, which she composed in high school:

I am Don Carlos Tadrid
And I'm a student in Madrid!

Each week the same Lidia, undaunted, carries fresh clothes to Beppino in prison and worries about having enough money to pay the bills. These people have reason to be afraid of what will soon befall them, and yet they remain open to mischief and absurdity, even to unexpected good fortune. Improbably, Beppino is released from prison, and though brother Mario has had to flee, he is *alive*, and the family can return for a time to what Beppino is always declaring to be their "boring" lives. While it is hard, in the era of Italian fascism, quite to believe in the good simplicity of normal life, Ginzburg's family can feel that things are, well, not so bad. Beppino openly mocks the fascists at his university and seems not to imagine what dangers his habitual antiestablishment demeanor might bring upon his family. The Levi family, for all its political savvy and sophistication, cannot conceive of what will come by war's end. Fascism, they are certain, cannot and will not last. Nor can the war. Or so they are assured by their informants and by those who speak in the name of reason and the reasonable. They *want* to believe these assurances, and Ginzburg's comic imagination lends itself to keeping the narrative close to that shared determination to believe that all will turn out well. The gift for a kind of cheerful stoicism, shared by all the Levis, endows the family members with what appears to be an almost genetically determined ability to withstand—or at least to avoid dwelling on—the worst.

Beppino, monumental in his *superbia* and buffoonery, is the most important figure in the book. He cannot suffer fools easily and yet it is his lot, he is convinced, to be surrounded by fools. But his unrelenting intolerance and irascibility are useful traits, it turns out, for surviving the challenges of his moment. Of course Mussolini and his fellow fascists are fools in a sense that has little to do with the mundane idiocies and delusions of family members and friends who are the objects of Beppino's practiced disdain. And yet there is in his readiness to pounce upon and hold up to ridicule every species of stupidity, including the most harmless and casual, a model for resistance to high-stakes injustice as well as small-scale incompetence and foolishness.

It takes a while to realize that Beppino is the strongest character in *Family Lexicon*, perhaps because from the start—literally, the book's opening—Ginzburg exposes him as something much less than an idealized paterfamilias. We meet him on page one as a routinely explosive—bordering on abusive—father who screams at his children and insults everyone at the dinner table, including his wife. Arrogant, overbearing, effusively opinionated, he habitually characterizes his family members as nitwits and "negroes." "Don't be negroes!" he admonishes them. "Stop your negroisms!"—by which he intends to exhort them all to use the language they speak in a way that seems to them (or rather to *him*) correct and reasonable. All behaviors of which he disapproves are *negrigure*, a term once commonly used in Italy, though bound by now, in the perfectly literal translation offered by Jenny McPhee, to seem outrageous.

And yet, one of the wonders of Ginzburg's book is the fact—it is a fact—that the portrait of such a father can seem to us somehow affectionate. To be sure, the man was, in the ways of his time and place, something of a racist, and there is no slightest suggestion in Ginzburg's book that this seemed to her, because commonplace, at all acceptable, or that the best thing to do when confronted by expressions of intolerance or abuse is to forgive or forget. If she never indicts Beppino directly for his use of *negrigure*, her decision to expose his use of this particular favorite vulgarism to correct the "mistakes" of his children is pointed.

By the time she was writing *Family Lexicon*, Ginzburg was already known to be—in her fiction and her journalism—a severe and unrelenting critic of hypocrisy and whatever else she deemed less than exemplary. Her frequent contributions to the Italian newspapers *L'Unita* and *La Stampa* had earned her a reputation as a gadfly and truth teller. Even in *Family Lexicon*, Ginzburg's gift for comedy in no way obstructs her cleansing, urgent will to chastise and correct. Though Beppino's virulence can make him seem grotesque and fearsome, his refusal to let stupidity pass or to keep his mouth shut about the criminally culpable and therefore stupid Mussolini is bracing and, for Ginzburg herself, clearly challenging. Can we find it in ourselves as readers to adore a man who tells his children to stop behaving like negroes? No doubt Ginzburg knew she was making it hard for herself in placing before us a man who would seem, much of the time, incorrigible and unbearable. But she knew, too, that her man was a Jew in fascist Italy and the head of a family of resistance fighters. Ginzburg concedes nothing in her portrait of Giuseppe Levi, exposing his worst features while allowing him to seem somewhat generous in the extravagance of his passion and in his refusal to be genteel or moderate. Ginzburg often found ways to praise and admire people who knew how to live within their limitations, but she had no patience for people who were timid when circumstances demanded something more. Her own father always reminded her that mildness, like correctness, was not—certainly not always—a virtue. Whatever our misgivings or reluctance, by the time we reach the end of *Family Lexicon* we readily acknowledge that Giuseppe Levi is the hero—lowercase hero—of the book. It is not easy to embrace such a man, but we come to love him as a great character without whom a great book would lack the essential drive and buoyancy that color its every page.

Odd, perhaps, to speak of buoyancy in a book that is also marked by the menace and presence of violence and oppression. But then *Family Lexicon* is an eccentric family chronicle, not a historical document. Mussolini's war and the fears and dangers it imposes are often referred to, but only insofar as they occasion another stretch of family narrative or enrich an existing one. There are references to political parties and figures by now grown obscure, but the character of the book derives more from the atmosphere of the Levi household, and the peculiar intensities that animate its family members, than from its historical context. Ginzburg knows how to make us hear and see her family. We experience the tumult and pathos of their strivings and rages and sudden accessions of tenderness. Politics is never primary in Ginzburg's world, not even when it threatens to overwhelm private life. The very enterprise of *Family Lexicon*—the insistent, loving, faithful construction of a family chronicle—may itself be said to be an act of fidelity and resistance.

After the initial portrait of the father and the variety of Teutonic hardships that he routinely imposes on his household, Ginzburg portrays the other family members, each with a pat phrase or other characteristic marker not unlike the attributes of saints in medieval and Renaissance paintings. Recalling her decidedly unsaintly family members in this ritualized way helps to make memory a devotional exercise, now a matter of consolation, now of praise. As Saint Catherine has her wheel and Saint Peter his keys, the paternal grandmother is emphatically associated with her chastising of the irreverent

Levi family for making "a bordello out of everything." A psychiatrist uncle is regularly cited as "the Lunatic" only by association with his patients, not because of any lunacy of his own. The notoriously coarse Uncle Barbison is so coarse that his nickname becomes an adjective with wide-ranging pejorative connotations. And his unfortunate, very red nose comes to stand, among the Levis, for all red noses. That nose there, says Lidia, is a Barbison. Uncle Barbison is also the author of the memorable formulation "Sulfuric acid smells of fart."

Lidia, the mother, is more of a mystery than Beppino. She has her sayings, some dating from before her marriage, but we know rather little about her past. We do learn that Lidia Tanzi knew a number of anarchists in Milan, that she isn't Jewish, that her mother is still alive and living comfortably in a lavishly furnished though increasingly shabby palazzo in Florence, where the family will temporarily take refuge after the war, but such information is never really developed. What matters is the way that Lidia accommodates herself to the Levi family tradition and finds her way to enrich the family lexicon and thereby to nurture the instincts for survival and resilience instilled by Giuseppe. At the same time, however, we gather that what is left out in the telling of Lidia's story is important and perhaps too painful to dwell on in this work.

Ginzburg is not an ostentatious writer. Her prose is famously terse and forceful, an instrument in which the smallest things are made to seem fresh and telling. In *Family Lexicon* she doesn't disclose much about her own thoughts or feelings growing up in the Levi home, but when we learn about everyone else in the family circle, in such extraordinary detail and gesture, we readily feel what it was like to be among them. Vulnerabilities and incoherencies are captured more or less as a matter of course, with only occasional commentary. The child, Natalia, as drawn by her adult self, is remarkably nonjudgmental; even when she reports her mother's preference for the company of her more gregarious sister, she does so without disdain or envy, perhaps taking consolation in obvious signs of her own difference, a difference that would eventually become distinction. In effect, Ginzburg conveys not only impressions but a fully intelligible way of thinking about them without underlining her views or striking edifying postures. For all the humor in *Family Lexicon* there is also an unmistakable gravity that is not to be confused with explicitly formulated ideas or convictions.

The voice of the narrator of *Family Lexicon*, marked by the self-deprecation that is prominently on display in Ginzburg's personal essays, is a voice with which Ginzburg fans will have long been familiar. She offers, for example, as sly proof of her early literary talent, a wholly unremarkable two-line poem written when she was very young to amuse her mother, who often complained of missing their sunny former home in Palermo:

Palermino Palermino,
You're more beautiful than Torino.

The Italian readers of *Family Lexicon* knew well that little Natalia would become one of Italy's leading women of letters, but the child growing up and coming of age in the Levi household, on an undistinguished street in Turin during the time of fascism, has no such sense of her future self. She tells her story through the innocent eyes of an ordinary child and resists any forecasting of things to come. When we arrive at the end of the book and Natalia speaks in her adult voice, revealing details about her life and her family in the aftermath of the war, the effect is therefore all the more powerful.

Although the book was written in middle-age, with the advantages of worldly experience and historical hindsight, Ginzburg chooses as her narrator a child for whom the prewar and war years pass mainly in the confines of the home. The Natalia whose voice is the main voice of the novel has very limited access to the outside world because to avoid contagion in a pre-vaccine era her parents keep her from school. She dislikes studying what her tutors provide, but she is a good listener and in this house of talkers whose conversations she overhears, she takes in a great deal of extracurricular information about the world. She learns about friends and relatives who die from natural causes and about others who disappear for other reasons. Eventually her parents' best friends are no longer fixtures in the house; people move because of the race laws or because of opportunities elsewhere. But even as war disrupts familiar routines, the sense conveyed is that life goes on more or less normally in ways that defy persistent expectations of besetting disruption and grief. Children are born, grandchildren are celebrated, friends appear, disappear, reappear. New stories are added to the standard repertoire while older ones are reiterated well into Natalia's adulthood. Where chaos threatens, Ginzburg's patient idiom clarifies, insisting that no virtue or incident is too small or too trivial to recount, no saying unworthy of repetition. Childhood unfolds slowly and lightly; the pliable net of language woven to contain it all is vulnerable but equal to the task. The effect is cumulative: the sum of absurdity plus absurdity is life.

In several respects *Family Lexicon* provides a kind of counterexample to the families Ginzburg chose to write about in her fiction, where the focus is almost invariably on the disintegration of conventional marriage and home life and the erecting, in its stead, of a new order in which the idea of family as she knew it was becoming a thing of the past, beyond retrieval. In books like *Valentino*, *The City and the House*, *Sagittarius*, and *Voices in the Evening*, Ginzburg describes one dysfunctional couple after another carelessly poisoning their marriages, misreading each other, and mistreating their children with more or less catastrophic results. These tales of dysfunction are told with a deadpan, often comic touch. The couples are unfaithful to each other in an almost exuberant way, reporting their infidelities with brutal candor. Everything is out in the open. Characters talk incessantly and well. They even joke—about each other, about each other's lovers, about their unfortunate children. Later they wonder how they managed to ruin things: *L'abbiamo sciupato tutto*. And throughout these tales we hear the familiar chiming of tags and attributes, each tale with its mini-lexicon of references, the lexicon contributing a layer of comedy without utterly neutralizing the inherent darkness of the vision.

Although Ginzburg's fiction is never programmatic, never reducible to social commentary or gloomy cultural prognostication, a central feature of her novels is the absence of strong parental figures who might be equipped to save the family and ensure its stability. Only *All Our Yesterdays* escapes this pattern, even though its central figure, Cenzo Rena (a vital and committed authority figure clearly modeled on Ginzburg's own father), in the end leaves the family to its own devices. He does so heroically, martyring himself to save a soldier he is hiding—and therefore to save the family who is hiding the soldier. He does not, however, manage to stay with the family to protect them for as long as they will need his protection, the way Giuseppe Levi *did* manage miraculously to do, against all odds. When compared with the weak, morally compromised, self-indulgent mother and father figures who populate the novels, Ginzburg's father might well seem to readers of *Family Lexicon* a paragon of strength and, in an old-fashioned sense of the word, character.

About halfway into *Family Lexicon*, very much in passing, Ginzburg allows herself occasional references to Leone Ginzburg, the man who becomes her first husband, but only as the friend and fellow resistance fighter of Natalia's brother, Mario. There is no reference to the wedding of Natalia and Leone, and we learn of children only indirectly, by way of Lidia having to take care of them, as if the fact of their having been born to Ginzburg during a time when she thought incessantly about the prospect of losing her husband was of little interest or importance.

Ginzburg had forewarned us of her intentions in the prefatory Avvertenza (Warning) she wrote for the original Italian edition of the book, where she indicated that she was not much interested in writing about herself. She follows through on her original intention with disciplined consistency, resisting—for the most part—intimate details about her own sentiments. If she denies her readers a full portrait of Leone and her marriage to him, she does devote considerable attention to the writer Cesare Pavese—using the one story, perhaps, as a stand-in for the other.

Pavese is first introduced as an energetic and opinionated co-editor at Einaudi, then as the intimate friend who commits suicide in 1950. Like the family members we come to know in *Family Lexicon*, Pavese, too, has his talismanic tags: his love of the first cherries in May, his stingy handshake, his abrupt, intolerant ways. In telling us of his death Ginzburg not only mourns the man but laments the impeccable logic with which he carried out the act of suicide, describing it all with a passionate regret she rarely permits herself:

> Pavese's mistakes were worse than ours. Our mistakes were born of impulsiveness, imprudence, stupidity, and naiveté. Instead, Pavese's mistakes were the result of prudence, guile, calculation, and intelligence. Nothing is more dangerous than this sort of mistake, which can be, as it was for him, fatal. It's difficult to recover from a mistake made through guile. Mistakes made through guile tie us up in tight knots. Guile puts down roots in us that are stronger than those put down by recklessness or imprudence. How does one get rid of those tenacious, firm, profound roots? Prudence, calculation, guile have the face of reason, the bitter face and voice of reason, presenting infallible arguments to which there is no response, nothing to do but submit.
>
> Pavese killed himself one summer in Turin when none of us was there. He had contrived and calculated the circumstances regarding his death in the way he planned a walk or an evening out. On his walks or evenings out, he didn't like to encounter anything unforeseen or surprising. Whenever the Balbos, the publisher, Pavese, and I went for a walk in the hills, he became very irritated if we strayed from the designated path or if someone arrived late to our meeting point.... The unforeseen made him anxious. He didn't like to be taken by surprise.

She returns to the loss of Pavese several times in this book, each time finding a new lens through which to see him and his act. She manages to mourn him and to chastise him at the same time, in classic Ginzburg style, loving him while exposing his faulty thinking in the same breath:

> Pavese's relationship with his friends always included an ironic banter that he called upon whenever he was talking with us. . . . This irony of his was perhaps one of his most wonderful qualities, but he never knew how to bring his sense of irony to bear upon those things most important to him; he didn't bring it to his relationships with the women he fell in love with, nor did he bring it to his writing. He was able to bring it to his friendships because friendship came to him naturally and he was in some ways careless about his friendships in the sense that they were something he didn't give excessive importance to. In love, and in his writing, he threw himself into such a state of feverish calculation that he no longer knew how to laugh or to ever be entirely himself. And sometimes when I think about him now, his sense of irony is the thing I remember best about him and I cry because it no longer exists. There's no trace of it in his books and it's nowhere else to be found except in that flash of his wicked smile.

That "wicked smile" is the Pavese attribute that surfaces with each iteration of his story, even as the picture is complicated by the alternating currents of love, admiration, frustration, and genuine grief that figure in Ginzburg's narrative. Pavese had been the dearest friend of her husband, Leone, and in losing Pavese, Natalia loses not only her own good friend but another part of Leone's world. Perhaps this is why Ginzburg allows herself a certain register of powerful emotion at the loss of Pavese, which she suppresses when referring to Leone's death. It's as if the loss of Leone is too great to express and so must be subsumed into the tale of Pavese; his grief at Leone's death is huge, as is Natalia's grief at Pavese's. But neither loss, we must imagine, can begin to match in depth or intensity what Ginzburg must have felt when Leone was tortured and killed by the occupying Nazis in Rome, very near the end of the war.

The news of Leone's death is recounted with contrasting, shocking economy, buried within a description of the Einaudi offices:

> On the wall in his office the publisher had hung a portrait of Leone: his hat slightly at an angle, his eyeglasses low on his nose, his thick black hair, his deeply dimpled cheeks, his feminine hands. Leone had died in prison, in the German section of Regina Coeli prison one icy February in Rome during the German occupation.

Of course *Family Lexicon* cannot possibly recover from this blunt, devastatingly terse report. Not even the Levi family can summon the voluble bluster and blab to lift their lives back onto the plateau of anxious comedy where they had once resided. Postwar Italy is in ruins. Everyone is older. There is not much to laugh about, and yet the book ends on something of a comic, but hardly resolved, note. The war has been survived, for the most part, but survival is a work in progress. *Si tira avanti.* The family moves forward, inching its way toward recovery. The losses have been enormous, but their instincts are to retrieve what they can, and as always recovery will be bound up with the recovery of laughter, or at least with recovering the reliable triggers for laughter: the sayings, spells, and familiar locutions forged by a shared experience which, though now marked by deep sadness, are the true mark of their identity and their common will to live.

As the book closes, Ginzburg returns to the domain of the parents. Beppino and Lidia are still, despite the ravages of war, refreshingly—doggedly, insistently—themselves. "Tragedy," Natalia writes of her mother, "had beaten her down and made her despondent . . . carved two deep hollows into her cheeks." Yet once the family apartment in Turin is repaired and they can move back in, Lidia takes her place at the table and begins her daily recitation of old saws and family tag lines: "An apple for the little ones and a devil to peel them for the big ones." And her husband's rejoinder—as always a complaint, "These apples have no taste!"—is answered with the same riposte Lidia has used for thirty years: "But Beppino, they are *carpandues*!"

Order is restored: the parents are back where we first met them, still arguing about the old characters, including the "lunatic" uncle who was not a lunatic—whether he was reactionary or bourgeois, a phony or a genuinely nice fellow, like Silvio, Lidia's deceased brother, a person she has been evoking as the gold standard for niceness throughout the book. Somehow the threads lead where they should, backwards and forwards, complicating and simplifying, confounding and reassuring. "How many times have I heard her tell that story!" Beppino cries, as if repetition and restoration were not the signal features of their experience—the keys to their survival. The two parental figures are old and have suffered greatly, their habitual sayings are tinged with an unmistakable melancholy, and yet the rehearsed lines continue to assert the vital importance of continuity in the face of devastation.

In the essay "Childhood," Ginzburg says about her family, "we were nothing," neither rich nor poor, Catholic nor Jewish. In that essay she characterizes her girlish apprehension of not fitting into any available category as a source of anguish, though in later years she came to prize this "nothingness" as a positive force. Noting in her education a certain "incoherence," the absence of any defining or comprehensive ideology, she was forced to fling herself into the task of clarifying—for herself and her readers—every issue that came her way: from abortion to the way we bring up children and mourn our dead. Ginzburg often appears, whether in her fiction or in her essays, to be considering her subjects for the first time, with almost childlike freshness, a result perhaps of never having had any reliable guideposts or authoritative sources drummed into her—no ideology, no handy prefabricated formulas to consult. She starts at zero, sees what is before her, and gets to work.

To read *Family Lexicon* is to be reminded, again and again, of Ginzburg's will to revisit the past not to find answers to questions but to furnish an alternative to carelessness, forgetting, and indifference. Ginzburg didn't know how to be uplifting or optimistic, but she clung to the hope that human beings might make something of their lives by being true—true as in honest, loyal, faithful, resistant to nullity.

—PEG BOYERS

TITLES IN SERIES

For a complete list of titles, visit www.nyrb.com or write to:
Catalog Requests, NYRB, 435 Hudson Street, New York, NY 10014

J.R. ACKERLEY Hindoo Holiday*
J.R. ACKERLEY My Dog Tulip*
J.R. ACKERLEY My Father and Myself*
J.R. ACKERLEY We Think the World of You*
HENRY ADAMS The Jeffersonian Transformation
RENATA ADLER Pitch Dark*
RENATA ADLER Speedboat*
AESCHYLUS Prometheus Bound; translated by Joel Agee*
LEOPOLDO ALAS His Only Son *with* Doña Berta*
CÉLESTE ALBARET Monsieur Proust
DANTE ALIGHIERI The Inferno
KINGSLEY AMIS The Alteration*
KINGSLEY AMIS Dear Illusion: Collected Stories*
KINGSLEY AMIS Ending Up*
KINGSLEY AMIS Girl, 20*
KINGSLEY AMIS The Green Man*
KINGSLEY AMIS Lucky Jim*
KINGSLEY AMIS The Old Devils*
KINGSLEY AMIS One Fat Englishman*
KINGSLEY AMIS Take a Girl Like You*
ROBERTO ARLT The Seven Madmen*
U.R. ANANTHAMURTHY Samskara: A Rite for a Dead Man*
WILLIAM ATTAWAY Blood on the Forge
W.H. AUDEN (EDITOR) The Living Thoughts of Kierkegaard
W.H. AUDEN W.H. Auden's Book of Light Verse
ERICH AUERBACH Dante: Poet of the Secular World
EVE BABITZ Eve's Hollywood*
EVE BABITZ Slow Days, Fast Company: The World, the Flesh, and L.A.*
DOROTHY BAKER Cassandra at the Wedding*
DOROTHY BAKER Young Man with a Horn*
J.A. BAKER The Peregrine
S. JOSEPHINE BAKER Fighting for Life*
HONORÉ DE BALZAC The Human Comedy: Selected Stories*
HONORÉ DE BALZAC The Unknown Masterpiece *and* Gambara*
VICKI BAUM Grand Hotel*
SYBILLE BEDFORD A Legacy*
SYBILLE BEDFORD A Visit to Don Otavio: A Mexican Journey*
MAX BEERBOHM The Prince of Minor Writers: The Selected Essays of Max Beerbohm*
MAX BEERBOHM Seven Men
STEPHEN BENATAR Wish Her Safe at Home*
FRANS G. BENGTSSON The Long Ships*
ALEXANDER BERKMAN Prison Memoirs of an Anarchist
GEORGES BERNANOS Mouchette
MIRON BIAŁOSZEWSKI A Memoir of the Warsaw Uprising*
ADOLFO BIOY CASARES Asleep in the Sun
ADOLFO BIOY CASARES The Invention of Morel
PAUL BLACKBURN (TRANSLATOR) Proensa*

* *Also available as an electronic book.*

FRIGYES KARINTHY A Journey Round My Skull

ERICH KÄSTNER Going to the Dogs: The Story of a Moralist*

HELEN KELLER The World I Live In

YASHAR KEMAL Memed, My Hawk

YASHAR KEMAL They Burn the Thistles

MURRAY KEMPTON Part of Our Time: Some Ruins and Monuments of the Thirties*

RAYMOND KENNEDY Ride a Cockhorse*

DAVID KIDD Peking Story*

ROBERT KIRK The Secret Commonwealth of Elves, Fauns, and Fairies

ARUN KOLATKAR Jejuri

DEZSŐ KOSZTOLÁNYI Skylark*

TÉTÉ-MICHEL KPOMASSIE An African in Greenland

GYULA KRÚDY The Adventures of Sindbad*

GYULA KRÚDY Sunflower*

SIGIZMUND KRZHIZHANOVSKY Autobiography of a Corpse*

SIGIZMUND KRZHIZHANOVSKY The Letter Killers Club*

SIGIZMUND KRZHIZHANOVSKY Memories of the Future

SIGIZMUND KRZHIZHANOVSKY The Return of Munchausen

K'UNG SHANG-JEN The Peach Blossom Fan*

GIUSEPPE TOMASI DI LAMPEDUSA The Professor and the Siren

GERT LEDIG The Stalin Front*

MARGARET LEECH Reveille in Washington: 1860–1865*

PATRICK LEIGH FERMOR Between the Woods and the Water*

PATRICK LEIGH FERMOR The Broken Road*

PATRICK LEIGH FERMOR Mani: Travels in the Southern Peloponnese*

PATRICK LEIGH FERMOR Roumeli: Travels in Northern Greece*

PATRICK LEIGH FERMOR A Time of Gifts*

PATRICK LEIGH FERMOR A Time to Keep Silence*

PATRICK LEIGH FERMOR The Traveller's Tree*

D.B. WYNDHAM LEWIS AND CHARLES LEE (EDITORS) The Stuffed Owl

SIMON LEYS The Death of Napoleon*

SIMON LEYS The Hall of Uselessness: Collected Essays*

GEORG CHRISTOPH LICHTENBERG The Waste Books

JAKOV LIND Soul of Wood and Other Stories

H.P. LOVECRAFT AND OTHERS Shadows of Carcosa: Tales of Cosmic Horror*

DWIGHT MACDONALD Masscult and Midcult: Essays Against the American Grain*

CURZIO MALAPARTE Kaputt

CURZIO MALAPARTE The Skin

JANET MALCOLM In the Freud Archives

JEAN-PATRICK MANCHETTE Fatale*

JEAN-PATRICK MANCHETTE The Mad and the Bad*

OSIP MANDELSTAM The Selected Poems of Osip Mandelstam

OLIVIA MANNING Fortunes of War: The Balkan Trilogy*

OLIVIA MANNING Fortunes of War: The Levant Trilogy*

OLIVIA MANNING School for Love*

JAMES VANCE MARSHALL Walkabout*

GUY DE MAUPASSANT Afloat

GUY DE MAUPASSANT Alien Hearts*

GUY DE MAUPASSANT Like Death*

JAMES McCOURT Mawrdew Czgowchwz*

WILLIAM McPHERSON Testing the Current*

MEZZ MEZZROW AND BERNARD WOLFE Really the Blues*

HENRI MICHAUX Miserable Miracle